FAE LEGACY

FAE LEGACY

The Titan and the Phoenix

BENJAMIN GOODWILL

Infinite Trinity

Contents

I

Chapter One: The War to Come.

At sunset, the seagulls soared overhead, their squawks blending with the salty sea breeze that whipped against Sam's face. The weight of the shackles on his wrists and the oppressive collar that the General added to prevent any chance of escape dampened his spirit.

As Sam headed up the gangplank to the looming galleon, he saw other groups of prisoners huddled on the pier. They were also waiting to be loaded onto the ship. All of them had their heads shaved the night before, a cruel reminder of their captivity. They chained Sam with five others, all unknown to him, but their eyes held the same fear and uncertainty he felt in his heart. General Criel approached General Ak'rah.

"General Ak'rah, you summoned me?" Criel asked.

"You're in command while I'm gone. I'm heading north to Remus's castle to secure my gem cutter. I'll return before the low moon of the Harvest festival. Move the wagons into place after the start of the festival. Have the humans visible and keep the rest of our forces hidden in the forest. Until then, keep everything out of sight. We need to keep the element of surprise. Understood?" General Ak'rah said.

"Understood," Criel replied. He saluted and left. Ak'rah saw Sam and caught up to him.

"I'm not stupid, Sam. I know you had something to do with that prison escape. You compromised my entire operation. I'm disappointed in you. I thought we had an understanding. You'll wear a collar now, so your fairy friends don't steal you away again. I'm taking you back to my castle, far from here. I hope we can put this behind us, and maybe we can even be partners," Ak'rah said.

Sam just looked onward. Several orcs escorted him into the ship through a door with all the other prisoners. Sam noted that orc troops and supplies were being unloaded. The prisoners were escorted through the vessel up to the main deck above. The goblin captain stood in front of the men. To Sam's surprise, the captain gave the order for them all to be unshackled. He waited for them to be released before he addressed the crew. Ak'rah insisted not to remove Sam's collar, so that was left on.

"I'm Captain Kavash. Whether you're a free man or conscripted, it is none of my affair. Onboard this ship, you'll work for your food and ale. If you're lazy or prove to be a problem, we'll see how good of a swimmer you are when we get to the middle of the sea. I spoke to all of your 'superiors.' They have agreed to sell some of you conscripts to me after our voyage," Captain Kavash's voice boomed across the deck, commanding the attention of the crew.

His sharp gaze scanned the crowd, daring anyone to challenge his authority. The salty sea air wafted over the new crew members as the captain outlined their fate aboard the Lightning Privateer.

"If you are a conscripted crew member. I will pay for your freedom if you work hard and impress me. Then, you are welcome to stay on as a crew member and earn wages. You lot on the right are part of the Forward Division or First Division. You lot on the left are in the Aft Division or Second Division. Food will be provided, and there will be a designated space for your belongings," Captain Kavash explained.

"You will be issued a work uniform, boots, and a knife. The knife is for cutting lines and doing your job. Suppose you pull your knife out for any other reason. I'll cut your throat with it and throw you overboard. There is no brig aboard this ship. Any offense I deem worthy is also punishable by death. I have no intention of killing off my crew, but I'll stop problems before they start. Exercise good judgment, and you'll thrive here. Get wise, and you will be sorry for it," Kavash paused before continuing.

"The men standing behind you are ranking crew members. When they talk, you shut your mouth and listen. They are here to teach and direct you, not babysit you. Please refer any questions you have to them. There is a warm meal waiting for you in the galley. You will be given your work and birthing assignments during your meal. Welcome aboard the Lightning Privateer, dismissed," Captain Kavash concluded.

Sam made his way down to the cramped galley. The scent of salted beef stew hung in the air. The clatter of wooden trays and the rattle of tin cups echoed in the narrow passageway. Sam joined the line, grabbing a wooden tray and a tin cup before shuffling through the line to receive his meal.

He was handed a hearty portion of salted beef stew, a side of hardtack, and a small ration of dried fruits. For dessert, there was a modest serving of dried apples. Sam filled his tin cup with water from a barrel and made his way to a table where three other young men sat, all of whom he recognized from the prison. However, he did not know them by name.

"Hi, I'm Sam," he said as he sat down. They went around the table and introduced themselves.

"I'm Augustus, but everyone calls me Augie. I worked at the military base in the kitchen and heard about what you did for us at the prison. Thank you for what you did at the prison. I wish it hadn't been my shift that day to work, or I'd be back in Seaside with my girl. That place was hell before you got there, thank you. This food is quite an improvement as well. Maybe life is looking up for us," Augustus said as he toasted with his cup.

"I'm Ivan, and this is my little brother Pavlo. He doesn't speak because an orc-guard slit his throat for talking back," Ivan said. Referring to Pavlo as his little brother emphasized their age difference, as Pavlo was much taller than Ivan. Pavlo untied the scarf from around his neck and showed the scar. He waved to Sam and Augustus. They waved back in acknowledgment. Ivan continued,

"If Drifa hadn't been there, he would have died. We worked as servers, and dishwashers in the deep sink, washing pots and pans in the bases officer's mess. We also appreciated what you did. I heard a rumor that the escape happened because you are related to the fairies. That's why you're wearing a collar, isn't it?" Ivan asked.

"I'd prefer if that would stay between us because that information can only jeopardize my situation. Ak'rah already suspects me," Sam whispered. They acknowledged with a nod. Ivan and Pavlo were taller and more muscular than Sam, but Augie seemed frail and shorter than Sam. He had likely been sick while imprisoned, but he looked healthy now. One of the crew approached their table.

"Gentlemen, good evening. My name is Petty Officer Volkov. You report to me now. You may just call me Volkov. I oversee the sails of the mainmast. I hope you are not afraid of heights. It will take me a little while to learn your names, but for now, you two are port topsail, and you two are starboard topsail. I know this may be confusing, but it will be explained in more detail later," Volkov said. He had pointed to Sam, Augustus, Ivan, and Pavlo, respectively. Sam was assigned the main topsail port side, though he had no idea what that meant. During the captain's speech, Sam recognized Volkov as a person standing behind his group.

"Do you all understand what I have assigned you?" Volkov asked.

"Not a single word, Petty Officer Volkov. I've never even been on a boat other than a canoe," Sam replied. The rest of the boys and Volkov laughed.

"This is a ship, not a boat. Don't worry. We will spend the next week or so training you to be sailors. We have at least as long as it takes to get unloaded and resupplied. The topsail is the highest sail on the ship. So, know that if 'Main Topsail' is called, that's you four. After dinner, go two decks down to the hold. You find the supply shop there. The cost will be deducted from your wages if you are a crew member. If you're a conscript, you don't need to worry about it. They will issue you two uniforms, boots, and a knife. In addition, you'll get a comb and a bar of soap," Volkov paused before continuing.

"Gentlemen, I'll warn you again about playing around with those knives. The captain is serious about that rule. If you get into a scrap, use your words or your fists. Any discussions of escape or mutiny and your deaths are assured, so do not even joke about such things. There is a ship's store, but it's coin only. If you're caught stealing from there, you'll lose a hand. After breakfast, tomorrow, report to me on the forecastle. That's the front of the canoe up top. Get cleaned up and get to sleep early. There is fresh water available for getting yourself clean and washing clothes topside. I suggest you get there quickly before it's gone. It'll be the last freshwater shower you get for a while. Take advantage of them when you can," Volkov continued.

"Eat your fruit while it's available. Out at sea, you don't want to get the scorbutus. When the fruit is gone, then it's just sauerkraut, pickles, or fermented cabbage to keep you from getting the plague of the sea," Volkov said as he sorted the items in a box.

"Here are your locks, and here are your hammock and locker numbers. Other than that, if you ever need anything, you can come to me, and I'll do my best to help you. Let's get your names," Volkov said as he wrote their names down. "Good luck, boys," Volkov said. He gave them each a lock, key, and a numbered wooden chip.

"Thank you, Volkov," Sam replied. The other boys responded as well. Volkov moved to the next table.

"Gentlemen, good evening. My name is Petty Officer Volkov. You can just call me Volkov. You work for me now," Volkov could be heard saying.

Two bee-sized fairies observed the discussion from the beams above the galley.

"Dugan, you stay with Sam, and I'll go report in. Make sure you nick us whatever they give to Sam so we can blend in with the crew," Gunay said.

"Why me?" Dugan asked.

"Because you're a water elemental, and I'm not. You must stay with Sam, especially if this boat goes to sea. You're his only hope of reporting where they take him. I'll just go back to camp, make a report, and get some supplies. I have to tell them we need a fire elemental to remove Sam's collar. Then I'll come straight back. Contact Sam only if it's safe, and he's alone," Gunay explained. Then he took flight and headed towards the exit.

Sam and his group finished eating and headed to the ship's hold. Dugan stealthily trailed behind them, flitting between the rafters and shadows. The group stopped in the ship's store to look around. They separated to look over the different aisles.

Sam looked over the books most intently. He found a book on sign language. That would be perfect for Pavlo. Pavlo also looked intently at a fancy harmonica. Augie was looking over a beautifully ornate concertina. Most of the items were luxury items targeted at the wealthy passengers. Since all of them were conscripts, no one had any gold on them, but Sam had something better. He had been skimming rubies from Ak'rah for months. He had sown a liner in the back of his pants to make a long compartment where he had hidden a dozen high-quality gems.

The group went to the supply shop, and each got their package of supplies. It was wrapped in a bath towel and tied with twine. Along with a small box of toiletries. Dugan flew behind the counter and shrunk two packages for him and Gunay. The group went and found their berthing area. It was at the foremost part of the ship. Near the ship's medical area. Dugan found a vantage point in the rafters to keep them under observation. He saw a roll of bandages on the shelf in the medical area. Dugan flew over and took them when no one was looking. He wrapped his ears. Sam went to the head (bathroom), which was nothing more than a room on the ship's side with a hole. As he entered the room, Dugan flew past his face and saluted. Sam almost slapped him out of the air. Dugan grew to full size.

"I'm Dugan of the Ocean. I'm here with Gunay of the Grasslands, but he's off making a report. Sam, we're here to protect and rescue you.

We've sent for a fire elemental to remove that collar, and then we can get you out of here. Let me test this collar of yours," Dugan said.

"Wait, I want you to hold on to something for me," Sam said as he removed his trousers and tore the rear liner to recover the rubies. Dugan had already sized them down to mid-height, but it stopped there. Pavlo walked into the bathroom and looked down to see Sam and the fairy at mid-height. Sam had his pants off. Pavlo looked on, stunned for a moment.

"Pavlo, don't let anyone in," Sam said. He laughed, but turned around and did as Sam asked. Sam handed Dugan the rubies. "Hold these for me. So, did Elnara, Drifa, and Tetyana make it out safely?" Sam asked as he handed the rubies to Dugan. He kept two of them and put them in his pockets. He put the pants back on. Dugan returned them to full height.

"Oh, that was awkward, sorry. I guess the collars do work. The only Fae injured were Her Majesty, your sister, and Princess Elnara. Princess Elnara took an arrow to each leg, but neither was too serious. Unfortunately, Her Majesty Princess Aysun suffered more serious wounds. She took an arrow to the chest and another deep in her leg. The last update I have is that she is stable and resting. Drifa is attending to her. Princess Elnara is acting regent now. I'll be nearby if you need me," Dugan said. He shrunk down and flew out. Sam and Pavlo returned to the berthing area. Pavlo was laughing so hard that he was doubled over. His face was bright red. Sam helped him to sit at a seat at the small table in their area. Augie and Ivan were already seated there.

"What's with him?" Ivan asked Sam as he pointed at his brother.

"Let's worry about that later. I'm going to go to the store. Is there anything that you want? I know what you want, Giggles," Sam said, looking at Pavlo. Pavlo started laughing harder and nearly fell out of his seat.

"If you get caught stealing, you know the punishment, so please don't do it. It's not worth it," Ivan said.

"Let's say I have the money for anything in the shop. What would you want to have?" Sam asked.

"A deck of cards for us and something to read," Ivan replied.

"And you, Augie?" Sam asked.

"Nothing for me, Sam, really," Augie replied.

"Okay, fine. I'll be back in a few minutes. Wait for me," Sam said. Then, he departed and went to the ship's store. He approached the cashier.

"I let your lot look around earlier as a onetime courtesy. This shop is for paying customers only. If you don't have any gold or silver to spend, I'll have to ask you to leave," the cashier said.

"What if I have something to trade?" Sam pulled out the rubies and showed them to him.

"Papa," the cashier called into the backroom. An older gentleman came out.

"I'm looking for a little store credit. I'll give you the deal of a lifetime," Sam said. Sam showed him the rubies. The man went and got a jeweler's glass and examined them.

"Where did you get these? Are they stolen?" The man asked.

"No, I found them in the river and made them. I'm a gem cutter. I can explain exactly how I made them if that would help?" Sam said.

"How much are you looking for?" the man asked.

"I'll start with the harmonica and the concertina," Sam said. He grabbed a sack from the side of the counter. Sam walked around the store and picked out two outfits with new shoes and a nice nightshirt. Next, he grabbed six books, a chessboard, three decks of cards, and a set of poker chips. Sam found a drafting kit with all the drawing tools. Finally, he grabbed a notebook and put them all in the sack. Next, Sam put bags of nuts, jerky, and candy in a separate sack. He placed it all on the counter. "I want forty gold pieces, too," Sam said.

"Ten," the man replied.

"Thirty," Sam countered.

"Twenty, and that's all I'm going," the man stated.

"Fine, with twenty silver and twenty copper. I also need a receipt. I also want store credit for more jerky, nuts, and candy," Sam said as he extended his hand.

***

At the berthing, the three waited for Sam. They had already changed into their nightshirts to get washed up for bed. Sam walked up to the table and set the sacks down. He pulled four fiction books out of the bag. He also put a pouch full of coins down on the table.

"This is for all of us to share. I'll keep the food in my locker, but just ask, and you can have whatever you want. Ivan divided the coins up four ways, but be quiet about it. Keep the coins in your lockers. Use it to buy your freedom when you can," Sam said.

Sam put his new clothes away except a new nightshirt much nicer than theirs and a better towel. He reached into the sack and pulled out the three decks of cards and poker chips. Sam placed them in front of Ivan. He put the harmonica in front of Pavlo. Pavlo picked it up and played a merry melody. Sam handed the concertina to Augie. Augie smiled and looked it over with excitement. A tear formed in the corner of his eye. He wiped it away quickly with his sleeve.

"Do you even know how to play that Squeezebox, Augie?" Ivan asked.

"A little," Augustus replied. He played a few chords.

"Here, give it to me, and I'll show you how to play," Ivan said. Augie handed him the concertina, and Ivan played a classic tavern song. Ivan played beautifully.

"I got a special present for you, Pavlo. I found this in the library in the ship's store. Consider this payment for your continued silence about what you saw earlier," Sam said. He took out the book labeled "To Talk Without Sound" and handed it to Pavlo. It was a book on sign language. Pavlo flipped through a few pages. Tears spilled out of his eyes, and his mouth quivered. Finally, Pavlo went over and picked Sam up, hugged him, and kissed his cheek. Pavlo put Sam down and made a gesture to lock his mouth.

"I bought a second copy so we can all learn with you. First, you become the expert, and then you teach us," Sam said. Pavlo nodded, and he mouthed thank you.

"Sam, how did you afford all this?" Augustus asked.

"You guys said it earlier. I won't repeat it. There are secrets I must keep. There are oaths I've taken. I can only tell you that it is better not to discuss anything, as you mentioned earlier. With all the orcs and goblins about, we are not safe here. We don't know anything about any of the other prisoners. It could put us all at risk if anything like that is overheard. I will be at risk most of all. We should look out for each other. I can tell you I didn't steal any of this. What do you say, friends?" Sam said as he put his fist out over the table. Pavlo put his fist in. Augie stood up and put his fist in.

"Ivan?" Sam asked.

"Oh god, help me with this group of crying girls. Okay, I'm in," Ivan said as he stood up and put his fist in. "Now, can we get cleaned up before we have to take salty showers?" Ivan asked.

They put their items away into their lockers and headed topside. Sam changed into his nightshirt. He threw his old clothes into the trash. The boys made their way up to the weather deck. Sam felt that he was crossing into a new chapter in his life. He had outgrown his clothes. He reflected on how much he had changed since leaving Farmers Mill. The boys bathed. They got there in time to get the last of the freshwater. They washed, dried, and redressed. As they returned to their hammocks, Ivan saw something was weighing on Sam. He put Sam in a headlock.

"Ok, out with it, Mr. Money Pants. What's bothering you? Don't say 'nothing.'" Ivan asked.

"It's just that I realized stripping off those things I've held on to for so long, those stupid raggedy clothes. Everything that I have been holding on to has been an illusion. So here I am, thinking I'm coming closer and closer to freedom, but in reality, I'm a prisoner, traveling farther and farther from being free. I just learned my sister was nearly killed trying to rescue me," Sam said.

"Well, brother, we are in the same boat, literally. Well, the same ship. She wasn't killed; be positive about that. So, let's try to find freedom together, but until then, let's persevere," Ivan said.

"Thanks, Ivan. I was just reflecting on all that's happened. I just got a little deep in thought for a moment," Sam said.

"Friends, remember?" Ivan said as he let go of Sam and punched him in the shoulder. They walked back to their berthing and settled into their hammocks. Each of them read one of the new novels, except Pavlo, who was practicing signing as he read his book. The bosun's whistle signaled lights out, and soon after, an attendant came around and extinguished the lamps. Pavlo imitated the whistle.

***

Aysun waved Hannah over as Elif's performance ended. "Hannah, please tell the King's valet. I request an audience with the King. Ask if he could please come to my room. The matter is urgent," Aysun said. Hannah went to inform the valet.

"Sebeli, I am ready to leave," Aysun said. Sebeli helped Aysun up. She helped Aysun down the stairs and back into the castle.

Hannah went to the King's valet and conveyed Aysun's message. The valet nodded in acknowledgment and moved to inform the King of Aysun's request.

Hannah caught up to Aysun and Sebeli and assisted. Aysun went back through the intelligence documents she had in a desk. She put the papers on the table and waited for the King. A brief time later. The guard knocked on the door and announced the King. Hannah opened the door.

The King entered the room. Aysun took a deep breath and prepared to share her findings with him. She offered him a seat at the table across from her.

"Aysun, what is it?" Alex asked.

"Alex, you asked me before if the orcs were planning to attack Seaside. I have never seen the north side of Seaside Castle before. Poor farm girls don't get invited to tournaments. I've never seen the castle from that side before. It matches the model of the attack plans. Seaside Castle will be attacked two weeks after the Harvest market starts. I'm sending out scouts. We'll watch your borders. As you and your army once stood by me. The Fae army will stand with you," Aysun said.

"Aysun, I don't know how to thank you," Alex said.

"I'm alive, and so is my family. I have you to thank for that. There is a secret transit system we are building near here. When it's completed, travel between our world and your kingdom can happen quickly. I'll return to my lands and summon my army. When I return, I'll need a couple of dozen rooms for my generals and their staff here at the castle," Aysun explained.

"Done. I'll open a wing. The main conference room will be available as our combined war room. I know I can't know its location, but I want to see where and how you live. Besides, I strongly suspect your nation is in my kingdom," Alex requested.

"I can indeed take you to our nation, but there would have to be some conditions. First, I can only allow you two guards, Valeria and Marcus. Those are the only two that I know and trust. You must be hooded, blindfolded, and flown to the station entrance. You can't know its location either. Trust me, and you'll be better off blindfolded. I got sick all the time, learning how to fly. Pack light and no weapons," Aysun said.

"No weapons? That doesn't seem very trusting," Alex said.

"Listen, it's not a matter of trust. Here, everyone carries a sword. It's not common for people to carry a weapon in our lands, especially not in my presence. The three of you being human, you will stand out, and my guards will already be suspicious of you. It's better just to avoid an incident. Your safety and well-being are my highest priorities during your visit," Aysun said.

"I agree with your terms. I need to send messages to my allies. Thank you, Your Majesty," Alex said. He bowed to her.

"You know that's not needed, Alex," Aysun said.

"I'm just practicing for when I am in your nation," Alex said.

"Your custom is to bow on approach. Ours is to kneel; everything else seems similar. There is another matter. To bring my military here, I must assert my right to ascend to Queen. There could be some drama.

I just want you to be aware," Aysun replied. The King nodded in acknowledgment and took his leave.

"Hannah, go find Shamus and tell him I wish to see him. Then, find Elnara and do the same," Aysun said.

"Yes, Aysun," Hannah bowed before she left. A short time later, the guard announced Shamus. Sebeli opened the door. Shamus came in and kneeled to the Princess.

"Princess Aysun, you summoned me," Shamus said. She motioned him to stand.

"How soon can the tunnel be useable?" Aysun asked.

"The tunnel's all done and dusted, but they're still laying the track, Your Majesty," Shamus replied, his voice tinged with a touch of Irish charm.

"I need to get to the Great Tree as soon as possible," Aysun said.

"Grant me a week, and I'll have something ready for you to use. Is there anything else, Your Majesty?" Shamus asked. There was another knock at the door.

"Aysun, it's Elnara," Elnara said.

"Come in," Aysun responded. Elnara and Hannah entered the room. They kneeled. Elnara sat at the table next to Aysun. She grabbed Aysun's hand.

"Elnara, in a week, the new tunnel will be opened. After that, I intend to return to the Great Tree to assume control of the military. King Alexander will accompany me with Valeria and Marcus. Shamus, you will come as well. Elnara, I'm taking Caria and Emira with me. I'm also taking half the guard," Aysun said.

"You shouldn't be doing this without consulting General Emir. Are you crazy? You're going to be deposed. You cannot invoke the Queen's right. The senior military staff treats us like little girls. You're only nineteen years old, and there is no direct threat to the Great Tree. We've been fairies for less than four years. Don't risk that. What will happen to Sam and me if you do this and get banished? What's going on? Explain it to me," Elnara said.

"My age has nothing to do with it. You and Sam are not involved.

You're staying here while I go. While investigating the military complex next to the prison, I discovered plans for an attack. At your competition, I realized the attack is coming here. It's coming from the west and potentially the east, supported by the sea. We may have stopped the potential advance from the South. I've pledged my support for Seaside to King Alexander. If I fail and I'm deposed and banished. I'll be walking out of the Great Tree alone. You will be coronated as the new monarch until another Moon Goddess is born and comes of age," Aysun said.

Elnara became furious. She paced about the room, searching for the right words.

"Leave us," Elnara said to all in the room with a raised voice. Hannah, Sebeli, and Shamus bowed and left the room.

"Aysun! Who do you think you are? What do you mean I'm staying here? The last person to take a choice away from me is currently being tortured and starved to death. You don't get to choose for me! The decision of whether I go back or remain here is my decision and my decision alone," Elnara said as she paced the room.

"Calm down. I'm only asking you to stay here while I exercise my right to be queen. I am not telling you to change. You still have that choice. If I'm exiled, I'll come back here and seek pity from the King, and I'll be here to fight when the orcs come. You can decide whether you stay human and live in exile with your precious Marcus and me or go back and rule fairyland. If you really want to come, then come. What's really bothering you?" Aysun said.

"Emir is like an uncle to us. You have to give him a chance before you exercise your right and force this into conflict. Once you do, one of you will likely suffer the consequences. If you push him, he will challenge you. You'll be deposed if you lose. If you win, you'll ruin his career. Taner will not be happy if you put him in a bad spot like that. You'll tear what family we have apart. Promise me you'll try to find a compromise before it comes to that," Elnara pleaded.

"I promise I'll make every effort. Now tell me, what's really bothering you?" Aysun asked.

"I shouldn't have done it. I wanted to do it so bad it burned me up inside, but now, how can I go through with it?" Elnara replied.

"What are you talking about?" Aysun said. Elnara stopped pacing. She sank to her knees and put her head on Aysun's lap. Aysun petted and teased her hair.

"How will Marcus love me after I have a man blinded and executed? How will I be able to look at him knowing what I've done?" Elnara sobbed.

Aysun picked her head up and looked into Elnara's eyes, "So it's love, then? Oh, you've got it bad,"

"I don't know. I planned to go back and live as Fae. Marcus complicates things," Elnara said.

"It's not complicated. You passed the sentence, and now you have a duty. It's not murder; Jerimiah is guilty of a capital offense. It's justice. I would have killed him myself. It's Fae law, and it's in motion. That has nothing to do with you and Marcus or your decision. Stay here and be the Fae representative to the humans. If, at some point, that no longer serves your wishes, then return to the world of the Fae. Whatever you choose, I'll support you. Couldn't Marcus also come to live at the Great Tree if you choose to return? It's you who will be stuck, not him. We can arrange something for him to live in both worlds," Aysun said.

"Thank you, Aysun. I love you. However, this goes and whatever you choose to do. I'll be behind you, cousin. Have Marcus stay at my house, or at least let him go through it," Elnara said as she got up to leave. She bowed.

"Your Majesty," Elnara went into the hall. Hannah, Sebeli, Mizzy, Caria, Emira, and Marcus stood in the hall a respectful distance from the door. Once Elnara exited and went into her room. Everyone sprang into motion. Emira, Mizzy, and Marcus went to Elnara's room. Marcus was granted entry.

"Elnara, what's happening?" Marcus asked.

"More than what I can talk about. Mizzy, you can have the rest of the day off. Emira out," Elnara ordered. Elnara pushed Marcus onto the sofa. Emira and Mizzy walked out and closed the door.

***

A few days later, Mizzy dressed Elnara in a beautiful white gown encrusted with jewels. At the center of the bodice was a large blood ruby. There was a knock at the door.

"What's the occasion? The tournament is not for a few more weeks," Mizzy asked as she styled Elnara's hair. Elnara didn't reply.

"Sergeant Edric of the Forge to see the princess," the guard announced. Mizzy opened the door. Edric entered the room and kneeled. "Princess Elnara, you sent for me," Edric said. Elnara motioned for him to stand.

"Edric, I need a favor from you, but I'll understand if you say no. It's time for the second phase. I need someone to melt the silver for Cinar," Elnara asked.

"It would be my honor, Princess Elnara. I thought you were upset with me?" Edric asked.

"No, I am not upset with you. I'm happy for you and Emira. The King's court is a gossipy bunch of aristocrats. You were repeatedly seen going into Emira's room. That added to that gossip, which was making me uncomfortable. You can blame me for having you moved. It was causing my reputation to be questioned. You were taken off our guard because I had to remove one of you. Emira has worked for years to get here. Caria selected you and Yusef, and Aysun and I trust you two. I even reserved a private room for you at the inn so you and Emira could spend time together, out of public view," Elnara said.

"I didn't know all of that. Thanks for clearing all of that up, Your Highness. I apologize for any inconvenience our relationship has caused. Excuse me for asking, but you're a more powerful fire elemental than me. Why do you need me?" Edric asked.

"I don't want to be there when it's done," Elnara said.

"I understand. It will be my honor," Edric said. Then, there was a knock at the door.

"It's Emira," Emira said.

"Come in," Elnara replied.

Emira entered and placed two stacks of silver coins in front of Elnara. Elnara put the coins in a small pouch. She tucked it into her waistband. Then, there was another knock at the door.

"Captain Marcellus, to see the princess," the guard said. Mizzy looked at Elnara.

"Tell him I'm busy, and I'll see him at dinner tonight," Elnara said. Mizzy went over and opened the door, and sent Marcus away.

"Emira, is my carriage ready?" Elnara asked.

"Yes, Princess. Cinar and Yusef are waiting out front," Emira said.

"Let's go," Elnara said and walked to the door. She grabbed the sword wrapped in cloth and carried it with her. Edric opened the door for her. Elnara descended the stairs to the entrance. Marcus and Valeria were there, standing outside of Marcus's office. Elnara looked at Marcus and shook her head at him. She took the last step down the stairs, and the pouch with the silver coins slipped out of her waistband. The coins sprayed out across the floor. Elnara gasped.

"Princess, go to the carriage. I'll pick them up," Emira said. She and Edric scrambled to pick them up as Elnara dashed for the carriage. Cinar held the door open for her. Marcus and Valeria helped pick up the coins and handed them to Emira.

"Not a word, Marcus," Emira said with a stern stare.

"I wasn't going to," Marcus replied.

She couldn't shake off the feeling that there was something more to Marcus's behavior. It was unusual for him to let the Princess pass without asking questions. Emira couldn't help but wonder what caused him to act this way. Marcus gave up too quickly. He had to know something. Emira joined the Princess in the carriage, along with Cinar. Emira handed the pouch back to Elnara. Yusef sat in the driver's seat. He drove the carriage onward. Edric followed behind with Elnara's guard detail. Marcus and Valeria watched the carriage head down the road.

"Should we inform the king?" Valeria asked.

"I gave my word. I'll be in my office," Marcus said. He turned around and headed back to his office.

"Cinar report," Elnara said.

"Your Highness, since his sentencing, the only time he has eaten is when people directly give him food in public. Otherwise, we make sure to stop him. He thinks he's outsmarting us. After today, he'll no longer know where 'in public' is, and his situation will worsen quickly. He sleeps in an alley not far from the tavern where he worked. He should be there now. The carriage drove past the alleyway. The carriage pulled outside the city gates and near a path in the forest. Edric jumped down and opened the carriage door. He offered his hand to the Princess.

"Princess Elnara," Edric said as he helped her down.

"My love," he added as he extended his hand to Emira, winking at her.

"Lieutenant, please," Emira responded.

"And you wonder why you two cannot work together," Elnara said.

"Sorry, Your Highness," Edric replied.

"Lieutenant Emira, you can take the Princess down this path to the river. I'll take two of the horses and get Jerimiah. Take the path until you reach a small camp. We set it up so Jerimiah can recover out of public view," Cinar said. He signaled for two of the Princess's guards to dismount. He then mounted a horse and grabbed the reins of the second.

"Thank you, Cinar. Very well, go get Jerimiah," Emira said as Cinar saluted and rode off to fetch Jerimiah. Emira then helped Elnara mount a horse, and they set off down the trail with Yusef and the other guards escorting them.

After a while, they arrived at a stunning campsite nestled beside the river. The camp was surrounded by tall trees that provided shade and seclusion, and the sound of the nearby river filled the air with a gentle hum. As Elnara dismounted and sat on a plush chair beside the fire pit, Emira noticed another member of Cinar's team was already at the camp.

The campsite was adorned with colorful fabrics and tapestries that draped over the tent poles and fluttered in the breeze. Various delicious-smelling dishes were laid out on a long table, along with crystal glasses and silverware. The fire pit was made of polished stone and was surrounded by comfortable cushions that beckoned people to sit and relax.

Emira's eyes were drawn to the device to hold Jerimiah, which lay on the ground beside the guard. It looked grotesque and intimidating, with blocks to keep his head still. There were cranks to secure it and straps to hold him still. Despite the luxurious surroundings, the device was a reminder of the gravity of the situation. Emira felt a wave of nausea at the sight, but she remained composed and comforting towards Elnara as Mizzy fussed over Elnara's dress.

***

Cinar rode up to the alleyway where Jerimiah was lying down. Jerimiah slept in a simple structure made of discarded boxes and scrap lumber. Mehmet sat nearby. Cinar knocked on the frame.

"Knock knock, time to get up, Jerimiah," Cinar said.

"Go away, leave me alone," Jerimiah replied. Cinar reached in, grabbed him by the ankle, and dragged him out. "Hey, let go of me!" Jerimiah demanded.

"The Princess has summoned you. I'm here to collect you. You can come willingly or not. The choice is up to you, but either way, you're coming," Cinar replied.

"You're just trying to trick me so you can get me back out in the woods to torture me some more," Jerimiah replied.

"The hard way it is, Mehmet, get him on the horse," Cinar ordered. Mehmet stood up and approached Jerimiah.

"Fine, I'll go willingly, but I need help to get on the horse," Jerimiah said. He used his crutches to go to the horse. Mehmet helped him up. The trio rode for the gate and down the trail until they reached the camp. Elnara was seated ahead. Her four guardsmen and Emira stood behind her. Mizzy served her tea. The men and Jerimiah dismounted. The three approached Elnara. Mehmet and Cinar forced Jerimiah to kneel. They also kneeled.

"Rise," Elnara commanded.

"Jerimiah, my worm prince. Will you join me?" Elnara said. She offered him a chair across from her. Jerimiah sat down. Mehmet held his crutches for him. Elnara signaled Mizzy to serve Jerimiah tea.

"I bought this just for you," Elnara said. She stood the executioner's sword up in front of her.

"It's very sharp. I'm ready to show you mercy. All you have to do is ask for it, and your suffering ends," Elnara said.

"I'll pass," Jerimiah replied. He gulped down the tea.

"This next part is going to be very painful for you. I prefer to swing the sword now rather than have you go through it," Elnara said.

"What are you talking about?" Jerimiah asked.

"I'm going to have you blinded," Elnara responded.

"I came here willingly. You should show me mercy by ending this constant abuse and torture. I'm starving! Call off your dogs," Jerimiah demanded.

"I told you before, I can't do that. What's been set in motion cannot be stopped. Your only mercy will be with this sword. Your torture and starvation will continue," Elnara said. She got up and walked over to Cinar. She looked down at Jerimiah.

"Your sentence is death. Do you ask for my mercy now?" Elnara asked. Jerimiah looked away.

"Cinar, I want to buy his eyes. Is this enough?" Elnara asked. She handed Cinar the pouch of coins. Cinar poured a couple of coins into his hand, and he felt the weight of the rest.

"This should be more than enough, Princess," Cinar replied.

"Wait until I am far enough away. I don't want to hear his screams," Elnara requested.

"Of course, Princess," Cinar replied.

"Emira, Mizzy, I'm ready to go," Elnara said. She went over to the horse, and Emira helped her to mount it. Elnara rode back to her carriage. Jerimiah protested and struggled. Cinar and Mehmet had to use force to lift him out of the chair and put him on his feet. They wrestled with him as he tried to break free, but eventually, they overpowered him and dragged him toward the harness.

"Let me go!" Jerimiah demanded, his voice laced with fear and anger.

"Listen, we're going to strap you in, so the silver doesn't spill all over that pretty little face of yours," Cinar said. They forced Jerimiah into the harness.

"Let me go!" Jerimiah demanded.

"I'd say I'm sorry or that I feel terrible about this, but every time I see her limp, it breaks my heart all over again. You feel like you're getting a bad deal. You're getting exactly what you deserve, so stop struggling," Cinar yelled as they finished strapping and clamping him in. Jerimiah resisted, thrashing and kicking against the restraints, but the Fae were too strong for him. The struggle lasted several minutes, with Jerimiah fighting until he was finally exhausted and was resigned to his fate.

Cinar waited until he thought Princess Elnara was far enough away. He then took out a handful of coins and handed them to Edric, a small smile of satisfaction on his face.

"Do you want me to melt them directly into his eyes, Master Sergeant?" Edric asked.

"No, Sergeant. Just melt them into the ladle, then get on your horse and leave," Cinar replied. Mehmet lit a fire.

"Yes, Master Sergeant," Edric responded. Then, Edric melted the coins, and the silver flowed from his hands into the ladle. Cinar set the ladle with the molten silver over the fire to keep it in its liquid state.

"Now get on your horse and ride out of here," Cinar said. Edric got on his horse and went down the trail.

Cinar was careful to only pour in the silver when the temperature was correct. He was careful to only pour in the minimum amount needed.

Despite being given time to put some distance between herself and the camp. Jerimiah's screams could still be heard within the walls of the city. Elnara's heart pounded with every agonizing syllable that escaped Jerimiah's lips. She pounded on the carriage, desperately pleading for Yusef to stop.

"Stop the carriage!" she shouted. Finally, the carriage stopped, and Elnara stumbled out the door, collapsing to her knees on the dirt road.

Elnara stumbled out of the door and collapsed to her knees on the dirt road. Her body heaved with sobs, each one more gut-wrenching than the last. In the distance, the piercing shrieks of Jerimiah echoed through the air. Mizzy and Emira quickly kneeled beside her, holding her hair back as she retched onto the ground. They stayed by her side, offering comfort and support.

Jerimiah's tortured cries echoed through the forest, sending chills down Elnara's spine. Her mind raced with a storm of emotions: guilt, horror, regret, and rage. What had she done? How could she have been so foolish and so naive?

Mizzy and Emira lifted Elnara back into the carriage, trying to soothe her as they rode back to the castle. Mizzy wiped away Elnara's tears and cleaned her face with a handkerchief. No amount of comforting could erase the traumatic scene that had just unfolded.

As they returned to the castle, Emira noticed Valeria and Marcus waiting in the lobby off in the shadows. They watched in silence as the distraught Elnara was escorted into her room. Elnara was haunted by the echoes of Jerimiah's screams ringing in her ears.

"Mizzy, help me get her out of the dress and then have a bath drawn for her. Once she is settled in the tub, have Drifa come in and check on her," Emira said.

"Yes, miss," Mizzy replied as they attended to Elnara. Aysun let herself in and came in and sat next to Elnara. Elnara was lying face down, sobbing into her pillow. She ran her fingers through Elnara's hair. Aysun looked at Emira with a questioning gaze. Emira pointed to her eyes.

"Jerimiah," Emira Fae whispered.

Aysun tended back to Elnara. Mizzy returned to the room, followed by maids carrying buckets of water. They filled the tub for Elnara. Mizzy and the maids helped Elnara into the tub. Aysun motioned for Emira to follow her as she returned to her room. Emira described all the events that had transpired for Aysun. Then there was a knock at the door.

"It's Caria. I have a scout with me, and he has news about Sam. It's urgent," Caria said.

"Let them in," Aysun said. Hannah opened the door. Caria entered with the scout, and they both kneeled. Aysun motioned them to stand.

"Caria report," Aysun said.

"Your Majesty, I will let the scout tell you what he has told me. Go ahead and report," Caria said. She looked at the scout.

"Your Majesty Princess Aysun, your brother, has been moved to a passenger and cargo ship called the Lightning Privateer. I'm pleased to report that your brother is alive and in good health. The ship's captain has incorporated the prisoners as his crew. They are treated fairly and appropriately fed. However, Sam has been collared like the Fae from the prison. We would have rescued him if it were not for the collar. We need a fire elemental to melt that collar off of him so we can shrink him down and fly him out of there. There is no time to spare if we are to get there before the ship leaves," the scout reported.

"Emira, I want Edric summoned immediately. Aysun said.

"Right away, Your Majesty," Emira responded. Then she bowed and left the room to search for Edric. She ran to the stables to get a horse.

"Caria, see that the scout is fed and resupplied. Get him a fresh horse. See that another horse is prepared for Edric and another for Sam," Aysun said.

"Your Majesty," Caria said. Caria and the scout bowed and left.

Emira was prepared to mount a horse when Edric rode into the stables.

"Oh great, there you are. Come with me quickly," Emira said to Edric.

"What is it?" Edric asked.

"There's no time to explain. Get down and follow me. It's urgent. I'll explain on the way, please," Emira said as she held out her hand for him. Edric dismounted and took her hand. Edric handed the reins to the stable boy. She pulled him toward the castle. Emira forced Edric to jog with her.

"What is it, Emira? What's got you so spooked?" Edric asked with concern.

"There's a chance to save Sam. Princess Aysun has summoned you for the mission," Emira said.

"I should run ahead," Edric said.

"Go!" Emira replied. Edric took off running. He arrived at Princess Aysun's room and announced himself to the guard. He was admitted, and Emira was right behind him. They both kneeled. Aysun paced the floor on the terrace. She waved them up.

"Edric, I have an important mission for you. A scout has reported that Sam is aboard a ship bound to depart soon. They need a fire elemental to remove his collar. Speed is of the essence. Find Caria and the scout. They are preparing to leave immediately. You might find them in the enlisted or officer dining halls. Go and rescue my brother, please," Aysun pleaded. She handed him a pouch of gold coins. Edric accepted the coins.

"If it's possible. I will get your brother and bring him safely back to you. I'll leave immediately," Edric said.

"Edric, I made a mistake by not rescuing my brother myself. He's a hero for the things he did in that prison. He refused to be rescued without the other prisoners being rescued. I'm ordering you to rescue him without delay. If he refuses on behalf of the other prisoners, take him by force if necessary. Go, and ride fast, Edric!" Aysun commanded.

"Yes, Your Majesty," Edric bowed and walked out the door. Emira bowed and followed him out. They walked down the stairs together. Near the entrance to the dining hall, Edric pulled Emira aside. "Emira, I love you. I'll be back as quickly as I can," Edric whispered.

"I love you too. Now go!" Emira replied. Edric embraced her. He put his head down to touch the crown of Emira's head to his. They savored a moment to share the same air. He kissed her.

"I need to go back and look after Princess Elnara. Hurry back to me," Emira said. She walked away as their hands lost contact, and their gaze broke. Emira turned and headed back toward Elnara's room. Edric was determined to save Sam. Edric went into the dining hall. He saw Caria sitting with the scout. He went over and introduced himself.

"Captain, Princess Aysun sent me to find you," Edric said. He extended his hand to the scout.

"I'm Sergeant Edric of the Forge," Edric said. The scout shook his hand.

"Corporal Neval of the Grasslands, nice to meet you, Sergeant,"

"Go get some lunch and come back and join us," Caria said.

"I'll be right back," Edric said as he went to get a plate of food. He returned a brief time later. He sat at the table.

"When you finish eating, three horses will be out front of the south entrance. I'll see they're packed with enough rations for the trip there and back. Make sure Sam has sufficient guards on his return trip. You have my authorization to sequester any non-officer to protect Sam. Stop by my office before you leave, and I'll ensure you have some gold for your journey," Caria said.

"That won't be necessary. Her Majesty has already seen to it," Edric said. He showed her the pouch Aysun gave him.

"Then good luck on your mission. Report back to me the second you return," Caria ordered.

"Yes, ma'am," Edric replied. Edric and Neval finished their lunch and headed to the horses. They finished packing the horses, and they set off to rescue Sam.

***

During dinner that night, Marcus noticed Elnara's absence. After dinner, he approached Elnara's room. He made a plate of meats, cheeses, and a slice of cake and headed to Elnara's room.

"Marcus to see the Princess. I brought her some dessert," Marcus said.

"She is not accepting visitors," the guard said.

"I'm sure if you announce me, she'll see me," Marcus said.

"I'm sorry the order came directly from her. She is not to be disturbed. You'll have to leave," the guard replied. Marcus reluctantly nodded and left.

2

Chapter Two: The Lightning Privateer

Two days later, it was all hands on deck as the captain and crew conducted drills to get the crew ready to sail.

"Unfurl the sails!" Captain Kavash ordered.

"Let's go. Boys climb the ratlines. Get up there, untie the gaskets, and let's free up those sails!" Volkov yelled. Sam and the others climbed up to the topsail. At over a hundred feet high, Augie called to Sam.

"I can't climb any higher. I'm scared!" Augie yelled to Sam.

"Augie, this is our assignment. We have to get it done. Don't look down. Keep three points of contact. Climb safely. Tie yourself on if you're tired, rest, and continue. We have to do this as a team," Sam yelled back, repeating the instructions Volkov had given them the day before. Sam had to overcome his fear of heights living in the Great Tree. So much of the city was vertically orientated. Augustus summoned his courage and continued after a brief pause. Finally, the four made it to the topsail. The boys spread out along the yardarm. They untied the gaskets around the sail, setting it free. There was no wind. Sam knew this was why the captain called for the drills now. They descended lines and positioned themselves on the deck, ready to handle the riggings for the topsail. Volkov called the order to lose the sails when everyone was in place.

"Lose the sails!" Volkov yelled.

Sam took the turns of line off the cleat, and Sam and Augie gradually let the line out. The sail unfurled. Ivan and Pavlo did the same tasks on a separate line.

"All sails unfurled, Captain," Volkov called out.

"Well done, Petty Officer Volkov. Furl the sails and secure them for port!" Captain Kavash ordered.

"You heard him, boys' heave-ho," Volkov yelled. Sam and Augie pulled on the line. Hand over hand, they drew the line back through the tackle. The topsail furled back up. The mainsail followed as the other teams completed their task. Sam and Ivan secured their lines back on the cleats. They repeated their climb back up the mainsail. They re-tied the gaskets around the sail to secure it.

"All sails furled and secured," Volkov called out to the quarterdeck.

"Well done, gentlemen. I'll make sailors of you yet," Volkov said to Sam and the others.

The crew stood down from sea and anchor detail. Volkov had the group stay on the forecastle to clean. Augustus and Pavlo swabbed the deck while Sam and Ivan polished the ship's bell and capstan. Sam dipped a rag in vinegar and polished the bell. Ivan sat on the capstan, watching Sam work.

"All right, Sam, out with it. No one can hear us out here. You want Pavlo and me to trust you. I need to know how you made the purchases and what Pavlo saw that's so secret. How can I trust you if you don't trust me?" Ivan asked.

"Ok, Ivan, you know I'm a gem cutter, and I cut gems for the General?" Sam asked.

"No, I knew you were responsible for building the restrooms and showers. I didn't know about the gems. I just knew you had a different job than the rest of us," Ivan replied.

"I leveraged my skills as a Gem Cutter to get the General to let me build that structure. I also bargained for the release of my cousin Princess Elnara of the Fae," Sam explained.

"The fairy is your cousin. Now, the story makes more sense. What about the phantom fairy? Was that her too?" Ivan asked.

"Slow down. Let me answer your questions before you ask more. I stole some gems from Ak'rah. Well, technically, I took gems that Ak'rah never knew about from my time collecting gems in the river. I told him I put gems next to my cell that were worthless and that the other prisoners were throwing priceless stones back into the river. That was not really the truth. I let a guard catch me polishing a nearly worthless stone. He thought I was putting junk stones next to my cell, but I was collecting quality ones. I evaluated the other prisoner's stones for them and kept the best ones for myself. They had no problem giving them to me. They hated the General. I made sure they turned in something good. An unpolished stone to an amateur looks worthless. I hid those priceless gems in plain sight for weeks and months. Before the escape, I sewed the gems into my clothes. Your brother caught me passing those gems to one of my Fae guards. He caught me with my pants off. That's what's behind the joke. I traded some of my cheaper stones to the store for credit and coins. That's how I made the purchases. As you call her, the phantom fairy is my sister, well, half-sister, Aysun. In human terms, she is the Queen of the Fae. That is why I have Fae guarding me, even now. I could buy this ship and more with the gems I have left. My Fae guards are over there, sitting on the railing. We can't see them, but they can see us. Go over and look. Dugan and Gunay, allow him to approach," Sam said.

"This is irregular," Gunay said.

"Are you going to defy Princess Aysun's brother?" Dugan asked.

"No, are you kidding me? Can you imagine being banished by a Moon Fae? What would even happen if she branded you? Would you sink into the earth or float away into space?" Gunay asked.

"He's coming over. Wave," Dugan responded. They both waved awkwardly as Ivan approached and inspected them. Ivan walked back over to Sam.

"Not much of bodyguards. I could've smashed them both dead like bugs," Ivan said.

"One of them is a water elemental. He could freeze parts of your body and snap them off. The other one could poison you to death if he wanted. Hitting them with your hand at that small size would only make them angry. If they decide to kill you, I can do nothing to stop them. I don't hold any rank over them. I am a royal family member, and they have orders to protect me. So, if you threaten them or pose a threat to me, I can't stop them from acting. So there, now you have the truth. Are you satisfied?" Sam replied.

"Yes, Sam, thank you for being honest with me. You have my friendship. Just keep me informed about anything you are planning from now on," Ivan said.

"You got it," Sam replied.

***

Elnara stood on her veranda, shivering in the darkness of the night. Suddenly, Aysun barged into the room, her eyes blazing with fury.

"We're leaving. The tunnel is completed. We're returning to our lands. I want you to come with me now. We are taking the tunnels back to the Great Tree. I'll not stay here and suffer another insult," Aysun said.

"What brought this on, Aysun? You cannot just ask me to leave here, to change. You do not rule me!" Elnara protested.

Elnara's heart sank. She had hoped to delay this day to spend a few more precious moments with Marcus. Aysun was having none of it.

"I do rule over you. Come on, we're going now," Aysun demanded.

Elnara's mind raced as she tried to find a way out of this nightmare. She couldn't leave Marcus. She loved him. As she tried to speak, Aysun cut her off.

"I rule the nation of the Great Tree and its citizens. You're a citizen. That makes you my subject. Would my own family dare defy me? Would you choose to live in exile, cut off?" Aysun demanded.

"No, but you can't just ask me to leave Marcus. I love him! Please, Aysun, be reasonable," Elnara said.

"I'm sorry about that. You must come with me now," Aysun commanded.

"I don't know if I can. I should consult with Drifa, and I need to say goodbye to Marcus," Elnara pleaded.

"There is no time for that. We must leave now. Here I'll help you," Aysun said. She put her hand on Elnara's shoulder.

"Ready?" Aysun asked.

"Yes," Elnara answered reluctantly. Aysun and Elnara shrunk down to near mid-height, and then they stopped. Aysun and Elnara pushed harder to shrink. Her wings ripped and tore as they emerged. Finally, Elnara cried and screamed as the mutilated wings finished coming out. She looked down to see the blood pooling at her feet. There was a knock at the door.

"It's Marcus. What's happening? I'm coming in," Marcus demanded as he began pounding on the door. Elnara cried. "No, stay out," she replied. There was another knock at the door. Elnara awoke.

"It's Mizzy. May I come in?" Mizzy said. Elnara sat up, realizing it had all been a dream.

****

A few hours later, Elnara walked into the King's dining hall for breakfast. The king's dining hall was a grand and opulent space. The walls were adorned with intricate tapestries depicting scenes from the kingdom's history. Elaborate frescoes of mythical creatures and ancient battles adorned the high ceiling. The room was illuminated by large crystal chandeliers, which cast a warm, golden light over everything. An enormous dining table, crafted from polished wood, featured silver candelabras and elaborate centerpieces. The finest fabrics upholstered the chairs.

"Her Royal Highness Princess Elnara of the Forge," Mizzy announced. The hall rose. Elnara bowed to the King, and the patrons re-took their seats. Mizzy escorted Elnara to her seat in between the King and Marcus.

"We have missed you at court, milady," Alexander said.

"I'm sorry I haven't been feeling well," Mizzy helped gather a lunch plate and poured Elnara's wine. She then stood behind her, awaiting Elnara's summons.

"I hope you are feeling better now," Alexander replied.

"A little, thank you," Elnara said.

"Princess," Marcus said.

"Marcus," Elnara replied.

"Maybe after lunch, we can go for a ride together if you are up for it," Marcus suggested.

"Sure, Marcus, that'll be nice," Elnara replied.

"You seem rather somber today, Princess. Is everything ok?" the King asked.

"Yes, just lost in my thoughts. Can I ask you a question, Your Majesty?" Elnara asked.

"Sure, what's on your mind?" the King replied.

"Could the Fae own land in the city? What if we also wanted some land outside of the city?" Elnara asked.

"Are you asking in an official capacity?" the King asked.

"No, Aysun has said nothing. I'm asking for myself," Elnara said. Marcus looked at her with a questioning gaze.

"I do not control the residentially zoned district inside the city. Therefore, you can purchase any property you like. I'm sure I can get you in touch with a realtor regarding owning and holding lands. As far as holding land outside of the city. I think that would be a conversation with Princess Aysun. Should she agree to permanent diplomatic relations, I would be open to setting some land aside," the King explained.

"It's not my place to address external diplomacy with her," Elnara replied.

***

Later, Marcus rode aside Elnara. "Are you planning to stay? Is that why you asked the King about owning property?" Marcus asked.

"I'm just thinking about my options. I have made no decisions. If I return home, I might buy my mother a nicer house. You know you could come live with me at the Great Tree. I spoke to Aysun, and it would be possible for you to keep your human lifestyle here. Not that you would need to. You could commute between the two worlds," Elnara said.

"I don't know, Elnara," Marcus said with some apprehension.

"Keep an open mind about it. You're going there next week. I told Aysun I wanted you to tour my house, and you could stay there if you like. I have a lovely wine collection," Elnara said with a smile.

"How do you know I'm going?" Marcus asked.

"Your King is going, and you and Valeria are going as his guards," Elnara said.

"Why the sudden trip?" Marcus asked.

"We have a hidden rail system. We are opening a station close to here soon. I think I've told you all that I can tell you. Watch out for Aysun while you're there,"

"What are you not telling me, Elnara?" Marcus asked.

"I'm not telling you the things I cannot tell you, Marcus," Elnara replied.

"You know this business with Jerimiah. You don't have to deal with this alone. We can talk about it," Marcus said. Elnara lowered her head and thought momentarily.

"I can't. I don't know how, not yet. When I'm ready, I will. Let's not dwell on this. I'll race you to the tree," Elnara said.

"You're on. On three, one, two," Marcus said.

She kicked her heels into Mia's side. "Hiya! Mia, let's go!" Elnara yelled as she shot off on Mia.

"Cheater!" Marcus called after her. Elnara beat Marcus to the tree. Marcus dismounted and then assisted her down. He spread out a blanket for them to sit on. He took wine and cheese from his saddlebag, and they sat down for a picnic. Elnara removed her cane from a sheath on Mia.

"I knew a ride would cheer you up," Marcus said.

"Beating you always brings a smile to my face," Elnara said as she laughed.

"That reminds me. I'm planning to compete in the upcoming tournament. I wanted to ask if I could ride Mia in the final race?" Marcus asked.

"Oh, I think that would be ok with me. I cannot race her with my leg. I might compete in the archery competition. What do you think, Mia? Do you want to carry around this handsome human in a race?" Elnara asked. Mia neighed and stamped about. "Oh, I would interpret that to mean she is excited, too. You know you are going to have to start running her. She is going to have to get used to your body weight," Elnara said. Marcus poured her a glass of wine.

****

Later that evening, Elnara awoke from a nightmare. "Marcus!" She said aloud and sat up in bed. Elnara got out of bed and poured herself a glass of wine. It was raining, which prevented her from going out on the veranda, as was her normal habit. The rain poured down hard. The sky lit up briefly, followed by a resounding clap of thunder. Elnara felt alone. She paced the room. What if she didn't convert to Fae form? She could stay and represent the Fae. She thought about Marcus. Was he asleep now? Elnara paced the room. She put her robe on and went to the door. She opened the door. Yusef was standing watch in front of her door.

"Yes, Princess, may I help you?" Yusef asked.

"No, you can have the night off," Elnara said.

"I cannot leave you unguarded, Princess," Yusef replied.

"Then be quiet," Elnara said. She walked down the hallway to Marcus's room. She knocked lightly.

"It's Elnara," Elnara said. She opened the door as Marcus sat up in bed. She let herself in and closed the door. Yusef stood watch at the door.

"Marcus, I can't sleep. May I lie down with you? Just for a few minutes," Elnara asked.

"Of course, come here. What's wrong?" Marcus asked. Elnara crawled under the covers with Marcus.

"Just a bad dream. It scared me," Elnara said.

"What's going on with you? I don't believe you're scared of anything," Marcus asked.

"I lose you in my dream. Aysun forces me to change into my Fae form, and you reject me," Elnara said.

"Why would I reject you? I care for you. I don't believe Aysun would take that choice away from you," Marcus replied.

"I know you're right, but I can't help what I dream," Elnara said.

Elnara snuggled closer to Marcus, feeling the warmth of his body against hers. The rain outside intensified, tapping against the window like tiny, insistent fingers. The room felt safe and cocooned from the outside world. Elnara closed her eyes and breathed in Marcus's scent. A combination of earth and wood mixed with the hint of his aftershave. She felt his fingers running through her hair, soothing her. Marcus was first attracted to her for her beauty and strength. She was now further endeared to him through her confession of vulnerability.

Elnara couldn't help but think about the weight of her responsibilities as she lay there. She had to take the actions she did based on the decisions she made. She felt overwhelmed. Marcus sensed her unease and pulled her even closer.

"You're not alone in this, Elnara. I'm here for you," he whispered.

Elnara felt warmed by his assurances, his embrace. This made her smile. Marcus meant his words, but her fears still felt heavy. She couldn't help but wonder if she would make the right choices and be truly prepared for the responsibilities and the consequences ahead. She was grateful to be in Marcus's arms, protected from the storm outside. Elnara's eyelids grew heavy with sleep. As she drifted off, she knew she felt safe with Marcus, no matter what happened. They stayed like that for hours until the rain finally subsided at daybreak. Elnara got up and went to leave.

"Leaving?" Marcus asked.

"Yes, I didn't mean to fall asleep. I need to get back to my room before anyone sees me here. I'll see you at breakfast," Elnara said.

***

After dinner, the boys returned to their birthing area as they were about to sit down to play some cards. The ship's bell started ringing, and the boatswain's whistle played an urgent tune. Volkov came down the hall.

"Sea and anchor detail, get up to the forecastle boys. Don't forget to bring your knives," Volkov said.

They put their knife sheathes on their belts. Volkov went around looking for other members of the division. He sent them to the forecastle. They followed him up the ladder well to the forecastle. There they were assigned positions on the mooring lines. There was a light mist of rain and a steady breeze.

"What's going on?" Sam asked Volkov.

"We're pulling out a couple of days early. The ship is loaded, and the winds are favorable. Be ready to pull the lines in as soon as they hit the water," Volkov explained. Sam looked down at the docks, and two men were stationed at the bollard holding the mooring line. When the signal came, the men took the line off the bollard and let it fall into the water. Sam and the others pulled on the line hand over hand. The line was so thick that Sam's hand couldn't fit around it. They pulled and pulled on the line.

"Come on, boys, let's get that line in. The longer she's in the water, the heavier she gets," Ivan yelled. The group got the line in, and Volkov signaled them to move the line below. They moved the line down to the main deck to allow it to dry before storing it in the line locker. They returned to the forecastle and took their position on the sail stations. The order was given to lower the sails. Swiftly, the boys unfurled the sails and secured their lines.

The sails caught the wind, and the ship pulled forward. Sam was amazed. He had never seen a ship outside of a book before boarding, and now he's actually working on one. The sense of him being a prisoner faded. He also realized that any plans to rescue him had failed.

As they worked, Sam couldn't help but feel a sense of excitement and adventure. Gradually, the ship lurched forward as the wind picked up, and the sails unfurled, billowing in the breeze. Alive with the energy of the sea, Sam could feel the vitality of the ship coursing through his bones. He looked up at the mast, where the lookout was perched, scanning the horizon. The sound of the waves crashing against the hull and the creaking of the lines and wood filled the air. It was the symphony of the sea.

Sam and the others continued to work to store the lines. The ship picked up speed. They had successfully pulled the ship out of its berth, and it was now sailing into the open sea. Sam wiped the sweat from his brow and took a deep breath of the salty sea air. He looked out at the horizon, wondering what adventures lay ahead on this journey. As the ship sailed into the night, Sam felt a thrill of excitement and anticipation in his chest.

The boys walked to the front of the forecastle. The wind blew in their faces. Gradually, the ship picked up speed. Sam realized this was the fastest he had ever traveled. The rain picked up, and so did the seas.

The boys returned to their birthing below. They got ready for bed. They washed their hands and face with water from a bucket. The ship's roll increased as they cleared the bay and entered the open sea. They had to brace themselves on the wall as the ship tilted back and forth. Sam and Augie didn't feel well and started looking pale. Volkov came around, checking on the crew.

"Crewman Ekici and Macer, put your rain gear on. I can tell you're going to be seasick. Go to the aft weather deck and lean over the railing to throw up in the ocean. If you puke on the boat, you clean it up. Bereza brothers, how are you guys feeling?" Volkov asked.

"We're fine. It's not our first voyage," Ivan replied. Pavlo nodded and gave a thumbs-up. Volkov moved on to the next group. Dugan looked at Gunay, and he looked very pale as well. His face was sweating.

"Let's get your rain jacket on. I think you should follow Sam and Augie. Come around the corner and take human form," Dugan said as he helped Gunay get his coat on. Ivan recognized the Fae as they passed by in human form. Dugan and Gunay wore stocking caps to hide their ears. He understood they were magical beings, not insects, as Sam had warned. They appeared more formidable now. Indeed, they are much older than the boys. Dugan noticed him back. Pavlo also noticed Dugan and laughed to himself.

Dugan led Gunay to find a place to get sick on the rail of the aft deck. Sam and Augie sat on the bollards suffering from motion sickness. They took turns throwing up over the rail. Dugan and Gunay kept their distance and sat on the other side of the ship.

"I think I'm going to die," Gunay said as he hurled over the side of the ship.

"You'll be ok. Your body just needs to adapt. You should be fine in the morning. Here, drink some of this," Dugan said. He handed him a small bottle.

"What's this?" Gunay asked.

"It's rum. I borrowed a few pints from the kitchen," Dugan replied.

"Dugan, that's stupid. A pint might go unnoticed. Three pints are going to cause an investigation," Gunay said as he hurled over the side again.

"Just drink it and be thankful. It'll help you go to sleep. I'm going to give a bottle to Sam. Don't fall overboard," Dugan said. He walked over to Sam.

"Hey, shipmate, I see you and your friend are chumming for sharks. Have a drink of this. It will help you sleep," Dugan said. Sam looked up to recognize Dugan.

"Thanks, shipmate," Sam replied.

"Don't bring the bottle back inside. Instead, drink it and throw the bottle overboard. You don't want to get caught with it," Dugan said. Sam took a drink and coughed.

"Ha-ha, you're a sailor now. Learn to drink your rum, boy," Dugan laughed and returned to Gunay. Sam took another drink and passed the bottle to Augie.

***

Edric set out after breakfast. "Come on, Neval, let's get going," Edric said. The pair broke camp and continued their ride. They rode through the day, arriving at the base camp in the evening. The camp was on a hill overlooking the harbor. It rained as they arrived. They tied up their horses and went into the main tent. Neval reported to the Sergeant seated at a table in the center of the room.

"Sergeant Hasan, this is Sergeant Edric of the Forge," Neval said.

"Sergeant Edric, I'm sorry to say you're too late. The ship set sail last night," Hasan said.

"Can we go after them?" Edric asked.

"I have two Fae with Sam. If they take him someplace, the water elemental with him is to report back here. If the ship comes back and Sam is still on board. We can stage a rescue with you here. Our best bet is to sit tight and wait for one of those eventualities. You're welcome to stay. Neval make sure that he gets a bunk. Come join me for dinner," Hasan said.

"Thanks," Edric replied. He and Neval grabbed trays, got food, and returned to eat with Hasan.

"We need to send word to Princess Aysun that we were too late," Edric said.

"I'll send a messenger in the morning," Hasan said.

"Have them report to Captain Caria," Edric replied.

***

A few days later, Caria approached Aysun at dinner. She kneeled and Aysun motioned her up.

"Princess Sam's ship departed earlier than expected. Edric did not arrive in-time. He's remained at the camp overlooking the harbor to see if the ship returns. I'll start a rotation and ensure that there is a fire elemental there at all times," Caria reported in a Fae whisper.

"Aysun, what is it? Caria wouldn't dare come in here unless it's big news," Elnara asked. Caria nodded to her in acknowledgment. She felt awkward when she walked in as the aristocrats at the table fell silent as she walked in and headed to the head of the table. Caria heard the whispers of 'Troll Killer' referring to her. Caria left as quickly as she had come in.

"The rescue attempt failed to get Sam. The boat left earlier than expected," Aysun said.

"Aysun, I'm sorry. It's only a matter of time. We'll get Sam back," Elnara said. Aysun nodded back to her.

"Excuse me, your Majesty, I've lost my appetite," Aysun said as she excused herself from the table. Hannah gave Aysun her cane to walk with, and she followed Aysun back to the Princess's room. King Alexander stood up as she left.

"Excuse me, your Majesty, I should go look in on her," Elnara said. Elnara excused herself, and Mizzy followed her out. She went to Aysun's room and knocked on the door.

"It's Elnara," Elnara said.

***

"Come in," Aysun replied. Elnara entered with Mizzy. Aysun sat in a chair in front of the fireplace. Elnara sat in the chair next to her. Hannah poured a glass of wine for Elnara, and she refilled Aysun's glass.

"Let's go play cards in the parlor," Elnara said.

"I thought you didn't like being around the other court members?" Aysun asked.

"I don't like their gossip, but I like taking their gold. They're not really good at playing cards. Come on. You won't do yourself any good by sulking all by yourself. You girls can have the rest of the night off," Elnara said.

"Are you ok, Aysun? I can stay if you want me to," Hannah said.

"No, that's okay. You and Mizzy enjoy your evening. Thank you, Hannah," Aysun said. Mizzy and Hannah departed for the evening. Elnara grabbed the vodka bottle. She poured a shot for herself and Aysun.

"Let's go be bad, fairies! Let's go drink and take their gold," Elnara said.

"I don't know, Elnara. I think we should keep a low profile while we're here," Aysun replied.

"It's too late for that, Aysun. We're seated next to the King at meals. Caria publicly beat up the king's advanced weapons instructor. Our guards have to be reminded constantly to cover their ears. All the humans in the castle know who and what we are. We stand out. Come on," Elnara pleaded. She poured another shot of vodka for Aysun and herself.

"Shouldn't you be spending the evening with Marcus? I heard about your middle-of-the-night visit to Marcus," Aysun said.

"What are you implying, Aysun? I had a nightmare about Marcus. I went to Marcus for comfort," Elnara said.

"What was the nightmare about?" Elnara asked.

"I don't want to talk about it now. I'll tell you about it over cards," Elnara said.

"Does he know yet?" Aysun asked.

"Does he know what?" Elnara asked.

"That you're in love with him," Aysun said.

"I see what you're doing here. You're trying to change the subject, so we don't go to the parlor. I'm going to put my earrings on, and I'm going to the parlor to drink and play cards, with or without you," Elnara said. She got up to leave.

"Come on, Aysun. You need a distraction, and what better way to distract ourselves than by beating the court members at cards?" Elnara said with a mischievous grin on her face.

Aysun sighed, knowing that Elnara was right. She needed to take her mind off the disappointing news about Sam and focus on something else for a while.

"Okay, fine. Let's go play cards," Aysun said, a small smile forming.

"Fine, Elnara, you win, but get Caria and Emira. At least one of them should escort us. Otherwise, we'll never hear the end of it," Aysun said. Elnara bowed and left.

***

Elnara went to Emira's room. She knocked on the door. Emira opened the door wearing a dress. Emira kneeled.

"Princess Elnara, I wasn't expecting you," Emira said. Elnara motioned her up.

"What are you all dressed up for? You got a new boyfriend now that Edric is out of town?" Elnara asked.

"Of course not, Princess. Valeria, Caria, and I are going out. We're going to see a play in the city. Was there something you needed?" Emira asked.

"Yes, but I didn't know you had plans. Aysun and I are going to play cards in the parlor," Elnara said.

"You'll need to have a guard with you. I can cancel my plans and let Valeria and Caria go," Emira said. Emira picked up her sword. Caria entered the room and kneeled to Elnara.

"That's not necessary, Emira. You go with Valeria. I'll guard the Princesses," Caria said.

"Are you sure, Caria?" Emira asked. Valeria entered the room with a knock on the door.

"Yeah, you're the one that's excited to go and see it," Caria replied.

"What's going on here? Princess Elnara," Valeria asked Caria as she kneeled.

"I'm needed tonight. So, you and Emira go on without me. I'll see you both in the morning for training," Caria said.

"Ok, come on, Emira, we have to hurry," Valeria said.

***

As Aysun, Elnara, and Caria entered the parlor, an air of anticipation settled over the room. Caria introduced Aysun and Elnara to the assembled guests. The room fell into a sudden hush.

"Her Majesty Princess Aysun of the Moonlight. The Moon Goddess. Her Highness Princess Elnara of the Forge," Caria announced.

Everyone arose to acknowledge the Fae duo. They gave a polite applause. If it wasn't for the canes, the two of them would have fully strutted into the room. While healing well, Aysun's injuries still required some assistance. Caria stayed close in case she was needed until Aysun was seated at the card table.

Aysun and Elnara, adorned with intricate earrings, proudly displayed their Fae ears, a captivating sight for those in attendance. The room buzzed with whispers and intrigued glances as the guests marveled at the non-human features revealed openly for the first time.

Choosing different paths for the evening, Aysun joined a friendly game of Gleek, her presence adding an enchanting dimension to the cards. Meanwhile, Elnara, with an air of confidence, sought the challenge of high-stakes Primero. The game involved a combination of skill, strategy, and bluffing. Caria purchased a set of betting chips for Elnara.

Once again alive with the sounds of shuffled cards and quiet conversations, the parlor became the backdrop for an evening that promised both camaraderie and intrigue, with the Fae at the center of it all.

***

Several days later. Shamus waited for Princess Aysun to return from lunch. As Aysun approached her room, she noticed Shamus waiting for her. He kneeled to her as she came closer. "What is it, Shamus?" Aysun asked.

"The tunnel's set, Your Highness. The station's all wrapped up," Shamus reported, a glint of accomplishment in his eyes as he shared the news. Aysun walked into her room and sat in her chair.

"Thank you, Shamus. Hannah, go tell Caria and Emira to come here. Sebeli, go inform the King's valet we leave for the Great Tree in the morning after breakfast if he chooses to come with," Aysun said. A short time later, Hannah, Caria, and Emira came in and kneeled to Aysun. She motioned for them to stand.

"Caria and Emira, I am returning to the Great Tree, and you are both to escort me. I'm going to challenge General Emir and the Council of Generals for my right to ascend to Queen. So, select half of the guard here to accompany me back and leave the other half to protect Princess Elnara," Aysun said.

"Hannah, see that Elif and Tetyana are ready to return to the Great Tree tomorrow morning. Make sure they're packed. Let Elnara know we're leaving tomorrow," Aysun said. Hannah bowed and left.

3

⸎

Chapter Three: Return to the Great Tree

The next morning in Aysun's room the King and the other listened as Aysun explained the trip to come.

"Alex, that's everything. Your luggage and the rest of the Fae are already at the station waiting for us. Now, I need to blindfold you. Once that's done, I'll let the guards in the hall come in, and they will carry you to the station. Your blindfolds will be removed once you arrive at the station and you're seated. The three of you should relax and don't struggle. We don't want to drop you. Questions before your adventure begins?" Aysun asked.

"No, I think you covered everything, Aysun," Alex replied. Aysun blindfolded him. Emira blindfolded Valeria. Elnara prepared to blindfold Marcus.

"Fae girls are quite pretty. Keep your eyes to yourself, Marcus. See that I am the only Fae girl you're thinking about while you're there. I'll hear about it if you don't behave yourself," Elnara said.

"Your card games in the parlor have reached my ears. Reports of men attempting to seduce you away from me, particularly Count Fabius, have not escaped my notice," Marcus said.

"Petran? He's harmless. I let him get away with flirting with me a little if it keeps him at the table. Don't play cards against someone who can hear your heartbeat from across the table," Elnara whispered to Marcus. He laughed while she blindfolded him.

"Shouldn't I be blindfolded too?" Hannah asked.

"You're being accepted into Fae society. You've taken your oath. You should know the locations of the tunnels in case of an emergency. I can put a blindfold on you, or you could just keep your eyes closed if you're afraid to fly," Elnara explained.

The guards came in, and they shrunk Alex and Marcus. With a Fae on either side, they flew them out the balcony door. Sebeli followed them. They flew into the courtyard, then back over the castle to the park inside the inner wall. Caria and Emira shrunk Valeria down and followed them.

Aysun, Elnara, Hannah, and Mizzy exchanged hugs before departing. Two more Fae guards came in, grabbed Hannah, and shrunk her down. Aysun and the final set of guards left with Shamus.

"How scary is this?" Valeria asked. As they flew over the castle. Caria looked down.

"For a Fae, it's not scary at all. We just have to watch out for birds and walls. If I were a human and couldn't fly. I'd be terrified. You wouldn't survive a fall from this height," Caria replied.

Hannah looked down as they flew her over the castle. Hannah screamed in terror before she passed out.

"See, terrifying, and fair warning, the Goblin trolly is probably not much better, maybe worse. This will be the first time any of us have taken this line. It's newly opened. It's a good rule of thumb. The newer the tunnel, the wilder the ride," Caria said.

They flew to a stream near the pond in the park. There was a small footbridge. Underneath it was a section of piping that came out of the ground. The Fae flew inside.

***

The Goblin station was still under construction. Aysun flew over to where Malcolm stood near the ticket booth, which was still under construction. Shamus was delivered next to her.

"Malcolm, I didn't expect to see you here," Aysun said. Malcolm and other workers in the immediate vicinity kneeled to her. She motioned for them to rise.

"Princess Aysun, it's a pleasure to see you again. I've been promoted to head of the trolley union and appointed myself head of new construction. Everything's prepared for you. The trolley ride on this ain't as polished as most others. It's also deeper than any other tunnel, so there's a wee bit of a drop-off. It has to go under the castle wall and then under the river. When you get closer to the Great Tree, there are some sharp turns to get around the roots there. Oh, and I think it's time I return this to you," Malcolm said as he took a necklace from around his head. He removed the ring from the chain around his neck. Aysun had given it to him some years ago. He handed it to her.

"I don't think you need me to have this anymore, Your Majesty," Malcolm said.

"I don't suppose so. Thank you, Malcolm," Aysun said as she accepted the ring back and once again placed it on her finger.

"This is Shamus. He is the Palace Financier," Aysun said.

"Aye, we're related. He's my second cousin. Shamus," Malcolm responded, nodding in recognition of Shamus.

"Malcolm will undoubtedly serve the opposition well. Yet, I have a more pressing matter at hand. I wish for this route to be expanded to support a military campaign. The details matter little to me. I expect it completed well before the end of the Harvest season. Can I rely on you two to figure it out?" Aysun inquired.

"Yes, Princess," Malcolm replied.

"Of course, Princess," Shamus said as he bowed to the Princess.

"Malcolm, send the cost estimates directly to me, and I'll make sure payments are expedited," Shamus continued. Malcolm nodded in acknowledgment.

They loaded into two separate trollies. Tetyana sat alone in the second trolley as everyone else was loaded into the first. Aysun walked over to Tetyana. "This is the last step to get you back into Fae lands, but the trolley is a wild card. Have you ever ridden in one before?" Aysun asked.

"No, never," Tetyana replied.

"There is magic, speed, and darkness. I don't know how your elemental abilities will react. I'm told the ride is scary, but I'll ride with you but try to keep calm. Don't be offended if I am in Moon form.

Elif approached the second trolley. She kneeled before speaking.

"Princess Aysun, I'd like to ride with Tetyana too," Elif asked.

"We've told you she's dangerous," Aysun replied.

"That's why you can't ride next to me, Princess Aysun. You're too valuable to risk. Here, I'll go ride in the back. That way, Elif can ride with you. If I need to discharge, I can do it to the sides," Tetyana replied. She got up and moved to the back. Elif sat down with Aysun. She looked back at Tetyana.

"Hey, we're Lightning and Arrows, remember? We're going to be fine. Just be calm and let's have fun. They say it's scary. I say that means it's fun. Don't be afraid. Have no fear," Elif said.

"No fear," Tetyana repeated.

"No fear? I'm practically shaking in me boots. Bringing a lightning elemental into the city, for the love of all things! What could go wrong?" Malcolm grumbled, climbing onto the trolley and taking the driver's seat. Aysun couldn't help but burst into laughter.

"Don't worry, Malcolm. I'll shield you and the girl," Aysun positioned herself between Tetyana and the other two. Caria stood outside the trolley, looking confused.

"Go ride in the other trolley. God only knows how this plays out," Aysun said to Caria. Caria boarded the other trolley and sat next to Hannah. The King and Marcus had their blindfolds removed. Valeria refused to have hers removed, considering the warning Caria had given. After she had been revived, Hannah grabbed the blindfold from the guard. She returned to her seat and blindfolded herself. Emira sat near Valeria and Hannah.

"Valeria, don't worry, you don't have to be scared. If anything gets really scary, I'll be the first to scream, and nothing ever scares me," Emira said.

Valeria reached out for her hand. Caria looked over at Emira with a questioning gaze. Emira winked back at her. Caria smiled. The trolley pulled out of the station. It slowly gathered speed as they approached the castle wall. The trolley had to dive underneath it.

As they went over the edge, Emira screamed, followed by Valerie and Hannah, and then by Tetyana. Tetyana lit up the tunnels as she pumped massive amounts of electricity from her fingertips. Elif too screamed, but soon Tetyana could see that Elif wasn't screaming because she was scarred but because she was having fun.

Elif held her hands in the air as they dropped into the near darkness. Soon, Tetyana also enjoyed the ride. She lost her fear and powered down. She joined Elif in raising her hands as they dropped.

They went deeper still as the tunnels navigated under the river. Then they went through the twists and turns of the underground forest roots. It did a massive double barrel roll around some large roots. Emira screamed again before they went into the rolls. Finally, as they approached the station, Emira screamed again, followed by Valerie and Hannah.

"Just kidding, we're here," Emira said. She and everyone else laughed hysterically. Finally, the conductor pulled on the brake to stop the car. Valeria tore the blindfold off.

***

"Oh! I'm going to freaking kill you, Emira," Valeria said. Emira and Ciara laughed. Valeria slapped and pushed on Emira's shoulder.

"I'm going to be sick," Hannah said. Sebeli handed her a bucket. Hannah cried into the bucket.

"I want to go back and live in the forest," Hannah sobbed. Aysun came over to comfort her. Sebeli was already attending to her.

"You don't mean that. Come, put the bucket down. Let's get you home. The worst is over. Wait until you see your room," Aysun said.

"I get my own room?" Hannah asked. Aysun nodded and smiled at her. Sebeli came over and helped Hannah get stabilized and cleaned up.

As they exited the station, Alex, Marcus, and Valeria paused a moment and stood in awe at seeing thousands of Fae flying around. Ahead in the bustling retail district, the shops went up to dizzying heights. Tier after tier of bleacher-style layers of shops and restaurants stacked on top of one another. They kept going up ever higher. There was a walkway out front of each level and a system of lifts that moved between all levels. Each tier is beautifully supported by the story below. The engineering was remarkable with its cross beams and supports.

Ahead of them was a giant mural across from the station, just as Caria had described to Valeria. It depicted the girl's and Sam's first moments in the Great Tree. In a rather Norman Rockwell-like way. Aysun barefooted, attempting to hide her red-stained dress. Elnara looking more like a farm girl in her overalls and boots. Everyone kneeled before them.

"See, I told you it was here. It's pretty accurate. I was there. That's me on the right. Oh, but Sam didn't have the teddy bear he is holding. The artist took a little liberty with that. When you get to meet Sam, ask him about the teddy bear. He absolutely hates it. People always ask him if he still has it," Caria said as she laughed.

Valeria could see that under the images of Sam and Elnara, people left flowers and candles. Even the image of Aysun gathered a following of candles and flowers. Valeria understood that these were shrines hoping for their safe return. She reflected on her intrusion on Elnara and the story Caria had told her.

"It's impressive, all of it. Oh my God, look at your wings. They're so beautiful. I can't believe all of this is in a tree?" Valeria asked. Caria showed off her wings, setting them in motion as she lifted off the ground a few inches before settling back down. The translucent color of Caria's wings astounded Valeria. Valeria also admired Emira's wings.

Aysun handed her cane to Hannah. She crossed the busy street and went over to the base of the mural near where the impromptu shrine had been set up. Aysun tried not to show the pain of walking without a cane. She didn't want her people to see her as weak.

Aysun fought against the pain and tried not to limp. Aysun picked up a candle and a couple of matches from a vendor's cart. She offered a gold coin for the candle, but the vendor refused to take it. Aysun smiled and nodded at the vendor in appreciation.

She walked over to the shrine of her brother. The surrounding crowd was silent and parted the way as she made her way to a table below the image of Sam. Caria and Emira were close at her sides. Sebeli, Hannah, and the rest of the group stayed back by the vendor. Aysun put the candle on the table and lit it. She stepped back, kneeled, and lowered her head to pray. The crowd kneeled and prayed with her. She arose, and she addressed the crowd.

"Sam remains a prisoner, but Princess Elnara has been rescued," she said, and the crowd cheered. She stayed a couple of minutes and answered some questions. Caria sent Emira to go flag down some carts. Aysun and Caria gradually made their way back to the group.

"Caria, this is amazing. I have so many questions. I can't believe I picked a fight with a fairy. The King was right. We know so little about you. My mind is blown by seeing your city. Your technology must be so much more advanced," Valeria said.

"That is why this is called The Great Tree. This is the city proper, but the nation extends underground to many other towns and cities. That's all I should say for now. I need to ride with Princess Aysun. I'll see you all at her estate," Caria said.

She departed and got in the cart with Aysun and Hannah. Sebeli rode with Tetyana and Elif. Valeria rode with Emira. She noticed that all the Fae had wings except the occasional goblin. All were going about their daily lives. She saw two female Fae with elaborate dresses. Their skin was very pale. They stood out from the others.

"Those two seem strange," Valeria pointed out.

"I'm not sure," Emira replied. Emira looked back again at the pair. The pair stared back at her.

"Yeah, I agree. There is something off about those two. Next time I see them, I'll question them," Emira said. They pulled into the park district among many magnificent estates. They entered a private guarded gate. The walled estates were quite impressive.

***

"That is Princess Aysun's estate on the right, and the other is Princess Elnara's. Their mothers were sisters. They wanted their estates to be equal and their families to be close. Unfortunately, that ended in tragedy. However, our hopes were renewed now that the princesses have returned," Emira explained. The houses were quite large and regal, yet warm and inviting. Aysun led the party into her house.

"Welcome to my home," Aysun said.

Aysun instructed everyone to get settled in. Sebeli organized the effort. Handmaidens and maids showed everyone to their respective rooms. Aysun pulled Marcus aside.

"Elnara wanted you to have unlimited access to her estate. Once we get people settled in, lunch will be served. After that, I can take you over there and let Elnara's staff and security know you have full reign of her estate. After that, if you wish to stay there, you may, or you can stay here," Aysun said.

"I'll go over there and look around, but I'll stay here with everyone else," Marcus replied.

***

Later that afternoon, after a lavish lunch, Aysun and Emira escorted Marcus over to Elnara's house. Aysun's house had been classically Western and conservatively decorated, but in comparison, Elnara's house favored a blend of Arabic and Indian décor. It had luxurious plush seating areas on the main floor and beautiful chandeliers. Aysun introduced Marcus to the staff.

"She has so much seating all around. Some rooms remind me of some of the parlor rooms at court," Marcus said.

"Yes, Elnara is quite the socialite. She hosts charitable fundraisers and frequently holds parties here. You can see she started constructing a recent addition to add a large area for ballroom dancing with a large pit for the orchestra. I think she's mad sometimes with her crazy ideas. She has a genuinely nice billiard room down the hall. I'm having mine renovated to imitate hers," Aysun said.

"Emira will stay here with you in case there is anything you need. I think I'll go gauge your king's skill at billiards back at my house. Join us when you're done here," Aysun said.

"Thank you, Princess Aysun," Marcus said as Aysun left.

"Are you here to babysit me or guard me?" Marcus asked Emira.

"Neither. I'm just here if you need something or you have questions. Other than Aysun, Caria, and Sam, no one knows Princess Elnara better than me. Outside of my duty towards her and the royal family, she is also my friend. I've spent many nights with her, reading and laughing over a glass of wine. So, unless you need something or have a question, I'll be in the library reading until you're ready to return to Princess Aysun's house," Emira said. Marcus nodded.

Marcus strolled throughout the estate. Emira had the staff make tea for her and Marcus. He drank his tea as he admired her tapestries and paintings. Marcus took great interest in Elnara's training room and extensive weapons collection. She had an entire wall with weapons of all sorts mounted on it. Another wall was covered in Elnara's sword competition awards and trophies. Grand Champion: The Great Tree, Enchanted Vineyards, Misty Moors, Whispering Woods, Emerald Serenity, and many other places Marcus had never heard of. The awards were beautiful and often encrusted with jewels.

Finally, he found himself in her bedroom. It was a magnificent affair. She had a luxurious golden-framed bed. The ceiling was painted with scenes of angels and a blue sky. All are surrounded by decorative etched gold. Lavished layered drapes decorated the many large windows. The floors were beautifully inlaid wooden floors.

The Fae clearly possessed superior artisanship in many regards. In the corner of the room, was an intimate sitting area. Marcus went to the table and opened a drawer. He found Princess Elnara's diary. Marcus sat down. He flipped to the last entry. Elnara had written:

> *Aysun and Emir surprised me at dinner tonight and announced my mission to find my mom and dad. I'm so excited, I should never have waited this long. Mom was spotted at the bank, of course. Dad is probably running it. I should have gone after my last birthday when I came of age. Aysun wanted me to finish my master's rating with the Dao sword before Master Wing left, and it's always 'not safe.'*
>
> *I asked Sam to go fishing with me tomorrow. I have so many fond memories of fishing with my dad. Hopefully, I'll catch some. I can't wait to bring my parents back here for a grand feast. I miss them so much. They won't even believe the feast I'll have prepared for them. Their daughter, the fairy princess. Ha-ha! I'll plan a grand ball in their honor.*

Marcus put the book back where he found it. He didn't realize that when he met Elnara's mother, she must have just learned of her father's death, yet she didn't show any signs at dinner. Marcus had not even thought to ask. He returned the diary to the desk despite his urge to read more.

Marcus poked around the lighting and the plumbing a bit. He was quite amazed by everything. Marcus then returned to Aysun's estate with Emira. He rejoined Aysun and the king in the billiards room.

*****

In the morning, Aysun traveled to the palace and placed guards at the entrance to the throne room. General Emir entered the palace a short time later and went to the throne room. Caria was there to greet him. Others who had arrived before him were waiting outside.

"Captain, what's the meaning of this?" Emir asked.

"Princess Aysun has returned. She is waiting for you inside. Please come with me, General," Caria replied.

"Why was I not given advance notice that the Princess was planning to return?" Emir asked.

"All I can say is that I am following her orders, sir," Caria said as she escorted him into the throne room. He approached Aysun and kneeled. Aysun wore the crown and wore her full royal cape. She didn't make a motion for him to rise.

"Your Majesty," Emir acknowledged

"Major General Emir, I'm prepared to demand my right to ascend; however, Princess Elnara has begged me to attempt a diplomatic solution first. She and I do not want to put a wedge between our adoptive Fae family. However, I have pledged military support for the humans at Seaside," Aysun said.

"The Goblin and Orc forces are planning a massive attack. I have given my pledge directly to their king. I know you would have opposed this if I had sought your counsel. Please help me solve this situation so I can honor my pledge. Elnara and I owe the humans our lives. You may rise," Aysun said.

"You're right. If you had sought my counsel, I would have told you to stay out of human affairs. However, there is no direct threat to the Great Tree, so you cannot ask for the right to ascend. The Generals would vote that down," Emir replied.

"If the Goblin and Orc army establish a foothold here again, it will reignite the Goblin Wars in this region, so I see this as a direct threat to the Great Tree. The resignation of any generals on the council can be demanded should they oppose me. If we cannot come up with a solution. My next move will be to march them in here, one by one," Aysun stated.

"So, you've thought this through. Let me get some coffee so I can think this through," Emir said as he retreated to his usual table. He waved Caria over, and he discussed the situation with her privately. He then re-approached Aysun.

"Princess Aysun, I am prepared to support your pledge to the humans, but I have some conditions," Emir said.

"I'll hear them," Aysun replied.

"First, no significant shifting of troops from the war in the north. Like you, I have committed troop strengths to our Fae allies. Second, I will not support the drafting or conscription of those unwilling to fight. Lastly, the Council of Generals is consulted before you make any further military decisions or commitments. If you agree to those terms, I am prepared to offer you my vote. I can also offer some options for how to increase the number of available troops. When is this attack to occur?" Emir asked.

"The second week after the start of the Harvest festival. How many troops would that give us?" Aysun asked.

"Maybe five thousand if I called in the reserves. We could also call for volunteers. That's almost three months away; therefore, there would be time to train incoming troops. The window is small, but it is there. Do you see this as a protracted campaign?" Emir asked.

"Not if we ambush their ambush. I have a counter-offensive plan. If successful, I believe we could cause their entire plan to collapse. Then, we can push them into the sea," Aysun replied.

"I could start rotating some elite troops in from the front, so I would say we could commit to around seven thousand troops," Emir replied.

"Send word to Queen Shey and any of our allies who are not fully committed to the war in the north. Ask for their aid. We need fighters, and we need weapons, and we'll need logistical support," Aysun said.

"Let's not get ahead of ourselves. I'll need to confer with the counsel of generals and get their support. You realize that our government is set up the way it is to prevent a dictatorship. Queens earn their titles and return military authority once the threat has passed. They keep the title as a sign of respect. If you had gone through with your plan, you would have eventually been deposed and likely banished. This is why the civilian police report to our government's judicial branch, not to you or the military. The only way you could try to stay in power is through fear and force. Eventually, you would lose the people's support and the military's respect and support. So, Princess, you have to ask yourself what kind of leader you want to be?" Emir asked.

"Well, thankfully, I have excellent advisors with you and Elnara. I want to be the kind of leader that serves her people with honor and dignity," Aysun replied.

"Promise me whatever the council decides, you'll abide by their decision," Emir said.

"I promise I will be on the frontline with or without the Fae army. I will be there, and Elnara will be there. We will be there fighting with our guard only if necessary. You may wish to inform the council of that. That they do not control," Aysun said.

"They will ask for you to retreat to the Great Tree," Emir stated.

"Elnara cannot, so I cannot," Aysun responded.

"Well, don't get discouraged before I've had a chance to ask. Please give me a couple of days. I have a good idea of whom I'll need to convince. This should come out as my idea. You reported the intelligence to me, and I came up with the idea to launch a pre-emptive attack. You came up with a suggested battle plan. It would be best if you were prepared to present the plan in a couple of days. Agreed?"

"Agreed, thank you, Emir," Aysun said as she came over and hugged him.

"How is Princess Elnara?" Emir asked.

"She's been badly beaten, so she is undergoing treatment for the scarring. If she shrank now to return, she couldn't return to human form," Aysun replied.

"What's so bad about that? You two are Fae, and your lives belong here. If Princess Elnara hadn't gone to the human world, none of this would have happened in the first place," Emir said.

"It's a little more complicated, and we are half-human. She's met someone, a human. She was also just reunited with her mother. Elnara is not sure if she wants to stay in their world or not," Aysun said.

"Princess Sarah is her mother and your aunt! She can't stay with the humans. It would be a tragedy all over again. The nation would suffer. You must order her to return," Emir said.

"I can't do that to her, but I agree with you. I think our lives are here now. If you try to force Elnara to do something, she'll do the opposite just to spite you. I'll try to encourage her when the time is right, but for now, she is stuck there. You might want to make sure the council really understands that," Aysun said.

***

The next day, after breakfast, Emira took the King, Valeria, and Marcus on a city tour. They shopped and had lunch on the fifth-tier layer. Emira and Valeria sat at a table in front of a café overlooking the expanse of the Great Tree. Emira didn't want to take them much higher since they couldn't fly. Valeria could see how everyone stared at them, not having wings and human ears. They stood out. She and Emira enjoyed a coffee. Marcus and the King admired the view high over the expanse of the Great Tree. This was a bustling metropolis.

"Valeria, you should come over here and take in the view," Marcus said. He and Alex stood at the railing.

"I'm ok over here. I've had enough of heights for a lifetime," Valeria replied. Emira laughed.

***

Aysun boarded the trolley with Caria and Elif. Aysun wore a simpler outfit. They returned to the meadow and went to Elif's house. Elif ran inside first. "Mom, Princess Aysun is here," Elif yelled into the house. Aysun and Caria waited on the porch. Elif returned with her mother. She kneeled, and Aysun waved her up immediately.

"Princess Aysun, I wasn't expecting you. You didn't have to come to bring Elif back yourself," Elif's mother said.

"That's ok. I wanted to apologize for keeping her longer. Once they arrived, I was told a tunnel was opening soon nearer to the castle. I figured it was safer to wait to have her return that way. Here I wrote her a note for school," Aysun said as she waved for her to stand and handed her the note.

"Thank you, Your Majesty. It's ok. I knew she was safe with you and Princess Elnara," Elif's mother replied.

"It smells delicious. What are you making?" Aysun asked.

"Chicken and dumpling soup. It's ready if you want to come in and have some?" She replied.

"I wouldn't want to impose," Aysun said.

"It would be my honor, and I made plenty. Come on in," Elif's mother said. She escorted them in.

"Mom, Princess Aysun said I can come to her house anytime, as long as it's okay with you. So, I can go over there and play with Princess Tetyana," Elif said.

"Princess Tetyana? I don't understand," Elif's mother asked.

"Tetyana is a young lightning elemental. We rescued her from the prison, and I plan to adopt her. She and Elif are close in age, and they seem to get along," Aysun replied.

"Aren't they dangerous?" She asked.

"She is still young, so she is still learning to control her ability. As long as she is just in the house, I believe the risk is pretty minimal. Elif knows she cannot touch her. You are certainly welcome to come and supervise any visits. I'll welcome you to my home also," Aysun explained.

"That is indeed an honor. I'm sure we can see how it works out," Elif's mother replied.

"I'll have passes made up and delivered to you. That will give you access to pass through the gate security and come up and knock on the door. We are having dinner tonight at the governor's estate. Why don't you two come along?" Aysun asked.

***

Later that evening, at the Governor's estate. Aysun sat in the living room talking to the other guests. Elif and Tetyana ran around playing.

Sebeli and Hannah helped Letty in the kitchen. Caria and Emira helped set the table.

"Alex, how was your tour of our city?" Aysun asked.

"Fantastic. Emira is quite the tour guide. We toured two museums and did some shopping. I loved the ability to be able just to tell them to bill it to your palace. Thank you for covering our expenses," the King said.

"Think nothing of it. You covered our every expense the whole time, while Elnara and I recovered. We're incredibly grateful to you," Aysun said.

"I really enjoyed the Royal Museum. I was fascinated to read about your family history going back so many generations. Your mother and great-grandmother are quite the heroines. I feel bad for the housing I provided you back at the castle and the lack of staff. I should have done better. I'll ensure that you have accommodations more closely suited to what you're accustomed to," Alex said.

"Please don't. Our accommodations are fine. I'm the seventh generation of the Moonlight. I haven't had the full museum tour, but I was taught Fae history in class. Caria dragged me into the museum when I first arrived, but just briefly," Aysun said.

"I spoke to my lead general yesterday. Thankfully, he supported my position to support you. I had to make some concessions, but I believe it worked out for the best. I still have to wait for a final decision from the Council of Generals," Aysun said.

"What concessions did you have to make?" Alex asked.

"We would not pull any troops from existing military commitments. I leave the military in charge and only function as an advisor," Aysun replied.

"Does that mean you do not ascend to becoming queen?" Alex asked.

"I only got the abbreviated version of Fae law since I came here. It seems safeguards are in place to prevent a princess from ascending and asserting autocratic rule. I should have known better, so no, I won't be queen," Aysun said.

"I understand even my grandfather established our government as a constitutional monarchy. It is important to have a democracy to represent the people. I'll understand if your council does not vote to support our aid," Alex replied.

"Regardless, I'll honor my pledge. I'll call for volunteers and finance it all myself if I have to. The only question is how much aid I will be able to provide," Aysun said.

Valeria sat next to Caria and Emira. Marcus sat next to Valeria, and on the other side sat a new Fae, then Tetyana and Elif.

"Marcus, Valeria, this is my younger cousin, Miray. She just finished her officer training," Caria introduced her.

"It's very nice to meet you. I've never met humans before. You look funny with those tiny ears. Should I talk louder? Is it weird to not have wings? Sorry, I don't mean to be rude. Caria says I need to learn to speak before I think. I mean, think before I speak. She says I'm a force of nature. I apologize if I have said something wrong," Miray said. Caria and Emira chuckled. Miray was embarrassed.

"Not at all. If you fight like Caria, then you are a force of nature," Marcus said. He looked over past Miray and noticed Tetyana working on a small piece of jewelry.

"I'm supposed to apprentice under Lieutenant Emira when she'll have me as a student," Miray replied.

"You're fine, Miray. We've had our stumbling blocks in communication between the Fae and humans. We find your ears just as strange, and we've never had wings, so we don't really know what we're missing," Valeria said. She continued to speak with Miray, but Marcus was more interested in what Tetyana was working on.

"What's that you're working on?" Marcus asked.

"It's a charm for a friendship bracelet. I'm making one for Elif and one for me. This is a charm to hang on the bracelet. It's a lightning bolt with a quiver of arrows," Tetyana replied as she handed the piece to Marcus. The work was exceptional.

"Princess Elnara told me you were studying to become a gem cutter like Sam. What else can you make?" Marcus asked.

***

The next day, Aysun took the group on a tour of the meadows. Aysun and Caria grew Alex, Valeria, and Marcus to full height. The town within the meadows was bustling with people. Alex was quite shocked at the sight. He looked around the edges of the meadow. It was surrounded by naturally occurring rock walls. It had an enormous pasture that went on beyond the stables. Farms dotted the landscape. The meadow was located inside a dormant caldera.

"Princess Aysun, you can't tell me this is not in my kingdom," Alex said.

"I can't answer that. You know the seriousness of that question," Aysun stated.

"Yes, yes, I know, but hear me out. If these are within my lands, I can gift them to you, and you can take control of them legitimately. I can make you a royal. You will be Duchess Alexandra Ekici or Aysun Ekici if you prefer. I can extend a similar title to Princess Elnara. That is the highest title that can be granted outside my family. She could be a Marchioness or Duchess Sachin. You can shut off your lands from human settlement and incursion. I think that would serve the interest of the Fae," Alex proposed.

They walked over to the café where Aysun had eaten when she first arrived. The staff immediately kneeled to her and cleared the table for her party.

"Why the sudden interest in giving the Fae land? The Fae have always lived in secret," Aysun said.

"Princess Elnara had asked about owning land, so I thought, what better way to establish permanent diplomatic relations," Alex said.

"I could grant you this land and the land around the Great Tree," Alex said.

"It's an interesting proposal, but it's unprecedented. Not something I could make a quick decision on. I'll have to make some consultations. I'll give your offer serious consideration. Now let's eat," Aysun replied. Dinner was served.

***

The next day, Shamus and Caria escorted Aysun to the military office complex. She met up with Major General Emir, who escorted her into the meeting. Caria announced Aysun. The generals and their staff kneeled as Aysun entered. Aysun laid out the materials she brought to present. Then she steadied herself at the head of the table.

"Generals, staff, ladies, and gentlemen. You may rise. Major General Emir, please let me know what I can contribute?" Aysun said.

"Princess Aysun, from your report to me. As you suggested, I have recommended supporting the humans against the upcoming invasion. You also indicated that there was a potential counterstrategy. I wish for you to propose that plan to the generals here," Emir requested.

Aysun unfurled a map of the king's castle and the surrounding areas. Outside the castle walls, to the west, was a forest. To the north are the tournament grounds, with a small dirt road leading toward the sea. East of the castle, there is a small patch of forest before reaching the river, which flows out of the mountains. To the south of the castle was the road leading to the house where they had built the mine.

"The orcs are planning to invade along the northern coast from the east. They'll pose as a human caravan coming for the Harvest festival when the moon is in its darkest phase. Two separate armies will march on the west and south gates. They are just a distraction from their plans at the north gate. They'll try to walk right in, and when they have sufficient numbers, they'll secure the gate to keep it open. While they flood in, causing chaos. They are planning a slaughter. If they cannot get a foothold in the north entrance. They are prepared to lay siege. They have three supply lines and a source of fresh water nearby, but that is where my plan comes in," Aysun explained. A general interrupted her.

"Princess, thank you for this information, but I think this is where you should leave this with the military, and we can keep you informed of our decision. This is not about parlor games and pageants. You can let us handle this," the General said with a chuckle. Aysun looked around the room at the other generals, and some chuckled with him.

Aysun's eyes glowed white as she spoke. She exerted her force on the table, cracking it.

"I wasn't done speaking. This isn't a social gathering. You will speak when I permit you to, and you'll show me the proper respect. If you interrupt me again, I'll make you wait in the hall like a child. If you ever condescend to me like that again. That will be the end of your military career. Do you understand what I have explained to you, General?" Aysun asked angrily. She stared at him darkly with the look of someone who had dealt out death. He recognized the icy stare from his days in the war. The General kneeled.

"Yes, Your Majesty. I apologize for the offense," he replied.

"You may rise. Your apology is accepted. This is a fair warning to you all. I am on a mission to get my family back. I know how you see me. A silly young half-human, but I am in no mood for games or insults. I'm not that young girl in the painting out there anymore. My brother is still a prisoner, and those orcs are another obstacle to getting him back. So, you'll hear my proposal. If you have a better plan, fine, we'll do that. You are the council. It's ultimately your decision, but you will hear me out now, so if I may continue," Aysun said as she looked around the room. No one was laughing anymore.

"My plan is to attack their supply lines. They have two routes by sea. First are the merchant fleets at the port city. We'll reach out to each captain coming or going into the harbor, letting them know if they have any cargo or troops going to aid the invaders. Then, they will be considered enemies of the Kingdom of Seaside and subject to sinking or seizure. The humans will take those warnings and deliver them. We will have every available water elemental sent with them to enforce the blockade. The other sea route is an old pier much closer to Seaside Castle. It's in poor shape. They plan to fix it the week before the attack. That way, they can move everything into position to supply the frontline troops. As well as deliver reinforcements," Aysun said.

"They have a fleet of six to eight galleons, which they will use to convoy supplies to the front directly. We'll let them repair the dock. The first two ships to arrive will be allowed to dock. After that, any vessel attempting to dock or supply the troops will be sunk or captured," Aysun said.

"The last part of my plan involves the water source. The large pond is located in the forest to the west. We are going to deny them access to the pond. Defensive positions will fortify it against use by the enemy. We will clear a road across the width of the forest. The road is not meant to be used as a road but as a firebreak. We'll set fire to the woods on the north side of the road. We'll use pitch to ensure the forest burns quickly. The clearing will also give them open ground to cross, making easy targets for our archers. At the same time as that offensive begins, the third aspect of the plan will be set in motion. To have all fire elementals and human archers attack the convoy with pitch and fire arrows. We'll have the archers on horseback to launch a surprise attack along the coast. Eliminating their supply line," Aysun said. She took a breath before continuing.

"We'll deny them fresh water, supplies, and sanctuary. That leaves them with only two options: retreat or attack. I now open the topic for questions," Aysun said. She took a seat. A general rose and applauded, followed by another and then another. Major General Emir stood up. When the applause subsided, he addressed the group and the Princess.

"Princess Aysun, thank you for sharing your presentation. I think your plan is a sound one. May I ask, why leave them any ships at all?" Emir asked.

"Even a cornered rat will fight. So, give them a way out and let them scurry away," Aysun replied. Emir responded with a nod and retook his seat; another general rose.

"Why not just fill the pond with salt? Orcs can't drink salt water any more than we can. That way, we do not have to divide up our forces. If they see there is no chance to penetrate into the castle, they may change their objective. Then they will put all their effort into gaining access to the pond to support their siege," the general asked and sat back down.

"It's a valid tactic, General. However, I am not comfortable with it.

I could only see it used as a last resort. I would not give that order to implement it. As Fae, we are obligated to protect nature, not weaponize it. If they change their tactics and go for the pond, we'll send the cavalry in to cut them down on the fire break road," Aysun replied.

"Thank you, Princess, but isn't burning the forest weaponizing nature?" the General asked.

"Fair point, but forests burn all the time. It's part of nature. I'm only proposing we burn a section of it. The forest will recover. Ponds don't salt themselves. The pond will not recover if we salt it. Everything in it will die. It may also contaminate the drinking water for Seaside," Aysun explained.

"Of course, thank you, Princess," the General replied.

"Are there any more questions for Her Majesty?" Emir asked. There was no response.

"Princess Aysun, again, thank you for all the intelligence data you have provided and your excellent battle proposal. We'll adjourn and meet again after lunch," Emir said. He and the rest of the Generals stood and applauded.

"Princess, you are welcome to return, but the rest of what we have to discuss is just logistics, and then bring everything to a vote," Emir said.

"Can you give me a report tonight at the Governor's house? There is another matter I need to discuss with you?" Aysun asked.

"Yes, I can come there. I also wanted to discuss another matter with you, but it can wait until tonight. I'll see you then," Emir replied.

"Until tonight," Aysun said as she departed.

***

Later that evening, Aysun, Taner, Emir, Shamus, and Alex sat at the table.

"King Alexander has offered the Fae land in the human realm. He would grant me and Princess Elnara titles that would pass the land down our family lines. So, it always stays under our control. To obtain this, we would have to exchange the relative location of our lands. I think that the expansion of the human population will eventually compromise our security. If we owned the land legally, then we could take control of our security. What do you think?" Aysun asked.

"I'm uncertain what kind of precedence this might set with the other nations. They might see the move as reckless. We ought not to be making this decision in isolation," Shamus cautioned.

"I think legally we are safe to do it, as long as we don't point it out specifically, then they don't know precisely how to find it. I can consult some of our attorneys to confirm," Taner said.

"What do you think from a military and security perspective, Emir?" Aysun asked.

"I think narrowing down our location increases our risk of discovery; however, if we could enclose the nation or a good portion of it behind the walls of a base or an estate, that could have multiple benefits. So, yes, I think we could support disclosing our general area. In addition, I think we should discuss the land we are farming in the meadow and outside the meadow. I assume disclosing that would not violate Fae law?" Emir asked Taner.

"No, I don't believe so. The farms outside the meadow pay taxes to the kingdom. The ones in the meadow do not," Shamus responded.

"May I ask why do they not pay taxes?" Alex asked.

"They pay taxes to the Princess. The meadows, you see, are a fair bit removed from the surrounding lands," Shamus replied.

"So, there is no way in or out other than your tunnel system?" Alex asked.

"There is another way in, but it's well hidden. Only one human ever stumbled upon the meadows by accident, and that stirred up quite a commotion. That access point is now guarded, mind ye," Shamus replied.

"What happened to the human?" asked Aysun.

"We burned him alive and ate him. We had to set an example," Shamus stated with a grave gaze in his eye. Aysun glanced at Alex, and he returned the look, his features perplexed. The moment hung awkwardly in the air. Soon enough, the other fellas around the table burst into hearty laughter.

"Do you not have a clue who it was? Here's a wee hint for you. His name was Adem," Shamus chuckled, adding a mischievous touch to the revelation.

"Oh, I see. I thought our diplomatic situation was about to get complicated. I assumed my mother met him in the human world," Aysun said. She blushed as she realized the joke was on her.

"Sebeli, come in here, please," Shamus requested as he called into the kitchen. She entered the room, drying her hands.

"Sebeli, how have you not told Princess Aysun how her parents met?" Shamus asked. Sebeli went around the table and topped off everyone's wine glass.

"If she had asked, I would have told her. Well, if you've already started telling the story, finish telling it," Sebeli replied snootily.

"Yes, please do," Aysun requested.

"Well, ye see, he'd barely taken a stroll for a couple of minutes before they nabbed him. He had a proper fright in his eyes as they shrank him down to fit the trolley station. I heard he screamed almost as loud as your human handmaiden," Shamus recounted, his Irish accent infusing the tale with a vivid touch of storytelling. Everyone laughed.

"Hey, I'm sitting right here," Hannah called out from the living room.

Shamus told the story of how the human was introduced to Princess Nuray, who disliked humans because they worked with goblins during the war.

"Having already taken the lives of a handful of humans herself, the Princess was leaning towards taking his life for the intrusion. Yet, I stepped in and swayed her to spare his fate. Adem was cast away to dwell within the bounds of the Great Tree. A punishment that sucked the very hope from his soul. He wasn't granted passage on the trolleys, seeing how he posed a risk of fleeing," Shamus elaborated.

"That would have been a death sentence for my father. He only came into the house to eat and sleep. If he wasn't farming, then he was hunting or fishing. So, how did he get by?" Aysun asked.

"He was granted a stipend and a wee apartment but wore a face of sorrow. He tried looking for employment, but no soul would take him under their wing. She kept an eye on him well through me, of course. Slowly, the reports darkened. He'd started drinking and gambling. The other gamblers would lay blame on the human for their ill luck. He ended up in a couple of tussles, which didn't end well for him.

Adem descended into the depths of depression. Then came a report, suggesting he might be entertaining thoughts of harming himself. He'd bought a length of rope, naught else. That's when your mother took him before her for the second time. She'd become queen by then, amid the war, but she made time to hear his tale. He'd been here two years, and yet not a single friend had he made.

Adem said the Fae scattered from him like a murder of crows fleeing a hawk as he walked the streets. He felt as if he carried the burden of a murderer or a traitor when all he was guilty of was curiosity. Adem was treated with disdainful looks. Adem spoke of the fights, and how he was constantly bullied. Gambling wasn't his fancy, but he felt it was all he had. His education was scant, and he could hardly read, yet his charm shone through.

That night, your mother invited him to dine with her, and they shared a meal before her entire court. A rare honor that did surely alter folk's view of him. His humor made her chuckle so hard tears brimmed in her eyes. A touch flustered, but the two had a grand time together.

Adem pulled her out of her usually regal, stoic self. He left quite a mark on her. Come, that morning she ordered that the restrictions on the trolley be lifted, so he could roam freely to the meadow. She also tasked me with purchasing' a proper patch o' land for him to build a home and till the soil. And she saw fit to employ him as an assistant accountant, a role I taught him," Shamus narrated.

"I'm sure he hated that. He would send me to Elnara's or Hannah's house if I needed help with my math homework," Aysun said with a laugh.

"He did, he did indeed, but he threw himself into his tasks with all his heart, and after a bit, we forged a bond. Adem truly treasured the opportunity to have a sense of purpose again. He didn't linger at my side for long. The moment that meadow house was fit for habitation, he moved right in. Adem called it his home for a couple of years as he and Queen Nuray kept sharing their meals, which grew into courtship. Yer father turned into one of the most renowned folks in the Great Tree," Shamus said.

"The Fae didn't scatter at his approach any longer. Restaurants would seat him at the best tables and not take a coin from him. He started making friends. Then, as fate would have it, Adem and your mother fell for each other, and the house where you live now was built. Adem didn't want the palace life. He gave Queen Nuray a bold choice: if she tried to make him move into that palace, he'd spend his time fixing it up, not minding who saw him at work," Shamus continued.

"As the houses neared their finish, the war came to a close. A grand wedding followed, and not long after, you were brought into the world," Shamus recounted, weaving the tale of Adem's journey with heartfelt detail. Shamus was noticeably saddened.

"If my father had a farm in the meadow, why did he move back to Farmer's Mill?" Aysun asked.

"I'm not rightly sure. I never asked him. He and Queen Nuray just made the move one day. I visited him a few times. The last time I saw him was to let him inspect Nuray's monument. I gave him the instruction to let you place the monument for your mother, as is our tradition. Many of us were there to watch, but we kept our distance. There's a painting of it somewhere in the palace. I'll make it a point to show it to you. It was your father's wish that you knew nothing about the Fae until you came of age. I reckon he maybe wanted to be closer to his human friends. Once they were wed, they split their time living here and there. Your mother loved farming. She did. I taught your father to play chess, while they wintered here," Shamus shared.

"Oh, so I have you to thank for that. We played all the time growing up. I taught Sam and Elnara how to play. We are still competitive playing with each other," Aysun said.

"I'd be delighted to have a game with ye. There's a game table in the great room. Are ye interested?" Shamus inquired, extending the invitation.

"Yes, but first, what did my father say to her that made her laugh so hard?" Aysun asked.

"I know it was a bit of a cheeky joke, but I asked him not to clue me in on the details. He mentioned it was something between them, anyway. Queen Nuray told me later that it was the fact he spoke to her like an equal that caught her attention. Unlike yourself, she only knew about being royal. No one would've dared to be so bold in her presence. He also shared that when he met with her, he felt like he had nothing left to lose, so he just spoke from his heart. So, shall we head over and have a game?" Shamus asked.

***

The next afternoon in Aysun's dining room. Aysun and the men from the previous night gathered to discuss the proposed lands. Taner had brought attorneys with him. Emir had brought military and civilian engineers. Alex was invited into the room after some discussion.

"Alex, we have a proposal. The lands here to the East of the river. The river and these roads would be our borders," Aysun said. She pointed out the details on a map. The map was spread out on the table.

"Most of these lands are woodlands, which are not normally granted. There is a portion of this land that is existing farmland. I can grant the woodlands. The farmland belongs to another lord," Alex said.

"Those farms are Fae farms already. Only the tax collector would change," Shamus said.

"I'll have to negotiate with the current lord, but I don't see this as a problem. Give me some time until I have his agreement," Alex said.

"I can't commit to anything until I hear back from the other nations. You should also realize that if we go forward, you'll be held accountable for keeping all of this a secret. If you leak any of this that leads to the Great Tree being discovered, you'll set in motion consequences I can't stop. That's not a threat coming from me. It's Fae law, and I am also subject to it. You have seen our city with your own eyes. Imagine what it would mean to us to evacuate everyone and burn it all to the ground. It would be best if you titled our human names, and no connection should be made between our Fae and our human identities. Not publicly or privately," Aysun explained.

"You will have the greatest care taken with this secret. You'll have the title of Her Grace Duchess Alexandra Ekici of Stormhaven. Princess Elnara will be Her Grace Duchess, Esra Sachin of Stormhaven," Alex said.

"Why Stormhaven?" Aysun asked.

"The woods you are asking for are named Stormhaven Forest. Please tell me if there is another name you prefer," Alex asked.

Aysun looked around the room. "Does anyone have any other suggestions?"

"I reckon it sounds grand to me, a name befitting Your Majesty, very elemental," Shamus said. It seemed there was agreement around the room.

"That name will be fine," Aysun confirmed.

"Very well. As soon as I get your approval, I'll legitimize the lands. Has there been any update on receiving military support?" Alex said?

"Emir, anything to report?" Aysun asked.

"Your plan has largely been accepted. It only remains to be voted on. Now, there are just some final discussions on how to bolster our numbers. There is also a debate on whether to salt the pond," Emir reported.

"What's this about salting the pond? Do you mean the pond in the center of the forest? I would say if it helps us in the battle, I don't have a problem with it," Alex said. Aysun stood up.

"I do. I have a problem with it! I thought I made myself clear to the council. Any Fae participating in that or ordering it would suffer corruption. I won't condone that for myself or any of our people. I'll defend the pond myself, against the orcs, and against any Fae attempting to dump salt in it," Aysun said.

"Princess, you will not be in command of the battle. I allowed you to lead the rescue because of your unique ability as a Cosmic Fae. Which had a very high success rate, but I cannot let you put yourself at risk on the front lines in this battle. You will be in the rear. All the General Council agreed with that. You were nearly killed. We won't risk that potential tragedy again," Emir said.

"Please give Major General Emir and me the room," Aysun said.

"I respectfully request to stay a part of this conversation. This is my kingdom; we're discussing, after all," Alex said. Aysun nodded. Caria and Emira escorted the rest of the people into the hall.

"Emir, I came here years ago and trained as a warrior. When I came of age, I was inaugurated as the leader of our people. When my leadership should matter, I have to defer to a council willing to commit an atrocity against nature. In your words, this is not a threat to the Great Tree. What makes you think we have the right to take that action in the human realm?" Aysun asked.

"What if the Fae don't do it? What if humans do? It is my land and my pond," Alex asked.

"I beg you to consider what we are discussing. This would not only make the water undrinkable. It would kill every living thing in and around the pond for decades, if not centuries. That area will be a dead zone in your kingdom," Aysun pleaded.

"Aysun, I understand your position. I also understand that the enemy will lay siege if our offensive fails. Eventually, they could breach the castle. That water cannot remain a viable resource for them. I respect your view on it, and I will only order it as a last option," Alex said.

"I respect that it is your right to decide, but if you do it. You will do so with my strong objection. My battle plan will not fail," Aysun said.

"I trust you, but it's better to have an option than none at all," Alex replied.

"Emir, I'll be damned if you think that you or anyone else can keep me from the front," Aysun said.

"You came with the intention of establishing yourself as queen. How many battles do you think queens in the past have participated in? The answer is zero. Well, nearly zero. If you want to lead, take command of the defense of the gate from behind the defensive lines. If you are beyond that, you are a target for the enemy and a distraction for all your people out there fighting. They're going to be worried about you and be distracted from fighting," Emir said.

"Fine, I'll take command of the gate," Aysun said. She sat down with a pout.

"There is another matter we need to discuss, Princess," Emir said.

"What's that?" Aysun asked.

"Lieutenant Emira must stand before a military tribunal and face up to the charges for fraternization. I must order all the members that were part of the rescue to return to the Great Tree so we can begin the investigation," Emir said.

"There are a couple of problems with that. First, Elnara will want to be present. She can't shrink down now. Two of the others are carrying out her sentence. So, they can't leave either," Aysun said.

"You can use the castle. There is a courtroom in the castle that's not in use. I can have it readied," Alex said.

"I'll let the judge and the council know. We'll plan to accompany you when all of you return," Emir said.

"I'm not returning," Aysun said.

"I thought you were coming back. We still need to finalize our arrangement," Alex said.

"I'll be of more value here. I can recruit volunteers. Plus, I need to see to Tetyana. She needs to get settled in. I'll return after I see to some things here. I'll be back before the tournament," Aysun said.

***

The following day, after breakfast. Sebeli and the staff cleared the table. Aysun and her guests were having coffee served.

"Sebeli, I need to take Tetyana to have a new prosthetic made for her. Can you go to the school and arrange for tutors for her? Can you also go talk to Fatima and see if she can't push the adoption paperwork through? Also, Hannah should begin her Fae education and combat training. Can you coordinate that with Shamus and General Emir?" Aysun asked.

"Of course, Princess," Sebeli replied.

"Princess?" Hannah asked with a questioning gaze.

"Yes, Hannah. Sorry, I probably should have warned you. You'll need to take some classes. There are some basics of Fae society you must learn about, our history and our culture. You'll also have to learn about Fae law, so you don't get into any trouble. Also, Fae receive combat training as part of their education. Even though you are an honorary Fae, you will still need to be trained," Aysun said.

"Of course, Your Majesty. That sounds fun, the combat training, I mean. Mizzy is going to hate it," Hannah replied.

"That reminds me. Alex, if we proceed with the Stormhaven project. Can you also see that Hannah and Mizzy are given titles of Countesses of Stormhaven? That would put them in the same standing as the rest of our handmaidens," Aysun asked.

"Of course, I'll see to it," Alex replied.

"Countess, does that mean I'm royalty?" Hannah asked with some excitement.

"Oh, I'm sorry. I didn't mean to speak out of turn," Hannah said.

"Hannah, this is your home now. Relax, you're not on the clock now. Your title is largely honorary, but you and Mizzy will be sent to take care of any human affairs associated with Stormhaven. Because you're human, you cannot hold any Fae title. You'll learn all this when you take the classes. In this house, your rank is my friend. So, relax. At court, it might be awkward for you. I doubt the other handmaidens will treat you as an equal, but they should address you by your title, even if it's a human one. If they mistreat you in any way, I am to hear of it," Aysun said.

***

At court the next day, Aysun tended to business. Having been away for so long, there was much to catch up on. Toward the end of the day,

Shamus came over and explained the next introduction. He made sure Aysun understood before allowing the petitioners into the room.

Caria stood behind Aysun, and Shamus gestured for Emira to take up a position behind Aysun as well. He handed Aysun a sealed letter of introduction for her to read. She broke the seal and opened the envelope. Aysun read the letter. Aysun motioned to the valet standing near the door to open the door. A pair of pale-skinned females entered the throne room. The same two Valeria and Emira noticed strolling through the Great Tree when they arrived.

"Countess Mathilde Ravencroft from the nation of Stonehenge, currently of the nation of the Enchanted Vineyard. Countess Veronica LaRue of the nation of the Enchanted Vineyard," the valet announced. Mathilde approached Aysun. Caria and Emira stepped out from behind Aysun. Veronica remained by the door.

"That's close enough, Countess," Caria said. The countess kneeled. Aysun motioned for her to stand. Veronica kneeled at her position by the door.

"It's rare to have a countess unexpectedly arrive at court, let alone two. What business do you two have here, and how may I be of assistance?" Aysun asked.

"Your Majesty, I've purchased a vineyard near the valley near here. I intend to manage it. My business partner and I already have a successful vineyard in the nation of the Enchanted Vineyard near Paris. My cousin Princess Marie reigns there. I wanted to announce my presence to Your Majesty and ask for your approval for me to reside in your lands," Mathilde asked.

"I know Marie very well. She attended my coronation. Marie insists on me calling her Auntie Marie; she's very sweet. According to your letter of introduction from her, there is more to the story. What more do you have to tell me?" Aysun asked.

"Yes, Your Majesty, forgive me. My business partner and I are, um, there is no easy way to say this. We have a condition that requires us to consume human blood to survive. We're vampires, as I am sure the letter says," Mathilde said.

"Vampires!" Caria said as she drew her axes and thrust herself forward in front of Aysun. Emira drew her short swords and did the same. The rest of the guards in the room also drew their weapons. Aysun's handmaidens next to Hanna pulled knives out from behind their backs. Hanna was startled.

"I knew there was something off about you two when I saw you earlier," Emira said. Veronica seemed to be annoyed by Emira's comments.

"Please hear me out. I am not a threat to the Princess or anyone else," Raven said as she kneeled again, demonstrating her submissiveness to the crown. Veronica appeared to find the display amusing.

"Stand down, Caria. Continue, Countess," Aysun said. Caria and Emira put their weapons away and resumed their position behind Aysun's throne.

"I came here for another reason. The medical school not too far from here is doing pioneering research on blood studies. I believe that I can find a source of nutrition for those infected like us that doesn't involve direct feeding," Raven explained.

"How did you become a Fae vampire? I have never heard of such a creature. I thought even human vampires were a myth," Aysun asked.

"Vampires exist. I do not know of any other Fae vampires other than myself and Veronica. Human vampires avoid us, but we are aware of them. I can sense them. We are stronger than they are because we are Fae. I can only say being turned is difficult. It's difficult to do and difficult to have done to you. So, I'm not surprised that there are not more of us," Raven replied.

"When did this happen to you?" Aysun asked.

"I was turned in the year 1348, but it happened even further back for her. My partner and I were afflicted with this illness unwillingly. I was twenty-five years old when it happened to me," Raven said.

"Who was your maker? Is she the one at the door?" Emira interrupted.

"Emira, you're out of line," Caria said.

"I'll allow the question. Who made you this way, Mathilde?" Aysun asked. Mathilde became noticeably uncomfortable.

"Um, forgive me, Your Majesty. I'm uncomfortable sharing exactly how we are made and who made us. Please forgive me," Mathilde said.

"I made her. She's mine! I drank her disgusting blood until she was dry as a bone. Then, I turned her. Tilly, my undead bride," Veronica called out from the back of the room.

"And who made you?" Aysun asked.

"Your Majesty, respectfully, that's my business," Veronica replied. Mathilde turned towards Veronica sharply.

"Don't be rude, and don't call me Tilly in public," Raven Fae whispered to her.

"Hurry and do whatever you need to do. Kiss her ring, and let's go! I'm hungry," Veronica whispered back. Aysun caught an echo and heard Mathilde.

"What should we call you then?" Aysun asked.

"I prefer to be called Raven, Your Majesty. I mean, my friends call me Raven. Please accept my apologies. I imagined this going much better. I've brought several cases of our best wines as a gift for you," Raven said.

"Countess Raven, please tell me how you've sustained yourselves. How many humans and Fae have you killed? Why should I overlook what you've done?" Aysun asked.

"You are as direct as my cousin, Your Majesty. As I said, this was not a disease of choice. The taste of Fae is unpleasant to us, so we don't target our kind. No Fae have died by my hands," Raven replied. Aysun looked over at Veronica.

"Just the one for me," Veronica said as she pointed at Raven. Raven continued.

"We must consume human blood. I've tried other sources. Nothing else is compatible. Our primary source is through donors or familiars we employ, the desperate, and the indigent mostly. We pay them to drain a little of their blood, but we don't need to kill them," Raven explained.

Veronica giggled in a fae whisper directed at Raven, but Emira also heard it. It sent chills down her spine. While Raven was sincere, she left out the fact that Veronica was not as restrained, sometimes hunting for the pure sport of it.

"When we kill to feed, we selectively target those who deserve it, never an innocent individual. We focus on murderers and other serious criminals. When I first became a vampire, we stayed in the heart of Paris. It coincided with the outbreak of the Black Death. The plague spread across Europe so fast that it was like the entire continent was on fire. We were immune to it, so feeding on the infected was a mercy. We've moved from city to city. Wherever we went, the plague slowed or stopped completely," Raven explained.

"What can you tell me about the origins of vampires?" Aysun asked.

"The origins of vampires are debatable. My understanding is that the original vampire was an angel named Lilith," Raven said. She looked back to see Veronica glaring back at her disapprovingly and shaking her head.

"You're speaking about too much, Tilly. Remember your place," Veronica said. Raven continued anyway.

"Lilith is the sword of God. His Reaper. She was the first. We perceived ourselves as her blades of justice, believing we were to serve him by ensuring the righteousness of humanity by culling evil, disease, and sin. To do God's work. Why else would we exist?" Raven paused to consider the question herself.

"I should take a step back. There are two versions of the story. In one version, Lilith, an original resident of the Garden of Eden, refused to submit to Adam. She abandoned the Garden of Eden to walk the Earth. So, God made a new plan for her. He chose her to be his reaper. His divine justice. In another version, Lilith was cast out of the Garden of Eden for failing to obey Adam and God. She was cast out in favor of Eve and was damned to roam the Earth as a Fallen Angel. Which of these versions is the truth? I don't know. I only know this is the story," Raven explained. This was an age-old debate between her and Veronica. One which Veronica was sick of.

Emira watched Veronica closely. Veronica rolled her eyes during Raven's story. She caught Emira's gaze. She became noticeably angered. This was the second time she felt Emira was trying to stare her down.

"If I catch you staring at me again, I'll tear your throat out, little bunny. Sleep," Veronica compelled her in a Fae whisper. The sleep command vibrated through the air before striking Emira. Emira lost her footing as her knees gave out. She grabbed onto the throne as she succumbed to the command. Raven and Caria rushed to Emira to see her safely to the ground. Caria caught Emira and looked off Raven, shaking her head. Caria attempted to keep her awake.

"Come on, Emira, don't let that vampire get the better of you," Caria said. Hanna brought over a cup of water and handed it to Caria.

Raven moved across the room in a flash. She drove at Veronica furiously. Veronica caught her arms by the wrists.

"Why would you do that? We traveled all this way. You always have to ruin everything!" Raven yelled. Veronica threw Raven to the ground with little effort. Raven was in tears. She raised her voice and yelled at Veronica as she picked herself off the floor.

"I need this! I need her sanctuary for my research. I don't want to be a killer anymore! Get out and wait outside. Now! Get out!" Raven screamed.

"Tilly, it was the guard who was rude. She should be told not to stare at her betters. I won't apologize for it. I do apologize for the scene, Your Majesty. You're always so cross with me lately, Tilly," Veronica replied. She bowed to Aysun and turned towards the door.

"Wait! You've attacked one of my guards in my throne room. That behavior is not acceptable. Leave the Great Tree and don't return until you've learned some manners. Countess, know I enforce the laws within my lands. Commit a murder here, and you'll find me in the darkness, and I'll exact justice," Aysun said.

"Message received, Princess," Veronica said as she bowed and left the room. Raven came over to Emira and said to Caria,

"The command to sleep is strong enough to have someone sleep through a bite. Spritzing water on her face is not enough. You'll have to let her sleep it off, slap her, or pour the whole cup on her," Raven said.

Caria looked at Raven and acknowledged the advice. She looked at Aysun to get her measure on it. Aysun shrugged her shoulders in deferment. Caria gave Emira a moderate slap across the face. Emira squirmed around as she attempted to wake up.

"Hey! What the... where's the vampire? Guards arrest her. She attacked me. Caria, did you just slap me?" Emira asked.

"If she attacked you, you'd be dead now," Raven replied.

"No sleeping. You're on duty. Come on, get up," Caria replied. Emira scrambled to her feet with Caria's help.

"Emira, I settled the matter for now. I doubt there's a cell that could hold her, anyway. Whatever they are, she accused you of staring at her, and she is a countess. Be more mindful in the future," Aysun said.

"That one is evil, and you didn't hear or see what I did, Your Majesty. That one is a monster. I'm sorry, Countess Raven, I don't sense that about you, but I have grave concerns about your business partner. You seem nice enough," Emira said.

"You can't judge us by your standards. Being what we are, surviving is all that we can do. It does not afford us any moral high ground. We're predators. Maybe someday, through my research, I can change that. I don't condone what she did, but that amounted to a warning. She's capable of a lot more," Raven replied.

"Let us continue our discussion. What's happened since Paris?" Aysun asked as they sat. She had a chair brought over for Raven.

"After the plague subsided, we couldn't stay in one place for very long. So, for the last one hundred and fifty years, we've traveled throughout Europe. I've increased sales for our vineyard. We visited many of the royal courts from Granada to Moscow. That's another reason I need to have this other vineyard. I can't keep up with the demand that I've created," Raven said.

"Over the years, I've also studied the sciences. I've studied medicine and the four humors. I know that somewhere, within the study of medicine, and some combination of chemistry, there must be a cure for my condition. It's just a matter of experimentation. I believed for a long time that I was doing God's work, but now I am not so sure. Maybe we are infected like a rabid rat, but I still believe we can serve the greater good," Raven replied.

"In your letter of introduction. It says in summary that Princess Marie has requested that you and Countess Veronica leave her lands. Not by banishment but by not being present during the investigation into some not-so-greater-good killings. What do you have to say to that?" Aysun asked.

"We were interviewed, and then my cousin suggested we take a vacation. Princess Marie has the right to conduct an investigation. It's her nation. She suggested it would be better for the investigation if Veronica and I were not around for a while. I chose to come here rather than return home," Raven said.

"As I said, there is some research going on near here. I don't believe we're evil. I have to believe that. We are infected with some form of disease like the plaque. I believe that someday, there can be a cure through my research. I've already proven that we can exist by blood extracted by medical means. This knowledge and technology are only bound to get better. I ask for your sanctuary so that I may pursue this knowledge and my commercial affairs," Raven concluded.

"Very well, you have it. What about Countess Veronica?" Aysun asked.

"She is not requesting sanctuary here. She accompanied me here at my request, but she'll return to France to attend to our business there," Raven replied.

"Does she always throw you around like that?" Aysun asked.

"Outside of murdering me, she has never been violent towards me. I know how this all must have looked, but I love her, and she loves me. We have been together for a very long time. I attacked her, so it was my fault. She was defending herself. I suppose I got off easy. It's a matter we'll settle in private. She has a way of ruining things. That's one reason we have to move around so much. I think another reason I want to have this vineyard is so I can have someplace to go to have some time alone. A hundred and fifty years is a long time to be together," Raven replied.

"Is she responsible for the killings your cousin is investigating?" Aysun asked.

"I would never betray Veronica like that. We're vampires, bodies tend to appear wherever we go. My first victim, when I was turned, was a well-off, respectable gentleman. A pillar in the community. Veronica insisted on him as the target, and my hunger was so great. As a fledgling vampire, I would have killed anyone. I had no control then. I was so young," Raven said. She seemed to be taken aback by the moment.

"We waited for him inside his home. I ambushed him. I bit into him, believing him to be a good man. My soul anguished as I thought my humanity would disappear. Finally, the monster I was to become would be unleashed. My soul be damned. Then I witnessed through his memories the three young girls he had recently murdered. He buried them in shallow graves in the woods, nude and defiled," Raven said. She paused for a moment to choke back the emotion before continuing.

"Did I feel guilty for killing him? No, all I felt was justice for those poor girls. We're vampires, but we're not indiscriminate killers. Veronica taught me the lesson that we don't have to be monsters if we choose not to be. They still hunted for his murderer for many years, but here I am, the murderer. That man was a monster, and it took a monster to stop a monster. I choose to be a servant of God, but I am still a vampire. My cousin can have her investigation. She had human friends of hers murdered, but I claim no part in it," Raven explained.

"Welcome to the Great Tree. You have sanctuary here, but you do not have my permission to hunt outlaws, kill, or feed off the unwilling. I am the blade of justice here, and me alone. If you break this agreement, I will banish you. Do we have an understanding?" Aysun asked.

"Yes, and thank you, Princess Aysun. I apologize for my partner's behavior. Our condition makes her arrogant, but she can be reasoned with when she's calm," Raven said. She stood and bowed.

"You are welcomed at court, and you may retain your title here as countess of the nation of Stonehenge. Countess Raven, if your partner wants to return here, she'll owe my guard, Emira, an apology. Her protest was excessive. If you require or desire an apartment here at court, seek out Shamus and arrange it with him. I'll send a letter to the Moon Goddess Marie and tell her you were well met and welcomed into our nation. Court dismissed," Aysun said. The court members stood as Aysun rose, and they bowed as she exited the room. Aysun went into her apartment at court, where she changed into something less formal.

"Are we going somewhere?" Hannah asked.

"Yes, Hannah. Can you go get Tetyana? We are going shopping for her," Aysun said.

Raven looked for Veronica, but she didn't find her outside the palace. She searched all the way to the exit of the Great Tree and at the Goblin Tunnels. There was no sign of Veronica, she had disappeared.

***

The atmosphere seemed to lift as Aysun and her entourage entered the storefront. Her mood lifted at the prospect of doing something nice for Tetyana. Aysun's gaze swept over the room, taking in the various prosthetic devices and tools scattered about. She and Tetyana surveyed the shop, taking in all the possibilities. There was a rustling from the backroom of the store.

"I'll be right there," the shop owner called out from the back.

"Take your time. We are having a look around," Aysun replied.

The store owner emerged from the back. His expression was surprised as he unexpectedly took in the group before him. Aysun, with her full royal contingent of handmaidens and guards, filled the small store. Aysun noted the prosthetic foot he wore. He had this in common with Tetyana. He also wore an old dingy hat, which she noted was odd to be worn indoors.

"Princess Aysun, Your Majesty, how may I be of service? I apologize for making you wait. I was about to close," the man kneeled, reverent to Aysun's presence. He was surprised by the group of evening guests. Aysun motioned for him to rise.

"I apologize for the late hour. I had a full schedule at court today. This is Princess Tetyana of the Clouds, my ward. She needs a new foot," Aysun said.

"I am Osmen of the Clouds. It's a pleasure to meet you, Princess Tetyana," Osmen said as he introduced himself with pride.

"There are no registered Cloud clan members here, Princess. He's from the Clan of the Dead. Explain yourself!" Caria demanded, grabbing Aysun and pushing her back towards the door. Placing herself between Osmen and Aysun, the contingent of guards covered the princess's awkward retreat. Caria's sudden outburst made a bit of a spectacle. Aysun protested, knowing that Osmen was highly referred.

"Caria, this is unnecessary. I need new prosthetics for Tetyana. The one Sam made is falling apart. Osmen comes highly recommended," she said firmly.

"First a vampire, now a lightning fae. What's next? Are we going shopping to get you a pet ogre, or perhaps a pink dragon? He could be an assassin," Caria said.

"I could have a pink dragon?" Aysun asked.

"No, they're extinct," Caria replied. She returned to talk with the shop owner.

"Why are you not registered? All elementals are required to be registered," Caria demanded, her voice laced with suspicion.

"I didn't want to be singled out. Unfortunately, some people fear us just because we exist," Osmen replied. His tone was calm and measured.

"I am one of them. I fear for Princess Aysun's safety, and you're a risk. You're not to use your elemental abilities in her presence," Caria said sternly. She expressed her concern and made it clear that she wouldn't tolerate any threats to Aysun or Tetyana's safety.

"You have my word. We make prosthetics here, not lightning bolts. So, the Princess is perfectly safe from me," he said, his eyes meeting Caria's with conviction. Osmen assured her he posed no danger. Caria stepped out of the way for Princess Aysun.

"Forgive my protector. She means well," Aysun said.

"It's all right. Your safety is our nation's highest priority," Osmen replied.

"So, you're from here and you managed to keep your abilities a secret?" Aysun asked.

"Yes, I grew up in the industrial district down the tunnels at the edge of the Great Tree Nation. It's still part of the Great Tree, but fairly remote. I was home-schooled. My parents were cobblers. Hence, this is how I got an introduction to making shoes. Limb replacements came later when I needed one myself. I wasn't happy with the available options, so I started making my own," Osmen said.

"How did you lose your foot?" Tetyana asked.

"Tetyana," Aysun scolded.

"It's ok. I don't mind. Everyone asks eventually. Why don't you have a seat here and let me take a look at your leg? I need to make a mold. It happened on a hunting trip when I was a teenager. A wild boar caught me. The wound wasn't healing properly. The healer thought it was better to remove it before the infection spread. How about you?" Osmen asked.

"A Goblin General chopped it off to free me from the tree I was chained to," Tetyana replied.

"Who made your prosthetic? The craftsmanship is pretty good. I'd like to know who my competitors are," Osmen said with a smile. He took an impression of Tetyana's leg. He also matched a color sample to her skin color.

"Sam made it for me in prison," Tetyana replied.

"Sam, the princess's brother? That's pretty impressive work to be done in prison. Your story is much better than mine. I'm going to have to add a dragon or a couple of zombies to my story," Osmen said, and Tetyana laughed. He smiled to himself. Osmen thought maybe the young princess was exaggerating. He looked at Aysun, and she nodded back at him to confirm Tetyana's story.

Aysun selected some of the more expensive prosthetics. She demonstrated them by holding them up in front of Tetyana as Osmen finished his measurements and completed the mold of her leg. Aysun would pose them in both serious and humorous positions. Tetyana chose two, and Aysun picked a third. They also selected some extra shoes to change out.

"I can produce those for her, Your Majesty. I can have them delivered by the end of the week," Osmen said. Aysun nodded, impressed by Osmen's confidence. She could see from the craftsmanship of the display pieces that he was a superb artisan worthy of his reputation.

"Thank you, Osmen," Aysun said. Osmen bowed.

"It's an honor to serve the Great Tree, Your Majesty. I'm sure you'll be happy with my work," Osmen said.

As Aysun and the group made their way out of the store, Caria kept a watchful eye on Osmen. His passion and skill left a good impression on her, despite her initial reservations. She whispered to Aysun.

"Perhaps I misjudged him. He seems good at what he does," Caria said. Aysun smiled.

"Indeed. It's important not to make assumptions about people. We should always give them a chance to prove themselves, but I appreciate your protection," Aysun said.

***

Osmen approached Aysun's estate. Sebeli admitted him into the house to find Aysun, Caria, Hannah, and Tetyana sitting in the great room. He greeted them politely and then set about to do a fitting for Tetyana. Osmen brought several completed foot pieces and shoes for Tetyana to try on.

"The shoes and prosthetics are insulated from the ground, which should prevent accidental shocks with your permission?" he asked before touching Tetyana. Tetyana nodded in reply. Aysun noticed how the two of their hair colors matched. Dark brown with streaks of white hair, distinguishing them clearly as Lightning Fae. He was also dressed up more formally than at his shop.

"No hat today? Would you care for some coffee or tea?" Aysun asked with a smile.

"No, I thought that if the Princess could walk around proudly as a Lightning Fae, then I can too. I would love a cup of coffee," Osmen said. Sebeli went to get him a cup of coffee.

"I think you look handsome without it," Aysun said without thinking it through. The man blushed. Did the Princess just flirt with him? He wondered. Osmen looked at her, and as their eyes met, they both blushed. He continued the fitting with a smile. Caria got up and started toward the kitchen.

"Excuse me," Caria said. Hannah followed her into the kitchen. They could be heard giggling, which made Aysun blush even more.

"You've learned to control your abilities? I'm not sure how to advise Tetyana. I just tell her to try to stay relaxed, but maybe you could offer her some better advice," Aysun said as she changed subjects.

"Yes, it is important to remain relaxed and passive, but sometimes practicing your abilities is good, too. Especially when she is angry or emotional, this teaches better control and is a lot more practical at avoiding mistakes. We build up a charge. It needs an outlet. I have some targets that I have made up at home. I could bring some by for her to practice on?" Osmen offered.

"We have plans for the rest of this evening, but maybe you could come over tomorrow evening and stay for dinner?" Aysun asked.

"Certainly, I think that would be great. Tetyana can learn the basics of learning how to practice safely. I'm honored by the invitation," Osmen said.

"I'll look forward to it," Aysun replied. Osmen cleaned up the packaging. Tetyana walked around on her new foot with a matching dress shoe. You could barely tell her leg was a prosthetic. Aysun walked Osmen to the door. He nodded and smiled at her awkwardly as he departed.

Tetyana's smile radiated as Aysun returned to the room. She was already changing shoes to try on the boots he had included. She set the formal prosthetic aside. Tetyana decided right away that the boots were her favorite. Caria and Hannah entered the room, laughing. Hannah immediately sat on the floor next to Tetyana and helped her change into the boots.

***

Later, the four girls boarded the trolley for the meadows. Several guards also escorted Aysun. Caria and Hannah were still laughing at Aysun's slip of the tongue.

"Will you two knock it off?" Aysun asked. The conductor boarded the trolley. Hannah put on her blindfold.

"This one is not that bad. You won't need the blindfold," Aysun said. Hannah put it on anyway.

"He was cute," Caria said. Aysun ignored the comment.

As they arrived, Emira was near the archery complex on a podium on a small stage. She introduced the King after giving a short recruitment speech. Alex spoke about his appreciation for meeting the Fae and visiting the Great Tree. Aysun ascended the stage and sat behind the King. Alex introduced Aysun before taking a seat. She approached the podium.

"Listen, good people of the Great Tree. You all know by now that we successfully rescued Princess Elnara from that hellish prison. But let me make one thing clear; we owe our lives to King Alexander. I owe my life to him. He stood by our side, and now it's our turn to stand by his. His kingdom is going to be attacked after the harvest. I will be there to fight at his side! Will you join me? Will you stand with me and fight? The choice is yours, my people, but I'm asking for your support. I call you to battle!" Aysun called out. The people listened intently as Aysun spoke of her pledge to defend King Alexander's castle. She waited for the applause to subside.

"There's one more announcement I need to make. I am proud to introduce to you all my soon-to-be adopted daughter Tetyana of the Clouds, future Princess of The Great Tree!" Aysun called out. The crowd applauded in support.

"Thank you all," Aysun said as she departed the stage, waving to her people. Tetyana also waved as she followed Aysun off the stage.

As Aysun finished speaking, the crowd erupted into a chorus of affirmations and calls to battle. The crowd of Fae gathered around Aysun and cheered and clapped at the news of the successful rescue of Princess Elnara.

Emira resumed her place at the podium. Emira continued her recruitment efforts, as large lines formed to volunteer. Aysun and Tetyana visited the Gem Cutter's guild section of the market and entered a large shop. An older Fae gentleman emerged from the back and kneeled to greet Aysun.

"How may I be of service, Your Majesty?" he asked.

"This is my ward, Princess Tetyana," Aysun said, introducing Tetyana.

"She would like to become a Gem Cutter. She began her apprenticeship with my brother, Sam. Since he is not here, I need a new teacher for her," Aysun said.

"Well, Sam was my student. I think he has learned everything I have to teach him, so I have an opening. I hope for his safe return, Your Majesty. My name is Neval," Neval said with a nostalgic smile.

"Despite her royal title, having a lightning fae come and practice here will be challenging. She'll need a more private learning place until she gets older," Neval said.

"I will have a workshop set up for her at the house. Can you come there to teach her?" Aysun asked.

"Yes, of course, Princess, that'll work," Neval replied. Tetyana listened intently, and when Neval finished speaking, she spoke up.

"I don't want to cause any trouble. I want to learn from the best. Sam said that was you," she said, looking up at Neval with determination. Neval nodded approvingly.

"You have the right attitude, young one. With hard work and dedication, you'll make a fine gem cutter. I'll take you on as my apprentice," Neval said.

"Thank you, and thank you, Aysun!" Tetyana said as she skipped along on her new leg.

"Tetyana, go pick out any tools or equipment that you'll need. Be sure to tell them to bill it to the palace but have it sent to the house. Caria stay with Tetyana. Then, when she is finished shopping, meet us at the café," Aysun said.

"By your leave, Princess, I'll escort Princess Tetyana around and get to know her better," Neval said as he bowed to Aysun. Aysun nodded to him in agreement.

"So, Sam taught you. How was he the last time you saw him?" Neval asked Tetyana as they went shopping for gem-cutting tools and supplies.

"He was fine. Sam is smart. I'm sure he will be ok," Tetyana replied.

"I'm glad to hear it. So, how many cuts did Sam teach you?" Neval asked.

"I've learned seven different styles. Sam said I was ready to cut diamonds. I would have learned more, but Sam makes me learn the math before attempting more cuts," Tetyana replied.

"He got that from me. I insisted he understood how the angles work. Your math homework has just begun," Neval said as he laughed. Tetyana rolled her eyes.

Aysun and Hannah laughed and broke off to head to the café with some of her other guards following. She noticed Osmen was at the café and went over to him.

"Are you following me?" Aysun asked.

"I could ask you the same question, Your Majesty. My workshop is here in the meadow. I came here directly after leaving your house. I didn't know you were coming here to give that amazing speech. The people really love you," Osmen said.

A hostess came up to Aysun and kneeled. "Your usual table, Princess?

"May I join you?" Aysun asked Osmen.

"Yes, of course. I'm surprised to see you at such a humble establishment like this," he said, as he offered her a seat.

"I'll sit here. The rest of my party can take my usual table," Aysun replied to the hostess. She pointed for Hannah to follow the hostess.

"This is my favorite place to eat in the Great Tree. I was raised a simple farm girl. The open barbeque, and the festive attitude here I just love. I feel closer to the people who eat here than to any of the fancy restaurants downtown. The singing here is so much fun. It reminds me of going to the Harvest market as a kid. I've even come here in disguise a few times. However, I am not sure if I fool anyone. I think they just humor me," Aysun said.

***

Later that evening, everyone sat down for dinner. "Thank you for your hospitality, Aysun. We'll be taking our leave tomorrow and returning to Seaside. I hope that you'll be rejoining us at the castle soon," Alex said.

"There is still a lot that I need to take care of here. I'll do my best to return soon," Aysun replied.

"Is it okay if I also return? My place should be with Princess Elnara," Emira asked.

"Very well, you may return," Aysun said.

***

At dinner the following evening, Mizzy announced Elnara's entrance to the king's dining hall. Marcus stood up and moved her chair out for her.

"I'm glad to see you all have returned. How was your journey to Fairyland?" Elnara asked.

"It's hard to come up with the right words. Very eye-opening. The capital city is so beautiful. I could hardly believe it was all there. The trolley ride was a bit terrifying," Alex replied.

"How about you, Marcus? Did you enjoy your visit?" Elnara asked.

"Very much so. I got to tour your party palace," Marcus joked.

"What? I host charity events," Elnara said as she sat down to eat.

"Of course, I'm just teasing. Your house is beautiful," Marcus said with a smile.

"In all seriousness, it was an incredible experience. The Fae are a fascinating people with a rich culture and history. I really enjoyed my visit," Alex said.

"I'm glad you enjoyed it, Your Majesty," Elnara said.

"Was Aysun successful in becoming queen and summoning the military?" Elnara asked.

"I believe there was a deal struck. She will not be queen, but we have assurances we will receive military support," Alex said.

"Oh, good. I was nervous about her going down that road. I know how grateful she is to you, as am I. I knew she would do anything to honor her commitment," Elnara said.

***

Later that evening. Marcus was admitted into Elnara's room.

"Come in, Marcus, come have a glass of wine with me. I've missed you," Elnara said as she poured a glass for him. He took the glass from her and followed her out onto the veranda.

"I have a confession to make. When I was touring your house. I found your dairy. I only read the last entry. So, I apologize for reading it, but I realized it the day I met your mother. You must have just learned about the death of your father. You haven't said anything to me about it. Why not?" Marcus asked.

"Honestly, Marcus, I am still processing it. I've never had to deal with losing someone before. It was my fault they killed him. I don't know how to talk about feelings. It's the one thing we weren't taught. We were taught to be warriors and taught to be royals. Expressing feelings was not on the list. In fact, we were taught to hide our emotions. Marcus, how do I live with that guilt? I need to visit his grave at some point, but that's impossible now," Elnara said.

"Why not?" Marcus asked.

"His grave is in East Mill, near where I grew up. That area is too dangerous to travel to. Aysun would never allow me to travel there. That orc army you fought could be back anytime," Elnara said.

"I have an idea. You can come with me to visit Felix. You could lay flowers there for your father. I'm sure Felix won't mind," Marcus said.

"I want my mom to join us if that's ok. Maybe we can make a picnic out of it, so it's not too gloomy. You can ask Valeria to join us. You must really miss Felix?" Elnara asked.

"Of course, I do. We definitely miss him. I live with the guilt of his passing. If it wasn't for me. He would have never joined the army. I miss mentoring him. That reminds me of the boys you told me to look after. They are both off to the university. One wants to be a teacher, and the other wants to become an officer. The king has seen to their tuition and expenses," Marcus said.

"Yes, I'm aware. Mizzy and the would-be teacher are seeing one another. So, I've been given updates. Thank you for seeing to that," Elnara said.

***

One hundred and fifty years ago, the nation of the Enchanted Vineyards overlooked the valley and vineyards from a rocky hillside. Deep within, the young Princess Marie sat awkwardly on the throne. The coronation of the Princess had taken place just a few weeks earlier. A year earlier, she was chosen as the new Moon Goddess. A valet announced a petitioner.

"Countess Veronica LaRue," the attendant at the door announced. Veronica entered the throne room and kneeled to the princess. She waited to be told to rise. The palace financier whispered the introduction to the Princess.

"You may rise and approach Countess Veronica. I've been told you were reported missing over a hundred years ago. Presumed to be abducted and likely dead. Now you've returned, and you haven't aged a day, it seems. Your lands and possessions have long since been redistributed. Where have you been, and what can I do for you?" Marie asked.

"Your Majesty, I was not abducted. I met someone in the human world. I fell in love, and we moved away. It's normal for us to live hundreds of years. I've been blessed to hit a pause in aging early," Veronica said.

"You left your station at court without permission and sent no word to excuse your absence. So, I ask you again, where have you been, and what are you asking of me?" Marie asked.

"Yes, of course, Your Majesty. It's true, I left without permission. I was given a choice to leave with that person, or she would leave without me. I beg the court's forgiveness. We moved to Portugal, near Lisbon, along the ocean. We lived as humans. No Fae nations were nearby, so it was impossible to send word. I didn't think I'd be missed. My humble apologies," Veronica replied.

"I mourn the loss of your great-grandmother, Her Majesty Queen Josephine. I congratulate you on your coronation, Princess Marie, Moon Goddess. After my relationship with that person ended, I moved back here and purchased a vineyard. I had hoped to offer you a successful vineyard, but I am inept at managing it. It will soon fall to the bank. I offer the vineyard to Your Majesty if you would consider allowing me to return to court. Perhaps someone at court would be more capable of managing it," Veronica said. She lowered her head as she waited for the Princess's decision. The Princess discussed the situation with her Financier. She reviewed the documentation about the vineyard.

"Grandmother, can you speak to Countess LaRue's character in the service of the Enchanted Vineyard?" Marie asked.

"Your Majesty, from what I remember, she served faithfully and loyally until her disappearance," her grandmother said.

"Countess Veronica, understand my position is to run a nation, not a vineyard. I will restore your position back here at court. If you cannot make the vineyard self-sufficient and are forced to sell, you will no longer hold any land in this nation. Without land for your family name, you'll forfeit your title and your place at court," Marie said ominously before changing her tone.

"I will provide you with a onetime grant. My financier will determine the size of the grant to compensate you for any assets you may have lost at fair market value. I am also prepared to extend you loans with favorable terms to aid in revitalizing your business. You must secure the support of another court member who will take on management responsibilities for this offer to be valid. I will ask for a seven percent stake in the vineyard once it is profitable as your tax to the nation. You can work out the details of any loan repayments with the financier's office. Is there anyone here at court who will manage this vineyard on my behalf?" Marie asked.

"I will, Your Majesty," Countess Mathilde said as she stood up.

"Countess Veronica, I present my cousin, Countess Mathilde Ravencroft. Tilly, you've barely been in France for a year. As far as I know, you've spent all that time at court with very little time in the human world. What makes you think you can produce wine better than the French? How much vineyard experience do you have?" Marie asked mockingly.

"I don't have experience in working at a vineyard, cousin. My expertise is in running a business. I have a proven track record running four companies across multiple industries in some executive capacity or another. I can hire someone who knows how to make the best French wine. If the Countess desires, I can produce references for her. Your Majesty," Countess Mathilde said.

"My apologies, cousin Tilly. I didn't know you were so accomplished. Countess Veronica, you will have two weeks to solicit offers from other nobles," Marie said. Mathilde bowed to the Princess and took her seat. Countess Veronica gave a slight bow to Countess Mathilde. She nodded in return.

Mathilde caught a flirtatious glance coming from Veronica. Veronica was beautiful, she thought. Veronica possessed an enchanting allure with her lustrous, chestnut brown hair. It cascaded in gentle waves, gracefully framing her flawless face. With a graceful nose and softly contoured cheeks, her face emanated a timeless charm. Her almost porcelain-like skin seemed to glow with a soft radiance. Adorned with a captivating smile that beamed right at Mathilde. Mathilde realized she had been staring. She nervously pulled the hair away from her face. Mathilde attempted to hide her face behind her fan, but she was smiling in return. Veronica noticed through the lace of the fan.

"If it pleases Her Majesty, I'll accept the generous offer of Your Majesty to be managed by the kind Countess Mathilde," Veronica said.

"Very, well. I wish you the best of luck, Countesses. Next order of business," Marie said. She handed the paperwork to the Financier, who brought it to Mathilde. Mathilde removed her glasses and reviewed the documents. Veronica bowed and went and found a seat off to the side. Veronica waited to speak with Countess Mathilde after the daily business.

"Countess Mathilde. Thank you for your offer to aid me with the vineyard. May I call you Tilly?" Veronica asked as she caught pace with Mathilde and walked alongside.

"No, you may not. Her Majesty and my close family are the only ones that may. My name is Mathilde Ravencroft. My name is not Tilde or Tilly. If you insist on referring to me informally, you may call me Raven. Otherwise, Countess Mathilde will do," Raven said.

"Please, Raven, call me Veronica. Perhaps we could go to dinner tonight to discuss our strategy. I am better at drinking wine than making it," Veronica said as she laughed. Raven came to a stop to face her.

"Countess LaRue, Veronica, I did not offer my services to Her Majesty and yourself to take this on as a half measure. I need to review all of this documentation. I need to get approval to get a guard detachment assigned for our trip. There's also the matter of packing. I expect us to depart for your chateau after breakfast tomorrow. We can discuss my cut for my services along the way. I hope you'll have a private room and a suitable office for me to work in," Raven said.

"Please forgive me, Countess Ravencroft. I pushed for informality too soon. I'm confident now, by your tenacity, that I have made the right decision. You and your cousin seem to have that in common. All things will be as you ask. You have your own room and office, but the chateau may not be what you are expecting. It's quaint," Veronica said with a bow.

"I'm sorry. I didn't mean to come off rude. My cousin likes to use the short of my first name in public because she knows I don't like it. She does it to irritate me. Her Majesty is paying me back for teasing her when we were little. I'm older than she is. She has been insufferable since her coronation. I appreciate you taking me on to manage your vineyard. I'm very good at what I do. Whatever the issues are, we'll work through them. Please call me Raven. All of my friends do," Raven said. Veronica renewed her smile. Raven's eyes met Veronica's, and there was a spark of attraction. They both felt it. Raven broke eye contact and lowered her head.

"If you'll excuse me. I need to go to the financier's office before it closes, Countess," Veronica said.

"Countess," Raven replied. They parted ways, and Veronica watched her walk away. Raven looked back a short way down the hall.

***

On the carriage ride to the vineyard. As they approached the entrance to the property. Raven opened the shade for the window. Veronica had requested earlier that they remain closed. Veronica quickly covered herself under a blanket.

"Please close the shade. I told you I have a skin condition," Veronica insisted. Raven complied.

"Sorry. Why does a countess with no knowledge of how to run a vineyard, and who cannot be out in the sun, buy a vineyard?" Raven asked.

"My ex, Lilith, bought it for me when we broke up. She knew I wasn't good with money. She wanted me to have a stable income. The vineyard was running fine at first. Then some of the staff left. The vineyard has been in decline ever since. I can only manage about a third of the production it once yielded," Veronica said.

"You did realize that the vineyard would require some management? Did you make any attempts to increase the size of your labor force?" Raven asked.

"I put up signs in the surrounding villages, but it doesn't seem to be enough," Veronica replied.

"So, why did your relationship end?" Raven asked. Veronica perked up.

"Oh, personal questions, finally. I hoped you would put down those stuffy papers and talk to me. Why does any relationship end? Differences of opinion and issues built up over decades. I loved her, but she called it off. It wasn't my choice. Since you asked me personal questions. I flirted with you at court. You smiled back at me. I know you find me attractive. Then, in the hall, you put up a defense. Why?" Veronica said.

"I was in a relationship, or so I thought. We broke up this morning. She didn't want to wait for me to get the vineyard on track, and she didn't want to come live in the human world. It's okay. We weren't together that long. It's not a big deal," Raven said. Veronica slid across the carriage and kissed her. After a few moments, Raven broke off the kiss.

"Please, Countess. I'd rather keep our relationship professional," Raven said.

"Ah, you poor thing. You're heartbroken?" Veronica asked.

"Yes and no, I'm serious about maintaining a professional relationship. Your family name hangs on our success: my family's reputation, my reputation, and Her Majesty's investment. We have to be diligent about this endeavor. I'm serious. Please back off," Raven said.

"Ok, I'm sorry. Strictly professional it is. ma chérie," Veronica replied with a smile as she sat back while waving her fan.

The vineyard was in a terrible state. Some rows had collapsed. The pickers left some vines unpicked. Only a few workers remained. Upon arrival, Raven immediately set to task. Interviewing the remaining workers. She listened to their concerns about the decline in their housing conditions. Several workers over the recent years have gone missing. A few others left out of fear of rumors and old wives' tales.

She contracted the construction of new housing facilities for workers. Raven ordered a modernization and expansion to the winery. She hung fresh signs in the surrounding towns, stating the vineyard was under new management.

***

The year was 1348 AD. Three years had passed. The vineyard thrived, fully staffed and flourishing under Raven's careful management. Not only had Raven successfully expanded the vineyard, acquiring some of the adjacent lands. She acquired the expertise of the vineyards she had purchased. The once bitter rivalry between two of the previous owners now fueled debates on improvements and expansion. Now joined by common purpose, the elderly drunken pair acted as Raven's advisors.

Nestled amidst rolling hills and bathed in the sun's warm glow, the vineyard stood as a testament to Raven's unwavering dedication. Vines laden with plump, ripened grapes stretched across the landscape, their lush green leaves shimmering in the gentle breeze. Rows upon rows of meticulously pruned vines created a mesmerizing tapestry. They painted the scenery with shades of emerald and amethyst sprinkled in a sea of green waves.

The air was filled with a symphony of scents, a harmonious blend of earthiness and sweetness, as the grapes reached their peak of maturity. Workers moved with purpose among the vines, their hands expertly tending to the delicate fruits, ensuring a bountiful harvest.

The vineyard itself had flourished under Raven's attentive stewardship. New structures had risen, blending seamlessly with the rustic charm of the original buildings. A grand winery now stood at the heart of the estate, its stone facade a testament to the artistry that went into crafting fine wines.

Expanding beyond the initial borders, they had seamlessly integrated the adjacent lands into the vineyard. Fields of wildflowers and aromatic herbs flourished alongside the vineyard. There were two bed-and-breakfast houses on the property. Visitors who stepped into the vineyard were greeted with warmth and hospitality.

The vineyard had become not just a place of work, but a sanctuary for those who sought solace and delight in the fruits of the land, a tourist attraction for the area. Raven's vision and dedication had transformed the once declining vineyard into a thriving business. The sun finally set, and all the workers left for the day or settled into the bunkhouse. Raven walked into the chateau.

"Ronny, are you coming? Come, take a walk with me," Raven called into the bedroom. She looked at the paper she was given earlier in the day. Raven stopped herself from crying. She folded the paper and put it in her pocket. She prayed to God for courage.

"Tilly, where is my umbrella?" Veronica called back.

"It's here by the door, but you don't need it. The sun is down," Raven replied.

"Where are my boots, the brown ones? They were under the bed," Veronica asked.

"They're in the closet," Raven replied. Veronica came out of the back of the chateau.

"Why the need to go for a walk all of a sudden? What am I in trouble for now?" Veronica asked.

"Just come walk with me," Raven held out her hand, and Veronica took it. They walked down the path along the vineyard.

"Why so serious, Tilly? Don't be mad at me. Whatever I've done, I can make it up to you, ma chérie," Veronica said. She pressed closer as they walked.

"I've done what I set out to do here. The vineyard is profitable and three times as large as when I came here. We have diversified into four new types of wine. The bed and breakfasts are booked out for the foreseeable future. Princess Marie is very pleased with the early loan repayment. The management I hired runs everything now. You can just live here and not worry about anything. My business is concluded here. I'm going to return to the Enchanted Vineyard. There is another job opportunity I plan to accept it. Then I'm leaving France," Raven said.

"Tilly, what are you saying? I love you. We're going to stay here at the chateau together as we planned. You love me. Why would you think about leaving?" Veronica asked.

"It's the lies. I can't handle it anymore," Raven said.

"What, what lies?" Veronica asked.

"Where do you go at night? I know you sneak out after I go to sleep. Why do I find blood on your clothing? What really happened to the missing staff before I came here?" Raven asked.

"I go for a walk at night to clear my head. It helps me sleep, and the blood I told you was from a poor little bunny I found alongside the road," Veronica said.

"It's just more lies. On and on, it goes from you. You must really think I'm stupid. I've watched you go on your 'walks,' one second, you're there. The next, you're not. The police came by this afternoon. They said they're investigating murders in the surrounding towns and that the indications are leading them to this area. They wanted to know if I had seen this person," Raven said as she shoved a folded piece of paper at Veronica. Veronica opened the piece of paper. It was a wanted poster from Portugal. It read, "O Demônio de Lisboa. Procurado por homicídio." There was a portrait resembling Veronica on it.

"The Demon of Lisbon wanted for murder," Raven said.

"I can explain," Veronica said.

"Don't bother. Veronica, I'm leaving in the morning. I'm not going to lie for you again," Raven said with a raised voice. She turned to return to the chateau. Veronica suddenly appeared in front of her and grabbed her by the neck.

"You're not leaving me. Now be quiet, don't struggle, and feel no pain," Veronica compelled her. Veronica's voice reverberated through Raven's body. Raven lost the ability to struggle. She could only bear witness to being attacked.

"I'm sorry, Tilly," Veronica bared her fangs. Her face changed, becoming sinister. Her eyes blackened. The corruption turned her beautiful face into something else, a Goblin Fae. Veronica bit into Raven's neck. She fed on her blood. Raven tried to scream, but nothing came out. She couldn't move at all. After a few minutes, the effect started to wear off, but Raven had lost too much strength to resist.

"Ronny, stop. I'm cold. I'm so cold," Raven begged. Veronica laid her down next to the vineyard row.

"Ronny, I'm dying. Please stop," Raven said.

"Shh, it's okay, my love. Tilly, I'm going to save you. I'm going to make you better," Veronica said. Raven struggled and tried to get up, but Veronica held her down.

"Ronny, let me go, please," Raven begged.

"It's too late for that now. I wanted to keep this from you. I wanted to protect you from it, but I need you. I love you. Leaving is not an option. You wanted to know the truth. I'm not Fae, not anymore. I'm an angel. Lilith chose me to be one of God's angels. Now, I chose you to serve at my side. I hope you can forgive me someday. You are in God's service now. We are his swords. I know he has chosen you for a reason. To be at my side forever. My beautiful Tilly," Veronica said. She cried tears of blood. Veronica laid Raven's head down. Raven could no longer stand or sit up on her own.

"Lilith was the first of us. She told me that she and Adam were the first to inhabit the Garden of Eden, but she left because God had a special purpose for her. To cull the herd of man and remove the sick and the weak. To bring justice where there is injustice. Lilith took me on as her apprentice. To be there to serve God during the coming apocalypse," Veronica said.

Veronica's appetites had proved too much for Lilith. She was attracting the attention of the police. Lilith ended their relationship, and she sent Veronica back to France. She purchased the vineyard to prevent Veronica from becoming destitute.

"Ronny, please stop. You're killing me. I don't want to die," Raven muttered. Her breathing became shallower. Her arms fell to her side. The stars blurred. She didn't feel the cold anymore. She didn't feel anything at all. Her life replayed before her eyes. Veronica listened to her heartbeat until it stopped. Veronica made an incision along her wrist with a small dagger. She held her wrist over Raven's mouth. The blood flowed down Raven's throat. Veronica continued to pour her blood into Raven's mouth.

Raven gagged on the blood and gasped for air. She sat up quickly. Her eyes blackened and matched Veronica's. Everything was blurry. Raven removed her glasses. She could see clearly again without them.

A red mist surrounded her. The fog came out of the vines overhead and out of the ground. She turned her head and spat out the rest of the blood.

"What is this red mist?" Raven asked.

She stood up and took a few steps. Her enhanced senses overwhelmed her, causing her to pass out. Veronica caught her. She quickly picked up Raven and brought her back into the chateau.

Over the next few days, occasionally, Raven awoke. Her senses overwhelmed her. She knew they were traveling. The sights and sounds buzzed and danced back and forth. Raven could hear conversations from other rooms and a bar down the street. The sound of people walking past on the street below. The sounds sickened her, but Veronica aided and comforted her. She helped her drink from a cup. Raven drank the broth Veronica offered her. It nourished her. It was delicious. She realized they were not at the chateau.

"Where are we? Are we in the city?" Raven asked.

"Yes, Paris, ma chérie," Veronica replied.

"I smell blood, and there is a faint heartbeat in the other room. Is someone injured?" Raven asked.

"It's just our dinner, a bunny, my love. Don't worry about it," Veronica said. Raven looked down to see the cup come into view. It wasn't broth or wine. It was blood. Raven smacked the glass from Veronica's hand.

"There's someone else here. I can hear her heartbeat, and I can smell her. Who else is here with us?" Raven asked.

"Juliette, come in here, my little bunny," Veronica said.

"Yes, Countess," Juliette responded.

"Juliette meet Raven, Raven meet Juliette," Veronica said.

"Countess Ravencroft, I'm glad to see you awake," Juliette curtseyed. She cleaned up the cup and spilled blood.

"I'll bring some more blood for you, madam," Juliette said.

"What have you done to me?" Raven asked.

"I've made you an angel of the night, like me. I didn't know if it would work. God, you tasted terrible. Like me, you are now the steel of

God's sword, here on the eve of the final apocalypse. You are immortal. Now, we must do our part to aid the Horsemen. Plaque and pestilence are already here. Our brother Death summons us to do his bidding. We are Mercy and Justice, and we must do our part," Veronica said with a giggle as she danced around with her dagger.

"Madness, you're talking crazy-talk," Raven said as she passed out again.

***

The next evening. Juliette helped Raven get dressed. Then Veronica and Raven headed down the affluent Rue Saint-Jacques. As they passed the bars and restaurants, Veronica held Raven close despite the looks they were receiving. Veronica seemed to relish in the attention. The somber streets were littered with the infected and the dead. A cart came along to collect the dead. Doctors tended to those anguishing along the roadside. The doctors wore dark suits with a long cone-shaped mask, a wide-brimmed hat, and goggles.

"Who is this, Juliette? Are you sleeping with her?" Raven asked.

"No, jealous one. She is just a familiar. I saved her from being attacked by a man, so she let us stay with her," Veronica replied.

"I can't believe you did this to me!" Raven said

"Tilly, don't be cross with me," Veronica said.

"Cross, cross. We're beyond cross, and stop calling me Tilly! You lost that privilege when you killed me!" Raven said.

"Countess Ravencroft, I only killed you for a moment. I transformed you. You were a bunny. I've made you a wolf. You asked me what the red mist is. It's the angelic ether. Only an angel of God can see it and use it. That is how I travel so fast. Come, let's go to the park. I have things to teach you. First, we'll start with speed," Veronica said.

***

A few days later, Elnara, Marcus, and Valeria met up with Elnara's mother in the garden next to the cemetery. Emira, Mizzy, and the rest of Elnara's guard followed behind.

"Thanks for coming with me today, Mother," Elnara said.

"I'm happy to spend any time with you, sweety. You're always so busy being a fairy princess. Too busy to come have dinner with your mother. Where's Alexandra? Why isn't she here with us?" Defne asked.

"She's away on business. She went home to the Great Tree?" Elnara replied.

"Home? Your home was with me and your dad. He would be so proud of the lady you've become. You know if you ever want to come home, there is room for you here," Defne said.

Elnara stood up and placed a small bouquet on Felix's headstone. Valeria and Defne did the same.

"I want you to come back to the house, all of you. I can make some coffee and some snacks. It's time I get to know this handsome young man that's courting my daughter," Defne said.

"We were planning to have a picnic," Elnara said.

"Don't be silly. I'm not sitting on the ground like a savage. My house is just down the street. It's not as fancy as your castles and dining halls, but it's what I call home. Come, Valeria and Emira, you're coming too," Defne said. She led them to her house. Marcus escorted Elnara. He lent her his arm, so she didn't need to use her cane to walk.

Defne led them inside. She insisted that Mizzy and Emira sit at the table with Elnara, Valeria, and Marcus. They both knew that it was not their position to sit and eat with the princess, but they obliged. They both looked to Elnara for her approval, which she gave in a polite gesture. Defne went into the kitchen. She stoked the fire in the stove and put a kettle on.

"Esra, help me set the table for your friends," Defne called out from the kitchen.

"Princess?" Mizzy asked. She was about to stand.

"It's okay, Mizzy. My mother is right. This is her home. To her, I'm still Esra, her human daughter with funny ears. She doesn't comprehend my position in Fae society. I can set a table for coffee, but please unpack the food," Elnara said.

Elnara got up and grabbed her cane. Elnara went over to a cabinet and opened it. She took out a teacup and a plate from the cabinet and turned around. Marcus was there to receive the cup and plate.

"I assume I can help?" Marcus asked. He gave her a flirtatious smile.

"Of course, thank you, Marcus," Elnara replied. Marcus helped her to set the table.

Valeria also got up to help, but Elnara waved her off. Valeria went over to the fireplace instead. There were two small trophies there, which had some slight fire damage. They were both for winning an archery competition.

"Those were all I could recover from the old house. The fire destroyed everything. Esra had so many awards for her horse riding and archery. It took up two walls in our sitting room and filled her room. Though she usually slept in the horse barn," Defne said as she poured the coffee.

"Mother, please, don't embarrass me," Elnara said.

"At four years old, you should have seen her with her pigtails climbing up Shadey's saddle like a little monkey. She had no fear. Shady was Mia's mother," Defne said.

"So, Marcus, tell me everything about you," Defne said as she sat at the table.

4

Chapter Four: The Voyage

TWO WEEKS LATER, Sam and Augie played chess as Ivan and Pavlo practiced sign language. The ship rocked back and forth. Sam was thankful that he had gotten over the motion sickness. He had become accustomed to being rocked to sleep. They had to spread their hands over the pieces as the ship dipped and bobbed in the other direction.

Two ranked crewmen came over. One of the two bumped the table the chessboard was on. Several of the pieces on the board were knocked over. The taller of the two grabbed the chessboard and went to pick it up, but Sam held it down.

"We have the next game," the other one said.

"Give me the board and all the pieces. This is my chess set now," the first man said. Pavlo went to stand up, but Ivan grabbed him and shook his head no. Sam held onto the chessboard. There was a stare-down as the man pulled harder on the chessboard. Sam pushed down harder and wouldn't give in.

"You'll have to beat me if you want to play anyone else on my board," Sam said.

"You catch on quick," the man said as he threw a punch at Sam's face. Gunay caught his fist and grabbed the other forearm that was clasped on the chessboard. He twisted his wrist, forcing him to release the chessboard. Gunay pushed the man backward. He poisoned him with his touch. Gunay then threw him to the ground. The man looked green and nauseous immediately. Dugan backed the other man into the wall and stared him down, daring him to get involved.

"I think you boys are in the wrong section of the ship. You should leave while you still can," Dugan said. The two men retreated down the passageway.

"You look a little seasick. I hope you feel better, sweetheart. Drink plenty of fluids," Gunay taunted the man he poisoned. The man got up and followed the other.

"Don't come back," Dugan said to them.

"What did you do to the guy?" Dugan asked Gunay.

"I gave him something akin to severe sea sickness. He won't die, but he might wish he had. He'll pay for the insult to Sam," Gunay replied. Volkov saw the confrontation and made his way past the retreating men. Gunay and Dugan saw Volkov coming.

"Let's get out of here," Dugan said. He turned around and walked around the corner. Gunay followed him. They both informally and discreetly saluted Sam as they went by. As they rounded the corner, they shrunk down, flew up, and hid in the rafters. Then, just as Volkov rounded the corner, they disappeared. He raced to the end of the corridor and looked both ways, but there was no sign of the men. He returned and addressed Sam and the others.

"Who were those men?" Volkov asked.

"The two men who tried to take our chessboard. They are in the aft division. They're petty officers like you, but I don't know their names," Sam replied.

"No, I know who those two are. Who are the other two?" Volkov asked.

"I don't know. I've never seen them before, but it looks like I owe them for stepping in," Sam replied.

"What about the rest of you?" Volkov asked. The rest of the group shook their head no. Sam and Augie restored the game pieces to their starting positions. Sam took the first move.

"How did you get that chessboard? That's from the ship's store. I've also heard you boys playing instruments. I know you came on board with none of that?" Volkov asked.

"We put our money together to get things we could all enjoy. Pavlo and I put in all of our tip money that we have been saving. Sam and Augie also chipped in. He has a receipt," Ivan said. Sam retrieved the receipt from his locker and gave it to Volkov.

"How did you get your money?" Volkov asked Sam.

"With all due respect, I don't believe that's any of your business," Sam replied.

"So, who is the leader of your little group?" Volkov asked.

"Sam is," Ivan replied.

"Sam, you'll report to the galley after the morning muster. We'll have a team leader's meeting. You can represent your team. Understood? If you see those two again, I want it reported to me," Volkov said.

"Yes, Petty Officer Volkov," Sam replied formally. Volkov handed Sam back the receipt. Then he turned and left back the way he came.

"I have a bad suspicion about that one. I'm going to follow him. You stay with Sam," Gunay said. He activated his environmental camouflage and flew after Volkov. Volkov went to General Ak'rah's cabin and knocked.

***

"Who is it?" Ak'rah called from inside.

"Petty Officer Volkov," Volkov replied.

"Come in," Ak'rah replied. Volkov entered and observed that Ak'rah was granted one of the more luxurious staterooms. It was at the aft of the ship, one deck below the captain's quarters. So, he had a window in the cabin, a small bunk, and a writing desk. Ak'rah was writing at his desk.

"General Ak'rah, you told me to keep an eye on crewman Ekici and that you would make it worth my time. There was an incident just now.

I believe you might be interested in it," Volkov said. Gunay landed on the top of the doorframe and listened in via the open door.

"Go ahead," Ak'rah said.

"Ekici and another crewman, Macer, were involved in an altercation with a couple of other crewmen. It looked like the two crewmen were attempting to take a chessboard from Ekici and Macer. Two other crewmen stepped in. It appeared as if they were defending Ekici and Macer," Volkov said.

"Did you get a look at their ears?" Ak'rah asked.

"Their ears? No, they were wearing stocking hats. I remember faces, and I haven't seen those two before. I think they could be stowaways. The other interesting thing is that Ekici and Macer were playing on a chessboard they purchased from the ship's store. I've also seen them in possession of other pricey items from the ship's store. They shouldn't be able to afford them," Volkov explained.

"I questioned them about it. One of the Bereza brothers claimed the four of them all chipped in to buy things. They even produced a receipt. The brothers said they chipped in their tip money. Ekici wouldn't say where he got the money to chip in. So, what's that worth to you?" Volkov asked. Ak'rah threw a small pouch filled with silver coins. Volkov caught the bag and looked inside.

"They're prisoners, not employees. Can you search their lockers? I bet Sam stole some gems from me. Recover those gems for me, and I'll pay you in gold. Take these, and if you catch those two men, stick these around their necks," Ak'rah said. He walked over to one of his bags and took out two collars and keys. He handed them to Volkov.

"Why the collars? These are like the one Ekici wears. What does it do?" Volkov asked with a questioning gaze.

"Don't ask. Besides, you wouldn't believe me. Make sure Sam doesn't take his off or try to cut through it. Keep me informed about anything out of the ordinary. Try to gain Sam's trust and see if he won't tell you about his other two friends, and make an introduction," Ak'rah said.

"I'll search their lockers tomorrow while they're working. General," Volkov said. He nodded to the General before leaving. Volkov left and went toward the port side of the ship. Gunay figured he was going to confront the other two men. He headed back to warn Sam.

***

Later that night, Sam was awakened by the night watch-man. "Ekici, wake up. It's time for your watch in fifteen minutes," said the watchman.

"Ok, I'm awake. Thank you," Sam replied. Sam got up and went to the quarterdeck to start his watch. That night, he started at the helm. Every hour, the watch rotated positions. The forward lookout relieved the helmsman. The helmsman relieved the aft lookout position, and finally, the aft lookout relieved the roving watchman.

After an uneventful hour at the helm, Sam was relieved to go to the aft lookout position to get some fresh air. This was his first night on the watch without a mentor. The roles were not very technical. Sam spent most of his time on watch, looking at the stars with the telescope. There was rarely another ship in sight.

The moon was exceptionally bright this evening and seemed closer than ever. It reminded him of Aysun. Sam marveled at the craters of the moon. He realized for the first time that the land was not visible in any direction. Sam knew they were heading north by northwest. Gunay came over and startled him.

"Prince Sam, I need to speak with you," Gunay said as he kneeled to Sam.

"What is it? There is no need to kneel," Sam replied.

"Sorry, I don't know how to interact with royals," Gunay said.

"I'm only royal by my relation to my sister, but I'm 100% human. I have no rank and no title. Any courtesy afforded to me is strictly informal. You can speak to me as a friend," Sam said.

"You can't trust Volkov. He's spying on you for General Ak'rah. He's going to search your lockers tomorrow while you're at work. The general suspects you've stolen some gems. I think you boys should give Dugan and me any money you have to hold on to," Gunay reported.

"I'll collect the coins in the morning and give them to you. It's so different from Earth. Do you think there is life on the moon?" Sam asked as he returned to stare at the moon.

"Yes, Inanna lives there, the Goddess of the Moon," Gunay replied with reverence.

"Do you believe in that Fae lore nonsense?" Sam asked.

"The Goddess of the Moon touched your sister. There can be no question of that. Her hair turned white when her mother died. That also happened with her mother and Moon Goddesses throughout history. How does that just happen? Those are facts. You can call it lore if you want. There are recorded accounts of the Moon Goddesses being visited by Inanna. Conversations have been documented. I'm surprised that you asked me about her. In my opinion, that's not the one you should be concerned about. It's the other one that I would worry about," Gunay said as he pointed to Mars, a faint red dot in the night sky.

"What do you mean?" Sam asked.

"The God of the Cosmos, the God of Chaos. Anu, his home, is Mars. That is his dimensional connection to the Earth. Why has he chosen to bless a Moon Goddess for the first time? He is known by other names. The God of Death, The God of Lies. Her Majesty, your sister should be cautious of him. If you make it back to her, warn her. She is being used as a pawn in some interdimensional game," Gunay replied. Sam smiled at Gunay.

"I don't really believe in any of that. There must be another explanation that actually involves science," Sam said. Gunay nodded.

"I understand your skepticism, Sam. Goodnight," Gunay said.

"Goodnight," Sam replied. Gunay grabbed Sam's shoulder and gave him a subtle, reassuring pat. Then he retreated off towards the berthing area.

***

The following day, Sam awoke to the sound of the boatswain piping of reveille. Augie and the rest were already up and getting into their lockers.

"Come on, Sam, get up. Let's get to breakfast," Ivan said. Sam got up and walked over to the group.

"I'm up," Sam replied.

"You look tired. Did you have the late watch last night?" Augustus asked.

"Yes. Listen here, guys. I've been told we can't trust Volkov. He's planning to search our lockers today. So, I'm giving my coins to my other friends to hide. Give me yours if you don't want Volkov finding it," Sam said. Pavlo and Augustus complied and poured their coins into the sack Sam was holding. Ivan just put some of his gold coins in.

"You're not putting it all in?" Sam asked.

"No, I've played poker a few times with Volkov. He knows I have money; some of it is his. He would be suspicious if he didn't find any money," Ivan said with a little laugh. Sam took the bag around the corner. Gunay was there to meet him. Sam handed him the bag. Gunay nodded, and then he shrank down and flew back into the rafters. Sam rejoined the others, and they went to the galley for breakfast.

***

Later that afternoon, Sam and Augie painted the railings on the forecastle.

"How did you end up getting captured?" Augustus asked.

"My cousin and I went fishing in the forest. When we got to the river, orc slavers ambushed us. They captured us and sold us to Ak'rah. How about you?" Sam asked.

"Our group was attacked during a camping trip. Five of us stayed to fight while the others escaped. They captured two of us. The others were killed," Augustus said.

"I didn't take you for a fighter," Sam said.

"I'm not, but I had to make sure she got away," Augie replied

"A girl? I'd like to hear the rest of the story," Sam said.

"My school had a camping trip. It's a tradition for the graduating class to go during spring break. It's a three-day canoe trip. The girls had their tents, and we had ours. The teachers chaperoned the trip. I spent the most time with Reyhan. She was my canoe partner. I started singing to her as we drifted down the river, past a patch of fragrant lilac trees. My heart sang out, and my voice followed. She sang along with me. It was magical. I've known her since we were little, but we connected on that trip. The orcs attacked us on our last night. Do you have a girlfriend, Sam?" Augustus asked.

"No, I've been focused on my studies and learning my trade. I notice girls looking at me, but I am not sure if that's just because I'm different. The human with no wings who walks everywhere. I never know what to say to them. Anyway, they're never alone. I'm just awkward around girls," Sam replied.

"What's it like living in the Fairy world?" Augustus asked.

"It's different from the human world. It's something you would have to see to believe. The Fae can fly, so the city's construction is very vertical. I can tell you it's all inside of a magical tree. So, what is this between you and this girl?" Sam asked.

"A magical tree? Wow, I can only imagine. I fell in love with Reyhan in that canoe, and she fell in love with me. It was kismet," Augustus said.

He had just finished his sentence when a giant tentacle smashed through the railing close to where they were painting. It sent wooden shards through the air. They ran from their station as more tentacles climbed aboard. They were uncurling and slamming about the deck.

A giant sea creature was attacking the ship. Its massive tentacles reached up and wrapped around the ship, trying to drag it down into the depths below. The railings splintered and shattered. The ship creaked and groaned loudly.

"Oh man, we just painted all of that!" Augustus protested as they ran.

"Never mind that, run!" Sam shouted back as they ran and tried to avoid the tentacles. The ship pitched to the starboard side. Sam and Augie ran towards the nearest exit, dodging the flailing tentacles. They could hear chaos and panic erupting around them. The other crew members scrambled to avoid the tentacles.

"It's a Kraken!" A crewman screamed. Whistles sounded, and the bells rang out. The boat listed hard over to the starboard side. More tentacles came over the side and grabbed onto the forward mast until the creature had pulled itself out of the water. Its eye scanned over the deck to view the ship's topside.

The ship leaned precariously to the side the monster was hanging on. Men and orcs charged the tentacles, chopping at them with swords and axes. The tentacles slapped them away. Sam and Augie clung to the railing; a tentacle wrapped around Augie.

"Sam, help me!" Augustus called out as he was being pulled away.

"Use your knife!" Sam yelled. Sam pulled out his knife and charged the tentacle. He and Augie stabbed at it. The tentacle lifted them both off the ground and flung them into the railings on the ship's port side.

Ivan and Pavlo came up on deck to see what was going on. When they saw Sam and Augie in trouble, they ran over to help. The four of them stabbed at the tentacle. Dugan and Gunay flew out of a nearby hatch.

"We've got to get to Sam!" Dugan yelled.

"No, wait, they're trying to save Augie. Be ready to jump in if Sam goes overboard," Gunay ordered.

"What about Augie?" Dugan asked.

"He's not our mission. Volkov is out on deck; look, he's carrying two collars. Sam is our mission. We can't risk exposing ourselves to save Augie. I'm sorry," Gunay replied.

The Kraken grabbed two small groups of men with its other tentacles. The foremast snapped in half under the strain of the beast's weight. It slid down the side of the ship and made its way back into the water. The foremast collapsed overboard. Crewmembers worked to cut the riggings free.

The boys worked to pull Augustus free. Sam pushed his knife deep into the tentacle and twisted it. At the last second, the tentacle released Augustus. The other men the monster grabbed were not so fortunate. They were pulled overboard, and under the water, screaming as they went. The Kraken returned to the abyss. Dugan dove over the side. He pursued the squid into the deep.

The boys went below decks to their berthing area. Sam, Ivan, Pavlo, and Augie were all in shock, their bodies trembling from the adrenaline rush. Gunay walked over to them, looking concerned.

"Are you all okay?" he asked.

"We'll be fine. What was that thing?" Sam asked, still catching his breath.

"It was a Kraken. A giant squid. A creature I thought was a myth," Gunay replied. Sam looked at him in disbelief.

"A myth? That thing was real enough," Sam said.

"Yes, it was, and it's not the only thing out here on the sea that's dangerous," Gunay replied.

"I thought I was going over with it," Augustus said, his voice shaking.

"You're bleeding. We need to get Augie to medical," Sam said.

***

A short time later, Dugan returned to Gunay on deck. He returned to human height. Dugan dried himself.

"What happened?" Gunay asked.

"I was hoping to rescue some of the men, but the creature swam too deep. None of them survived," Dugan replied. Dugan surveyed the damage. Debris littered the forecastle. The starboard railing was in tatters. The missing mast and sails left an awkward opening in the scenery.

"Any of the boys hurt?" Dugan asked.

"Augie's probably got a couple of cracked ribs and a nice cut on his head. Sam's taking him to the doc to get stitched up," Gunay replied.

***

King Alexander sat on his throne as Aysun entered the throne room. The court members came to silence.

"Her Grace Duchess Alexandra Ekici of Stormhaven," Hannah announced. She approached and bowed to Alex.

"Aysun, it's wonderful to have you return. No more limping. I'm happy to see you healed," Alex said.

"I did promise to attend the tournament. The time I spent at home was very healing," Aysun replied.

"Cousin, welcome back!" Elnara said as she came over, kneeled, and then hugged Aysun. Alex led them to a seating area.

"What news do you have from the Great Tree?" Alex asked.

"I've heard from the other nations. There is no significant opposition to moving forward with the partnership. Most view this as a potential model to follow for the future of the Fae. At any rate, they figure we are taking all the risks. I'm taking all the risks. I need assurances that if we build an estate on the property, it's not searchable. It's beyond human laws. I'll deal with trespassers according to Fae law. We're only agreeing to this arrangement to protect our lands. We'll consider any uninvited approach as a direct threat and act accordingly. Any direct assault as an act of war," Aysun said.

"Whatever assurances you require. I will provide it. Our alliance is very important to me. I'll identify your lands as diplomatic lands. Your lands will be a sovereign nation within the kingdom," Alex said.

"Elnara, if you choose to stay in the human world, the estate we build will be yours. You cannot stay in the castle after we resolve this battle and get Sam back. We will use the titles given by the king, and we will blend in. No more 'bad fairies.' The other nations are upset with how public we have made our presence. They have eyes here. You are to take charge so that we fade back into being nothing more than a myth again. We will maintain relations with the humans via proxy. I'll expect you to hire a human representative and manage that relationship," Aysun said.

"Of course, Aysun. I'll see it done. Did any of the other princesses mention me?" Elnara said.

"Yes, of course they all did. I also wrote you a brief on

two visiting countesses. I think you should be aware of it. Hanna, give her the letters," Aysun said. Hanna handed Elnara a packet containing the letters.

"Alex, what will my human title be?" Elnara asked.

"You will be Duchess Esra Sachin of Stormhaven," Alex replied.

"I don't want to be Duchess Esra. My birth name is Elnara. Only my human mother calls me Esra," Elnara replied.

"Whatever your preferences are, that is what you will have," Alex replied.

"Thank you," Elnara said as she noticed Caria whispering to Emira.

"Excuse me for a moment," Elnara said. She went over to question Emira. Meanwhile, the king continued.

"Aysun, the lands we discussed are all yours. Build on them as you see fit. I bow to you as my friend and ally," Alex bowed to Aysun.

"Please, this is your court. As long as our agreement holds, then I am your friend and ally as well," Aysun responded. She returned the bow to him. Elnara went over and questioned Emira and Caria.

"Okay. What are you two talking about while Aysun is addressing me and the King?" Elnara said.

"Apologies, Princess," they both said.

"Well, out with it, Emira. What is it, news or gossip? You know you can't keep a secret from me," Elnara said as she stared Emira down. Emira stirred uncomfortably under the weight of Elnara's glare.

"Princess Aysun has been seeing someone," Emira said as she buckled under the pressure.

"Emira! I told you that in confidence," Caria scolded.

"Sorry," Emira replied.

"Okay, I want details," Elnara changed her glare from Emira to Caria.

"Princess, if Her Majesty finds out, I've been gossiping about her. She'll be upset with me. I can't risk my position," Caria pleaded.

"Caria, Aysun would never do anything to you. She loves

you. Me, on the other hand, I could give Mizzy the month off and have you serve me during meals. I'm sure the rest of the court would love to see you there. Troll Killer. I could also use my feet rubbed nightly," Elnara said.

"You're an evil princess! Okay, fine. She met a Lightning Fae named Osmond. He owns a shop in the upper district. Princess Aysun had some replacement prosthetics made for Tetyana. He's an excellent craftsman," Caria said.

"I want all the details. Tell me everything," Elnara said.

"There is not much more to tell. He came over to the house to deliver the order and do a fitting. Now, he comes over to teach Tetyana how to control her abilities. He usually stays for dinner. Aysun seems to enjoy his company," Caria said.

"Is he handsome?" Elnara asked. Caria blushed.

"Yes, he's handsome. He's tall and has the same white streaks in his hair as Tetyana," Caria responded. The three of them laughed.

"Did Tetyana like her replacements?" Elnara asked.

"She loves them. He made her a pair of boots, and she always wears those," Caria replied.

"I should have kept her here with me. Is she happy?" Elnara asked.

"Yes, she and Elif are inseparable. Aysun lets her decorate her room any way she wants. Her room is currently split between a fortress and a crime-fighting office. Elif wants to teach her to ride, but Aysun has told her no for now," Caria said with a laugh. Elnara laughed with her.

"I can understand that. She has progressed in her control, but I would fear for the horse. I miss her. I want regular reports on her," Elnara said.

"Of course, Princess, the adoption has gone through. You're officially related," Caria responded. Elnara smiled.

5

Chapter Five: The Tournament

The next morning. Elnara and Aysun walked into the courtyard where Valeria was leading a class. Emira and Caria followed behind them.

"What's this I hear about a date with a particular crafts-man?" Elnara asked.

"It wasn't a date. He came over and did a fitting for Tetyana," Aysun replied.

"I heard there was a bit more than that," Elnara said with a smirk.

"He stays for dinner sometimes. I'm just being polite. He's coming over twice a week to work with Tetyana. Osmen went out of his way to bring some equipment to help Tetyana. He is also volunteering to spend time with her. I think it's good for her to have a Lightning Fae she can go to with questions. I must get to know him a little to trust him with Tetyana," Aysun replied.

"Are you going to keep seeing him?" Elnara asked.

"I have other priorities right now," Aysun replied.

"That's not a no," Elnara said as she tickled Aysun in the

ribs. Aysun discreetly slapped her hand. Elnara laughed. Aysun stopped, turned around, and looked at Caria.

"You're in so much trouble," Aysun told Caria sternly. Caria lowered her head and kneeled. Aysun continued into the courtyard. Caria continued to follow behind her.

"I'm never telling you anything ever again," Caria said to Emira. Emira sulked.

Valeria came over and greeted the group.

"We came hoping to use some of the equipment to get some sparring in. We've been idle too long," Aysun asked.

"Yes, of course. Your Majesty, use whatever you like. I'm glad to see you've recovered so well," Valeria said.

"Thank you. It's nice to see you again," Aysun replied.

Elnara and Aysun sparred with swords. Elnara struggled without her cane. She was forced to hop and limp. Aysun ducked her charge and pushed her to the side. Elnara fell after she tried to turn to face Aysun. Her bad leg gave out. Elnara winced in pain. Aysun extended a hand to pick her up.

"Maybe it's too soon? You should give yourself more time to heal?" Aysun said.

"It's fine! I just stepped on it wrong. I just have to learn to get my balance," Elnara replied as she got up, a bit embarrassed. She tightened the laces on her leg brace.

She charged Aysun, showing off her sword skills. Aysun was forced to back up to dodge her attack. She recognized Elnara was coming at her full-on. Elnara knocked the sword from Aysun's hand.

Caria and Emira also sparred. Valeria's class took a break to watch the action. Valeria quickly saw that Caria and Elnara were more equal in sword skill. "Caria, why don't you spar, Princess Elnara? She seems like more at your skill level?" Valeria asked.

"Gee, thanks, Valeria," Aysun said.

"Oh god, Your Majesty, I meant no disrespect," Valeria blushed and bowed her head.

"Relax, Valeria. I'm not offended. Elnara is the finest

swordsman in our nation. We are just trying to get some exercise in. We don't want to turn this into a competition. Besides, I'm more of a dagger or hammer girl," Aysun said.

After a short time sparring with each other, they paired up with the humans and sparred. Valeria could see now that the Fae's speed and agility made a difference in combat.

***

The setup for the tournament had begun. In concert with that, Aysun's plan was also being implemented. She and Elnara stood outside, not really concerned about the tournament setup. That was a subterfuge to Aysun. Aysun pointed out the fire road to Elnara. They were logging the trees.

They had also constructed a spear wall. Although it currently lay flat on the ground, its base would rotate downward when lifted. The spears would then secure themselves at approximately chest height, with another set locking in beside them at waist height. The design pleased Aysun. She pointed it all out to Elnara with Caria, Emira, and a large contingent of guards in tow. This would give a significant advantage to the Fae archers.

They walked and toured the pond. The defensive wall was being built as more than a dozen masons constructed a chest-high archer wall. Once completed, they would place a similar spear wall in front. Aysun was satisfied with the progress. She saw the line of wagons containing the salt to salt the pond. It bothered her they were there.

"Elnara, you'll command this section and decide when to ignite the forest. Once lit, you are to transfer command to Caria and retreat to the castle," Aysun said.

"Retreat when I'm needed most? Don't be silly," Elnara said.

"Yes, we are to stay in the rear by order of the Council of General," Aysun said.

"That's ridiculous. We're trained warriors," Elnara said.

"I know I made the same argument, but General Emir overruled me," Aysun said.

"He overruled you? Was he wearing your tiara?" Elnara teased.

"He said they won't risk losing either of us again. I think we should respect their wishes, at least, as long as the situation doesn't require us to get directly involved. So, is Marcus competing in the tournament?" Aysun asked.

"Yes, He's entered all the events. I was thinking about entering just the archery competition myself," Elnara said.

"About that. I don't want any Fae to participate. We need to take the other house's concerns seriously. I'm sorry," Aysun said.

"Oh, you're no fun, but fine. Yes, your Majesty," Elnara replied.

***

Finally, the day of the tournament was here. Aysun came out of the castle, escorted by the King. His valet announced him first. Hannah announced Aysun as Duchess Alexandra Ekici of Stormhaven. She wore a magnificent gown of deep royal purple, a color fit for royalty. She wore pearl jewelry. Her white shoes and gloves matched the partial veil on her hat.

They announced several couples before Elnara, and Marcus came out. Elnara wore a dress similar to Aysun's but crimson. While Aysun's dress was open-shoulder, Elnara's had a high neckline that gracefully encircled her neck. This helped to cover her scars. Elnara walked with the aid of an ornate redwood and silver cane, matching the accents of her dress and jewelry.

The dresses were a gift from the King. Mizzy announced Elnara as Duchess Elnara Sachin of Stormhaven. The paperwork listed Esra as her middle name. She allowed it because she knew her mother would never adapt to calling her Elnara. Marcus escorted Elnara to their seats next to Aysun. Marcus excused himself to prepare for the competition. Aysun and Elnara thanked the King for their dresses as they were seated.

"Wish me luck," Marcus said as he kissed Elnara on the hand, which was no surprise to anyone at court, as their relationship was common knowledge.

The archery competition took place on the opening day of the Seed market, marking the beginning of the four-day tournament. It's worth noting the Seed market was smaller than the expansive Harvest market. It symbolized the beginning of the planting season. Stretched out along the cobbled streets, the Seed market was a vibrant tapestry of pastel spring colors and fresh scents. Stalls adorned with brightly colored canopies showcased an array of seeds, bulbs, and farming equipment.

Tomorrow would be the joust. Following the next day was the melee competition with a hand weapon of choice. The last day was the horse race. This was the most prestigious event for the nobles. Aysun noticed there was additional seating around the edges of the fields, and the public was filling in. She gave a questioning gaze to Alex.

"Did you let the public in?" Aysun asked.

"Yes, I made it so even a poor farm girl could come and watch," Alex smiled at her.

"Well done, Your Majesty, well done," Aysun smiled back. Then, she got up and went and walked among the crowd. She paid extra attention to the children. How much would it have meant to her as a little girl to have a royal lady of the court acknowledge her? Caria and Aysun's guard contingent stayed close to her. Elnara joined her. Eventually, seeing the positive attention they were getting, some of the other noblewomen got up and went about the crowd. They resumed their seating when the horns for competition signaled its beginning.

***

After a long first day of competition, Aysun, Elnara, and the rest of the nobles returned to the castle. Marcus had won the archery competition. A castle guard intercepted Aysun at the foot of the stairs to her room.

"Duchess Ekici, a party, is here and requests an audience with the Moon Goddess," a guard reported.

"Who is it?" Aysun asked.

"It's a blind man. He announced himself as Jerimiah," the guard replied. Aysun looked over at Elnara.

"I'm sure he is here to contest his branding," Elnara responded.

"Very well, I'll see him. Bring him into the courtroom. I need to bathe and get changed. I'll hear him out when I'm done," Aysun said. Aysun and her guards and handmaidens departed toward her room.

Marcus carried the trophy he had won as he escorted Elnara.

"Can I come with you?" Marcus asked Elnara.

"This is a Fae matter, so I'd rather you didn't. This is your castle. I can't stop you from attending. I'm going to meet him. Attend if you wish. Either way, we'll celebrate your victory afterward. The King is going to have a party in your honor, after dinner," Elnara said as she kissed Marcus and then followed the guard. Elnara went to meet Jerimiah. Cinar and Mehmet were with him.

"Welcome to the castle, my Worm Prince. Cinar, bring him along," Elnara said. She escorted them into the courtroom. Elnara walked alongside. The tap of Jerimiah's improvised woodland walking stick tapped in unison with her cane. The tapping made her laugh to herself, but it also made her sad.

"It looks like your eyes are healing well. I hope you're not still in pain," Elnara said.

"His eyes are healing fine, Princess," Cinar replied.

"I wasn't speaking to you, Cinar," Elnara snapped.

"Apologies, Princess," Cinar said.

"Your dog's let me have some poppy oil. It's manageable," Jerimiah responded.

"I'll let the dog comment slide, but do not refer to the Fae as dogs again. Otherwise, I'll have Cinar teach you some manners while you wait for my cousin," Elnara said.

****

"Have him seated there. Her Majesty will be joining us soon. I'm going to freshen up. I'll return with her," Elnara said. She sat Cinar and Jerimiah at the prosecutor's table.

After an hour, Aysun entered the courtroom. Hannah announced her.

"Her Majesty Princess Aysun of the Fae Nation of the Great Tree, the Moon Goddess," Aysun sat at the judge's desk. Elnara followed behind her. She whispered to Mizzy before being announced. Mizzy announced her. Elnara dragged the sword in, letting its tip scrape the ground as she went by Jerimiah.

"Her Royal Highness Princess Elnara of the Fae Nation of the Great Tree, the Dragon Princess," Elnara smiled at Mizzy. Everyone kneeled to Aysun. Elnara saw Marcus sitting alone in the back of the courtroom. She didn't acknowledge him, but went and took a seat at the defendant's table. She set the sword on the table loud enough for Jerimiah to understand that she had brought the sword.

"Ok, Jerimiah, you've come to challenge your branding, I take it?" Aysun asked.

"Moon Goddess, Your Majesty Princess Aysun. I came to beg for the mercy of the Fae. I have suffered savage beatings. My eyes were burned out. It was a pain unlike I have ever known!" Jerimiah said with passion, raising his voice. Cinar cracked Jerimiah on the side of his head with the back of his hand.

"Never raise your voice to her!" Cinar growled in Jerimiah's ear.

"I'm sorry. My apologies for getting excited. I'm gradually being starved to death. I know I deserved a lot of this, but I beg for my life. Please, Your Majesty, put this to an end," Jerimiah pleaded.

"Jerimiah, I'm sorry you've come all this way. Fae law is clear. I could only intervene if there remained some doubt of your guilt, but there isn't. Everything you are suffering is to force you to starve to death. That is your sentence. I would have given you a quick death like I did your henchmen, but Princess Elnara stayed my hand. It is she that you wronged. She had you branded. The only mercy she can give you is a swift death. Otherwise, you will eventually die of starvation. That I cannot change; I have legitimized her brand. Make peace with this life and your deeds and call for her mercy. I hope you find peace in the next life," Aysun said.

"I request an audience to speak to the King! This is a human kingdom. Your law doesn't exist here," Jerimiah demanded, as his demeanor changed to a seething rage. Aysun raised her hand and kept Cinar's hand from striking Jerimiah.

"Emira, can you please see if His Majesty King Alexander is available to hear his plea?" Aysun asked.

"Of course, Your Majesty," Emira said as she bowed to Aysun and left. A short time later, she returned with the King. The king's valet announced his entry. Valeria entered behind the king and took a seat next to Marcus. Seeing that this was clearly a Fae matter, he addressed Aysun as Fae.

"Aysun, what can I do for you?" Alex asked.

"This is Jerimiah. He has been sentenced to death for violent crimes against the royal family. My family, specifically for his role in the beating and maiming of my cousin Elnara. He came to appeal his sentence, but this is not possible under Fae law. His sentence will stand. He's requested an audience with you," Aysun said as she stood up from the judge's podium and offered the seat to the king. He sat down and addressed Jerimiah.

"Jerimiah, you have my attention. You may speak," Alex said.

"Your Majesty, these foreign invaders are torturing me, your loyal servant. Please, I beg you to give me sanctuary and protect me from these evil fairy invaders. They use evil fairy magic to poison your mind. Look what they have done to me. Please, Your Majesty, grant me asylum from them," Jerimiah begged as he came around the table and dropped to his knees.

"I'm sorry, Jerimiah. There is nothing I can do for you. I respect the Fae rule of law in this matter. I will not intervene. For the record, I would have you executed for what you've done to her. If you will excuse me," Alex stood up and politely bowed to Aysun and Elnara, then he left. Aysun stood up and returned the bow. Elnara stood up and went over to Cinar and Jerimiah. Elnara approached Cinar as she addressed Jerimiah.

"Jerimiah, you have exercised your right to challenge the branding. Your only course of action now is to call for my mercy or starve. I'm ready to show you mercy. Do you ask for my mercy?" Elnara asked.

"No," Jerimiah grumbled.

"Cinar, show him out," Elnara said.

***

The tournament continued throughout the week. The last day was the day of the race. Marcus looked for Elnara in the morning. She was not in her room. A guard told him she had gone to see Mia. He walked out to the stables. Elnara was grooming Mia. Marcus walked up and petted Mia.

"There are people to do that for you, Princess," Marcus said.

"Mia is my horse. If you want to ride her today. I want to make sure it's done properly. No one can groom her better than me. You know she's probably the oldest horse in the race," Elnara said.

"You're always bragging about how fast she is. Do you doubt her now, Dragon Princess?" Marcus asked.

"I'm just not sure if you can handle her if I unleash her. She was one of my father's fastest horses. That was before I could talk to her as a Fae," Elnara said.

"I'm sure I can handle her," Marcus said.

"Are you sure? You seem to have trouble handling me sometimes," Elnara said.

"You didn't just say that! What do you mean? You're going to regret saying that," Marcus said. Elnara dropped Mia's brush and dashed around Mia to put Mia in between her and Marcus. Elnara jeered at Marcus as she tested to see what side he would approach on. Emira struggled not to laugh. She giggled.

"Security detail. It's time for a perimeter sweep. A very slow perimeter search," Emira said, leading the other three guards out of the stables. Marcus stalked her around Mia. Elnara kept Mia between them.

"Mia, today is an important day. Girl, run as fast as you can. Run like the wind. Carry my champion to victory!" Elnara said as she let Marcus catch her. Mia responded in acknowledgment with a snort.

***

Marcus sat mounted on Mia. He and the other riders paraded past the King's stand. Marcus saluted the King. He waved and winked at Elnara. Elnara stood up and started cheering. She was making a bit of a spectacle of herself.

"Elnara, remember your position!" Aysun called over to her. Elnara glared and smirked at Aysun as she retook her seat. She continued to root for Marcus and Mia.

The officials led Marcus and Mia to the starting gate. Mia got excited upon entering the gate. Marcus could tell Mia was breathing deeper, and her heartbeat picked up. She was excited. Marcus stroked her neck.

"I know you don't understand me like you do her. I want you to run fast, but run safely. We don't have to win. I want us both to finish unhurt," Marcus said softly to Mia. Mia seemed to reject the notion as she became restless at the starting gate. Marcus didn't need to win. He had won these tournaments in the past. Marcus didn't want Mia to get injured or for himself to get injured. He had lost the joust in the first round, being unseated. Marcus had done better in the melee but finished in fourth place. He needed to finish first to win the overall tournament. Mia reared up and neighed.

"Ok, fine, have it your way. Let's see if we can win this, then. Don't hold back and give it all you got. I'll hang on for dear life. Let's see how fast you really are," Marcus said.

Marcus gave her a firm slap on the shoulder, and then he hunched into position. An official came and checked the gate. He looked to make sure it was locked and then went along and checked the next one.

Mia pressed her chest against the gate and set her feet to run. Marcus understood whatever Elnara had told her that Mia was going to run.

Mia's muscles tightened in anticipation. Her breathing deepened, nostrils flaring as she readied herself for the race. This was not her first race. Elnara's father raced her for many years.

The announcer announced the contestants and that the race was about to begin. The officials ran banners across the track, then stood to the side of the track. A bell sounded, and they waved the flags down. The gates flew open, and the horses were off. Marcus started from the outside position.

Mia was off like a shot. She almost ran out from underneath Marcus, but he held firm. Marcus tried to work her toward the inner rail. Some rubbing with other horses made him have to settle for the fifth position as they passed the first half of a lap. He and Mia moved into the third position by the start of the second lap. Marcus moved Mia to the outside on the last half of the lap.

As the thundering hooves echoed through the stadium, the race was reaching its electrifying climax. The crowd's roar grew even louder, and the tension in the air was palpable. Marcus knew this was their moment. The crowd silenced as the anticipation grew.

"Now's our chance. Go, Mia!" Marcus yelled. With a surge of power, Mia responded to the urgency in her rider's voice. Her powerful muscles flexed and propelled them forward as she tapped into an inner reserve of strength and determination.

In a breathtaking display of speed and finesse, Mia kicked into high gear, her every stride covering more ground than the one before. She rapidly closed the gap between herself and the frontrunner. The tension was palpable, gasps hanging in the air, a collective breath held.

Mia, with a heart full of fire and an unyielding spirit, overtook the lead. The gasps of the crowd turned into jubilant cheers. With each powerful stride, she pulled ahead, gaining precious inches and then feet. The finish line was in sight, a tantalizing ribbon of hope.

For the last quarter of the lap, Mia gave it her all. Her every muscle burned with effort, and her breath came out in hot, misty puffs. Mia stretched her lead. The exhilaration was palpable as Mia and Marcus raced over the finish line, breaking the ribbon. Marcus was the local favorite. The crowd erupted in an explosion of applause.

Elnara cheered and rushed down to celebrate with Marcus. He and Mia were being led to a stage. They were led to a stage to be awarded. Aysun walked with the King toward the award ceremonies. Caria walked alongside Aysun.

"I don't think I've ever seen Princess Elnara so excited. So, who was she rooting for, Marcus or Mia?" Caria asked with a snicker. Aysun also laughed.

"I don't advise that you ask her," Aysun said. They approached the stage. Elnara had already ascended the stage and stood next to Marcus and Mia.

Marcus was presented with a trophy. Elnara was presented with a decorative wreath adorned with colorful ribbons. Marcus and Emira helped her to place it around Mia's neck.

***

Two weeks later, the tribunal for Emira had begun. As Emira walked into the courtroom, she could feel the eyes of everyone in the room on her. Elnara walked in with her by her side. Emira stood tall and composed, but she was nervous and uncertain inside. She knows what she's done is wrong, but she also knows that her actions were driven by her love for Edric. Seeing Edric sitting on her side of the courtroom brought her comfort. They rotated him back for questioning and the trial. However, he hadn't seen Emira before the trial.

"I love you," Edric Fae whispered to Emira. She smiled and blushed. Emira took her place at the defendant's table. Then she put her head down and waited for the judge.

"All rise," the bailiff commanded as he introduced the presiding Fae judge. The judge entered, and everyone rose to their feet. He sat at the bench, and the courtroom retook their seats.

The judge called the court to order with a couple of taps of his gavel.

The prosecutor listed the charges against her. Emira waited patiently, her eyes fixed on the judge as she tried to maintain her composure.

"You may present the charges," the judge said. The prosecutor stood up and addressed the judge.

"Your honor, you can see from the depositions submitted the defendant is accused of fraternization and showing favoritism. Throughout their mission to rescue Princess Elnara, Lieutenant Emira allegedly showed favoritism towards Sergeant Edric. The charge is fraternization with the enlisted, and conduct unbecoming an officer," the prosecutor said.

"Sergeant Edric was given separate work assignments, as the depositions clearly show. He was also permitted to stay in the housing reserved for the officers and Her Majesty. Additionally, their cohabitation has led to their ongoing relationship and her subsequent pregnancy," the prosecutor explained. He retook his seat.

"How does the defense plea?" the judge asked. Emira and her attorney rose from their seats.

"As to the fraternization charge, the defendant enters a guilty plea, your honor. As to the charge of conduct unbecoming, we enter a plea of no contest. We ask for leniency given the remote nature of their mission and the importance of their mission. Such a relationship developing is not inconceivable. I would also like to enter into the record a letter of recommendation for her service from Her Highness Princess Elnara and Her Majesty Princess Aysun. I also have letters of support for the Lieutenant from every member of the mission. They all state that Lieutenant Emira did her job and acted professionally at all times," the defense attorney stated. He and Emira returned to their seats. The judge reviewed the evidence.

"Before I pass the sentence, would the defendant care to make a statement?" the judge asked.

"The defense rests, your honor," Emira's attorney stated.

"You realize that these are serious charges and can result in your dismissal from military service?" the judge said to Emira. Emira stood up.

"I want to make a statement. Your honor, I understand that what I did was wrong, but I do not regret that it happened. Edric and I love each other, and I'm happy we will have these babies together. My duty to the royal family has always been my highest priority. I have served the princesses faithfully and accept whatever consequences the court deems appropriate. I only ask that I'm allowed to continue my service to the royal family," Emira said. She retook her seat.

"Being part of the Royal Guard is among the highest honors for our military. Your lapse in judgment cannot be overlooked. However, I will grant your request for leniency and allow you to remain in the royal family's service. As to the charge of unbecoming an officer, it is dismissed. I accept that there were extenuating circumstances as to the fraternization charge. I accept your plea of guilty. You are sentenced to a reduction in rank to second lieutenant and forfeiture of twenty-five percent of your pay for six months. I would also like to add that the nation is grateful to you for the successful rescue of Princess Elnara, as am I. Consider that you have gotten off easy because of this. Princess Elnara, we are all happy to see your safe return. Court adjourned," the judge said with a bang of his gavel.

Emira thanked her attorney and cried. Edric went to her and wiped her tears aside.

"What's wrong?" Edric asked.

"Nothing, I'm happy. I'm so glad that it's finally over. I was so worried I would be dismissed from the guard. When did you get back?" Emira asked. Emira tore up a folded letter she had sitting on the table and threw it in the trash.

"I got back the day before yesterday. Your lawyer advised me to wait to see you until the trial, in case I was called to testify. What was on the piece of paper?" Edric replied.

"My resignation. I was only going to use it if they removed me from the guard. Any news on Sam?" Emira asked.

"No, there has been no sign of the ship," Edric replied.

Elnara waited for Emira as the court emptied. Elnara hugged her.

"Come, follow me. There is a surprise for you," Elnara said. She led Emira and Edric to a room near the main dining area.

Aysun and Caria were already there. In addition, Alex and Valeria were also there. The room had a lavish assortment of cookies, cakes, and champagne. The room was decorated festively. There was a sign that said 'Congratulations' on it. Marcus and the Fae officers, along with the members of the human court, also entered.

"Come on in, Emira. We're having a celebration. Come have some cake," Elnara said.

"I lost my rank, so it wasn't much of a win. You didn't have to do this for me, Princess," Emira said.

"I'm happy for you that the consequences were not more severe. I may have implied a minor threat in my recommendation letter if he removed you from our service. General Emir and I will discuss your rank. I'll see what I can work out. Oh, and Aysun and I didn't arrange this. Though we helped," Elnara said.

"Emira, I did," Edric said from behind her. Emira turned around, and Edric kneeled. He pulled a small box out of his pocket. He opened it to show her a ring. She covered her face as she cried.

"Emira, I love you and want to spend the rest of our lives together. Will you marry me?" Edric asked.

"Yes!" Emira said with excitement. Edric stood up and kissed her. They embraced, and then Edric placed the ring on her finger. Those in attendance applauded. Mizzy and Hanna poured champagne for all. Hannah poured juice into a champagne glass for Emira. They toasted to the engagement.

"I have an engagement gift for you," Aysun said.

"Princess?" Emira asked. Aysun handed her a scroll.

"It's from General Emir. He's officially assigned you to Princess Elnara as her protector. You are now in charge of her guard. We have divided the guards between us. Edric, you are back in the Royal Guard. You'll report to Yusef under Caria for my guard. Emira, you will have Cinar and Mehmet under your command. Try not to sleep with either of them," Aysun said. Everyone laughed.

"I have the man I want. I've learned my lesson," Emira said.

"You better have," Edric said. Emira smiled at him.

"And Edric, you'll remain at the hotel. You're not to come up to this floor unless it's required for your duties," Elnara said.

"Understood, Your Highness," Edric replied. Edric pulled Emira to the side.

"When do you want to do this? I was thinking of something small and private. Maybe we could get it together here in the courtroom in a couple of weeks?" Edric asked.

"Yes, I like that idea. We should do this while I can still fit in a dress. We should have our immediate family there. Let's let Caria and Princess Elnara know of our plan," Emira said. They walked over to where Aysun, Elnara, Caria, and Valeria were talking.

"Excuse me, Princesses. Edric and I have decided to get married as soon as we can. With your blessing, we would like to return to the Great Tree for the weekend to invite our families to the wedding. If the judge agrees, we'll have the wedding the weekend after this one. Just something small, no celebration. At least not until Sam is rescued. Then, we can have a nice dinner. We just want to be married when the twins arrive. So, is it ok?" Emira asked.

"Of course, it's okay. Do whatever you two need to do to make it happen. I think you can make it a little bigger. Shamus can perform the ceremony. Aysun and I would expect to be in your wedding party. You two will be excused from your duties and for a reasonable honeymoon, not in the castle. Let me know if you run into any problems," Elnara replied.

"Okay, thank you, Princess. I have one problem, then. I can't decide on who my maid of honor should be. Princess Elnara and Caria, you're like my sisters and aunts. Valeria is my new friend. Your Majesty, I could not even believe in the honor of you being my maid of honor. How do I decide?" Emira asked.

"I have too much to do, but I'm honored. Your honeymoon expenses will be covered as my gift to you," Aysun replied.

"I have to plan the construction of Stormhaven. Sorry, I'm going to be too busy. I'll cover all of your bridal and wedding expenses as my wedding gift to you and Edric," Elnara said.

"Don't look at me. My wedding gift to you is to show up and wear the stupid dress," Caria said.

"What do you say, Valeria? Will you be my maid of honor?" Emira asked.

"I would be honored. Do you know where you'll go on your honeymoon?" Valeria asked.

"Edric and I have talked about going to Cyprus. Edric's uncle has an olive orchard there close to the sea. He says it's beautiful there," Emira replied.

"A human honeymoon? I didn't expect that. Let's go dress shopping tomorrow, all of us," Valeria responded.

***

Elnara met with the housing designers and landscapers in the king's large conference room. It's been a week of planning. Emira sat in a chair near the door. She had nodded off. Marcus entered the room and walked past her. Mizzy was slumped over in the chair next to Emira. Emira's head was on Mizzy's shoulder. Mizzy barely took notice as Marcus entered the room.

"Marcus, you can't be in here. Shamus, turn the documents over. This information is not for you. What do you want?" Elnara asked. The Goblins and Fae scrambled to turn the documents over, and Shamus collected them.

"Your security detail seems to be on high alert," Marcus laughed at Emira.

"Ha-ha, leave her be. Let her sleep. The bride-to-be has been busy getting ready for the wedding and entertaining her family. She doesn't share my interest in design," Elnara laughed. Emira stirred from her sleep.

"I'm awake. You try to listen to hours of conversation about bushes and wall colors. I was up late planning my wedding and honeymoon," Emira said. Marcus acknowledged Emira.

"I was curious about how the progress on Stormhaven was going.

You've been spending a lot of time on this project. Dinner has started. I thought I would escort you in, Your Grace," Marcus replied.

"Shamus, are there any plans that I can show Marcus?" Elnara asked. Shamus shuffled through the documents. He selected a rolled-up document.

"Here's the schematic of the residence. This ought to be safe for human eyes," Shamus answered, unfurling the diagram and placing it on the table.

"Thank you, Shamus," Elnara said.

"Aye, I'm starving. A grand dinner is calling my name. Will there be anything else, Your Highness?" Shamus inquired.

"No, Shamus, that's it for the evening. Thank you everyone. Everyone, have a good evening. Shamus, I want construction to begin immediately. I will come and visit in a month to check on your progress. Coordinate with Caria on the security," Elnara said.

"Yes, Your Highness," Shamus replied. Everyone bowed and left. Marcus and Mizzy remained. Emira closed the doors as she exited. Music played from the adjacent dining area.

"Marcus, come over here. Look at what we have been working on. This is just the main building with the outer walls. Inside the walls, there are going to be horse stables, a guest house, and a large farm. There is going to be a rose garden and an orchard. It's going to be beautiful," Elnara said. Marcus looked over Elnara's shoulder at the drawing. He grabbed her by the waist, pushing her side to side to the music.

"You're beautiful. You're glowing. I haven't seen you this excited since you popped out of the bushes," Marcus said.

"Stop there, human," Elnara replied, recounting her first words to Marcus. She set her cane on the table and turned around. Marcus continued to dance with her.

"You're happy, and you're in love. Anyone I know?" Marcus asked in jest.

"Yes, maybe, and probably not," Elnara replied. Marcus spun her around as he engaged her in a waltz. Marcus held her close to support her weight for her bad leg.

"Say it," Marcus demanded with a smile.

"No, you say it first," Elnara replied.

"Ladies, first," Marcus said.

"Age before beauty. Are you afraid to say it first?" Elnara retorted.

"No, I'm not afraid to say it," Marcus replied.

"Then say it," Elnara said. She spun herself around and then back into Marcus's arms.

"Say it," Elnara demanded.

"I love you," Marcus replied. Elnara spun back out, picked her cane up, and walked toward the door.

"I'm hungry. Mizzy, I'm ready for dinner. Please announce my entrance," Elnara said. Mizzy could barely contain her laughter.

"Elnara, don't you dare leave," Marcus said.

"That's Duchess Elnara to you, Major," Elnara said. She nodded to Mizzy.

Mizzy opened the doors to the dining hall.

"Her Grace Duchess of Stormhaven Elnara Sachin," Mizzy announced. Elnara entered the room and bowed to the king. Marcus pulled out Elnara's chair for her as she sat. Marcus took his place at her side. Hannah poured more wine for Aysun. She looked over at Mizzy. Mizzy was smiling and trying not to laugh. Her face was red. Hannah looked at her directly and gave her a questioning gaze. Mizzy glanced down at Marcus. She mouthed the words,

"He said he loved her," Hannah snickered. Aysun took notice.

"What did I miss?" Aysun Fae whispered to Elnara.

"Marcus told me he loves me," Elnara whispered back.

"What did you tell him?" Aysun asked.

"I told him I was hungry," Elnara replied. Aysun nearly spit the food from her mouth. They both broke out in intense laughter. Aysun covered her face with a napkin but could not stop laughing. Marcus became noticeably irritated.

"I just remembered I have some work to finish in my office. If you'll excuse me, Your Majesty, Your Graces," Marcus said as he hastily split a roll open and stuffed it with meat and cheese. He filled the rest of his plate and then started to walk out.

"Have a good night, Major," Elnara said. Marcus paused for a moment and then continued without looking back.

***

Later that evening, in the stables.

"Laydown girl" Elnara said. Mia laid down when Elnara asked her to. Elnara climbed up and laid on top of her.

"Marcus said he loved me. Do you believe it, girl? Hey Fat Dog, are you listening to me?" Elnara asked. Mia's ears perked up.

"Are you expecting her to reply?" Marcus asked. He appeared suddenly from around the corner, startling Elnara.

"She answers me in her own way. I'm still learning to interpret it. You startled me. Don't you know better than to sneak up on a Fae Princess by now? My guards could have killed you. How did you get past them?" Elnara asked.

"Emira is easily bribed with a little chocolate. Besides, she knows you're safe with me. Why didn't you say it earlier? You embarrassed me with Aysun. I know you did the whisper thing," Marcus asked.

"I'm sorry, Marcus. That exchange was not my fault. Aysun asked me a direct question. I was just having a little fun with you. The four of us grew up together, and we could never keep secrets from each other. Save one," Elnara replied.

"Being fairies?" Marcus asked.

"Being different," Elnara replied. She rolled over on Mia onto her side, facing away from Marcus.

"Do you come out here to sleep often?" Marcus asked.

"Sometimes, when I have nightmares. Mia comforts me," Elnara replied. Elnara's thoughts briefly turned to her dreams about Jerimiah.

"I've slept with her ever since she was born. Her mother died at birth. I'm her mom. Other times, when I have nightmares, I crawl into my wardrobe and close the door. Marcus, maybe we should slow things down," Elnara said.

"No, you don't get to do that, not now. You can't break up with me for fear of letting me in. Let me in, drop your wall, and tell me what's holding you back," Marcus pleaded.

"There is a darkness in me. I can't shake it," Elnara said.

"The nightmare about losing me?" Marcus asked.

"No, it's much more than that. Yes, I had that dream. Thank you for letting me lie with you and for being a gentleman. Aysun is not going to let me live that down anytime soon. In my dreams, I'm back in that small box they imprisoned me in, squatting in the filth. My skin hurts when I move as the scabs crack and break open. I blocked so much of the experience out of my mind since then, but in my dreams, I re-live every moment. I was beaten and brutalized for months," Elnara explained.

"I'm sorry. You know, I have no idea what you went through. I can't imagine how terrifying it must have been to be locked in that box. You always put up a front. Princess, Warrior, or Duchess. I don't care for any of them. I see through it all. Elnara, I love you," Marcus said.

"It's not being in the box that terrified me. It's when they would come to take me out of it. They would drag me back to that pole to whip me because I couldn't work. I screamed as my leg was dragged across the ground. They wouldn't believe me. I was safe in my box! I wake up at night afraid. They are coming to take me out of my box. You're asking me to come out of my box," Elnara explained. Mia stood up, and Elnara slid off of her.

"I'm not being dramatic. Nobody asked your opinion. You lumpy horse!" Elnara said as she jeered at Mia. Mia walked out of the stable. A stable boy opened the door for her and let her out into the corral.

"It seems Mia is on my side. Come on, let's go lay under the stars. It's a perfect night," Marcus said. He pulled Elnara up by her hand. Marcus grabbed a clean blanket.

"I just want to make sure that you know what you're getting yourself into," Elnara said.

He and Elnara left the stable. Emira was sitting outside the door eating a bar of chocolate.

"Emira, you should have announced Marcus, but you betrayed me for a bar of chocolate," Elnara scolded Emira.

"Actually, it was two bars, and I voted to tell you, but the twins out-voted me," Emira said. Elnara snatched the remaining bar from Emira's hand. She took a bite of the chocolate bar.

"You can tell your traitorous twins they have forfeited the rest of this chocolate bar," Elnara said.

"Taking candy from babies. Fae, justice is cruel," Marcus joked. Elnara and Emira laughed.

"Where are you going, Princess?" Emira asked.

"Just up the hill a bit to see the stars. You can stay here," Elnara responded. Marcus escorted Elnara up the hill and laid the blanket on the ground for them. They lay down and looked up at the stars.

"See the series of stars there? That's the Big Dipper. It points to the Little Dipper. Polaris, the North Star, is at the end of the little handle. My Grandfather would tell me fishing stories when I was a boy. He would use that star to navigate his fishing boat to his secret fishing grounds. Then, he would use it to find his way home again. When I can't sleep, I come outside and gaze at that star and remember all of his crazy fishing stories, like how he made friends with a giant squid," Marcus said. He and Elnara laughed.

"If this is your way of asking me to go fishing, the answer is no. It didn't work out so well for me last time," Elnara said.

"No, that's not what I meant. I mean, I am here for you when the darkness comes. You don't have to face it alone anymore. Say it," Marcus said.

"Your, my North Star?" Elnara asked sarcastically.

"You know what I mean. Say it," Marcus demanded.

"You're asking me to come out of my box. It's difficult, Marcus," Elnara said.

"Maybe you're right. Maybe we shouldn't see each other anymore.

Goodnight, Your Highness," Marcus replied. He got up and started to walk away.

"I said difficult, not impossible, my love. Come back and sit with me. Tell me more about your grandfather's fishing stories and the stars," Elnara Fae whispered to him. Marcus came back, sat down, and faced her.

"Say it aloud, Elnara," Marcus demanded.

"Fine, I love you too. You smelly, hairy, oversized human, as much as I have tried not to. I hated all humans in prison. You and my mother have made me realize I can't escape my human side. You're a good person, Marcus. I saw it when I climbed into that carriage when we first met. Felix's death was my fault. I thought you would hate me for it," Elnara said, and Marcus kissed her.

"You're not to blame for Felix. I fell in love with you the moment I saw you emerge from the woods," Marcus replied.

"Okay, I confess. I was also attracted to you from the beginning. I went to ride in the other carriage so I wouldn't give it away. Marcus, I'm leaving in a month to go oversee construction at Stormhaven. Come with me," Elnara said.

"Yes, I heard you earlier. What about Aysun? Is she going too?" Marcus asked.

"Our coming and goings are now a guarded secret. If you want to join me, you must swear an oath," Elnara said.

"Okay, what is it?" Marcus replied. He and Elnara sat up and faced each other.

"Repeat after me. I, Marcus Antonius Marcellus, swear an oath to the Fae. That I am being entrusted with Fae secrets, I will keep them secret," Elnara said. She paused and waited for his reply.

"I, Marcus Marcellus, swear an oath to the Fae. That I am being entrusted with Fae secrets, I will keep them secret," Marcus replied.

"I will protect the location of all Fae nations and their entrances or forfeit my life," Elnara continued to recite.

"Wait, what? Forfeit my life," Marcus asked.

"Yes, Marcus, you know the law. Don't play dumb," Elnara insisted.

"I will protect the location of all Fae nations and their entrances or forfeit some pay," Marcus said.

"Marcus, be serious about this. Say it properly, so I know you understand the consequences. It's not a laughing matter for us," Elnara demanded.

"...or forfeit my life," Marcus replied.

"Good, now I can have Shamus enter it into the records," Elnara said.

"That's it. That's all I had to do to learn the secrets of the Fairies. We don't need to have witnesses?" Marcus asked.

"I'm sponsoring you personally. No one will question my word," Elnara replied.

***

Emira had only wanted a small ceremony, but the princesses insisted on a proper wedding. Valeria, Aysun, Elnara, and Caria stood beside Emira. Caria felt awkward in the dress. Yusef, Cinar, Mehmet, and Lucius stood beside Edric. The chapel was packed. The king and many of the royals were also in attendance. Emira's and Edric's families filled most of the pews. Shamus read the vows from a book as he stood in front of the couple.

"Do you, Edric Demir of the Forge, take Emira Sansiz of the Ocean to be your lawfully wedded wife, to have and to hold, from this day forward, for better or for worse, for richer or for poorer, in sickness and in health, to love and to cherish, until death do ye part?" Shamus asked.

"I do," Edric replied.

"Stop crying, beautiful," Edric said. Edric could see that Emira's makeup was running under her veil.

"I can't. I'm so happy," Emira sniveled. Her makeup was a mess because of the tears. Edric handed her a handkerchief. She used the handkerchief to keep her eyes clear.

Yusef handed Emira's ring to Edric. Edric placed the ring on her trembling finger.

"And do ye, Emira Sansiz of the Ocean, take Edric Demir of the

Forge to be your lawfully wedded husband, to have and to hold, from this day forward, for better or for worse, for richer or for poorer, in sickness and in health, to love and to cherish, until death do ye part?" Shamus asked.

"I do," Emira replied.

Valeria handed Edric's ring to Emira. Emira placed the ring on Edric's finger.

"I now pronounce you husband and wife. You may kiss the bride," Shamus announced. Edric pulled Emira in, pulled back her veil, and kissed her. The congregation applauded.

***

A month later, the late-day sun waned in the sky, and the moon was called forward. Elnara, Marcus, and her guard contingent entered the construction encampment near The Great Tree. The second story was being framed for the main house. A tent city filled the forest floor. The carpenters' symphony of saws and hammers intermingled with the ambient sounds of the forest. Hundreds of workers were hard at work constructing the house and the grounds.

Taner and Fatima were there to greet them. Elnara and Marcus dismounted and approached the couple. Elnara walked with a noticeable limp, giving away her identity. She was dressed as a normal soldier. Elnara's cane sank through the ground. Marcus noticed and quickly fashioned a walking stick from a nearby pile of tree limbs for her. Elnara used the walking stick. She removed her helmet and hung it on Mia's saddle. Fatima and Taner kneeled as Elnara approached.

"Princess, welcome home," Fatima said. The workers in the area stopped and noticed her when Fatima and Taner kneeled. They stopped working and began to applaud and cheer. Elnara waved to them. The workers kneeled.

"My trip was supposed to be a secret," Elnara said. She motioned for them to rise.

"I received a letter from Shamus this morning announcing your arrival. The communication was authorized by Her Majesty. Fatima and Sebeli are aware of your arrival, and now all the workers here are. Your presence here will not remain a secret for long. The news will spread through the Great Tree quickly. We never gave up hope that you would return. How's your leg?" Taner asked. Elnara approached them and embraced them.

"It's fine. I'm still getting treatments. This is my friend, Major Marcus Marcellus, and Countess Miranda Acar of Stormhaven, my new handmaiden. She will be the human face of Stormhaven," Elnara said.

"Yes, Your Highness, we've met Marcus. Nice to see you again. It's nice to meet you, Countess. Marcus, how's Valeria and the rest of your family?" Fatima asked.

"Please, just call me Mizzy. I'm not used to titles and such," Mizzy said.

"Nice to see you again, and you too, Governor. They are all well," Marcus replied.

"I'm so happy to see you again, Princess. I'm having a tent prepared for you. It should be suitable for you to freshen up in now, but we are still bringing furniture from the Great Tree. Sebeli should be along in a little while. She's coming with some of the girls. I'll have them draw you a bath," Fatima said.

"Please have a tent prepared for Marcus next to mine. The countess should also have reasonable accommodations," Elnara said.

"Of course, Princess, would there be anything else?" Fatima asked.

"Yes, see that the men are fed, and the horses are stabled? Show Emira where the men can set up camp. Maybe you can get some people to help them. It's been a long ride. I'd like a meal in my tent for Marcus and me. Make sure a bath is prepared for Marcus, and he has proper clothes to change into. He smells worse than Mia. Marcus and I are going to take a walk to the Great Tree," Elnara said.

"Has he taken the oath?" Taner asked.

"Yes, and Shamus recorded it. Have the table set for four. I want you two to join us," Elnara replied.

"Come, Marcus, let's take a tour. If you will excuse us," Elnara said.

"Your Highness, Marcus," Taner replied. He and Fatima bowed. Elnara and Marcus went to the back through the gardens that were being planted. Then, they walked through an orchard and down a hill. They approached a stream. Ahead in a clearing was the Great Tree.

"There it is, Marcus. This is why I had you take the oath before we came here. It could be dangerous if you had stumbled upon this without it. You are only the third human to know its location," Elnara said. She sat on a log facing the tree. Marcus sat next to her.

"It's beautiful," Marcus replied.

"We landed just there behind the tree. In front of the tree, there is where we slept that night. Up the stream, a bit is where Sam and I were captured," Elnara said. Marcus sat next to her and put his arm around her.

***

Summer was almost at an end. Raven entered the tasting room where her vineyard manager was waiting for her. A variety of wines were neatly arranged on the bar. There were plates of grapes fresh from the harvest.

"Rafael, how is the harvest progressing?" Raven asked. Rafael poured them both a glass.

"Countess Ravencroft, so lovely to see you again. The harvest is progressing smoothly. I wish you would come to see our operations firsthand during the day. I've prepared a selection from the cellar for you to taste. We've got several batches that have matured well and are ready for market. A salute to the owner of this great vineyard," Rafael said.

"Then you should pour me a glass as well," Veronica said as she entered the room, seemingly from nowhere.

"Madam, this is a closed session. You can't be in here," Rafael called out.

"Who's the bunny Tilly? Is he a familiar?" Veronica asked.

"No, he's not. This is Rafael. He's our vineyard manager. Rafael, this is the Countess Veronica LaRue, my business partner," Raven replied.

"My apologies, Countess LaRue. A pleasure to meet you. I was not informed of your existence," Rafael said. He took out another wineglass for her. He poured a glass for her.

"Rafael, would you excuse us for a minute? We need to catch up on some things," Raven said.

"Of course, Countess. I'll be in the back room," Rafael said as he excused himself into the back room.

"Where have you been all these months? Why did you abandon me at The Great Tree? I traveled back to our vineyard in France looking for you," Raven asked.

"The Moon Goddess told me to leave, so I left. I took the tunnels north. Then, I booked a passage across the sea, and I went and visited an old friend. You were being cross, so I felt we needed a break. I didn't think you would go searching for me," Veronica replied.

"You could have waited for me and told me. Did you go back to her?" Raven asked.

"No, I don't know where Lilith is. She disappeared a long time ago. I went to visit a friend. He has asked for our help. There is a battle coming, and he needs reapers. I came back for you to join me," Veronica said.

"What? No, I'm building our business, and your place is here with me. I've made a breakthrough in my research. The blood can stay viable for over a month. I add a touch of a wine and vinegar mixture so it doesn't clump. I have a reserve now that can sustain us both. We don't have to get blood directly from humans. Here, try some," Raven said. She took a flask out of her bag and filled a wine glass. She gave it to Veronica. Veronica took a sip and spit it back in the glass.

"That's disgusting, ma chérie. Stop this nonsense of yours. You're a wolf, not a dog, or should I buy you a collar? Bark bark," Veronica teased.

"Stop it. I can't keep killing. We have to find another way," Raven replied.

"We're killers. The sooner you accept it, the better," Veronica said.

"Keep your voice down!" Raven demanded.

"Let's go for a hunt," Veronica said.

"We can't. The Princess prohibited us from hunting here," Raven replied.

"She can't forbid us from feeding. We must feed to survive. Who is she to dictate to an angel of the night? I've fed freely for hundreds of years. I'm not changing for her," Veronica said.

"We're vampires, not angels. Change is inevitable. I'm not going to any battle with you. I'm not killing anymore. Don't go back. Stay with me. You'll get used to the blood," Raven pleaded.

"I leave in three days. I don't want to get used to that blood. Fresh and warm is how blood is meant to be drunk. Let's not argue, ma chérie. You can drink that blood if you want to. Let's get on with the tasting. Rafael, you may come back and serve us," Veronica called out and clapped her hands.

****

Two days later, Raven and Veronica strolled through the park. The village streets next to the park were bustling with horse and carriage traffic. Veronica pointed out a carriage stopped ahead. A female prostitute on the side of the road was talking to the occupant of the carriage. Veronica pointed it out.

"So, what? That happens all the time on this street," Raven said.

"Listen to them," Veronica said.

Raven focused on the pair. Her eyes blackened. She conjured the ether to become visible. Through the ether, she could listen in on their conversation. She focused her vampiric hearing on the pair.

"They're discussing price and service, as expected. Nothing unusual. It's quite disgusting," Raven replied.

"Look deeper. See his intentions," Veronica said.

Raven reluctantly complied again, using the red mist to amplify her vampiric senses. Images appeared in her mind. Passionate images of the two of them flooded over her. Then, the images turned violent. She could see his intentions. He's strangling her. Then he's selling her body at the back door of the surgical hospital.

"Do we do nothing, or are we angels of the night, mercy and justice? Now read her," Veronica asked.

Raven focused in on her, seeing her memories. She sees a young girl and an infant at a dinner table. The infant is hers, but the girl is her sister. The girl is talking about school. She is not aware that her older sister is soliciting herself to support them. Now, she is about to meet her fate. Raven's eyes returned to normal.

"What can we do? I gave my word," Raven said. The woman climbed into the carriage.

"You can taste his blood on your tongue. Deliver her from evil, or let her and the children become victims. It's up to you. How long has it been since you fed on a live human? Warm, fresh, delicious blood," Veronica asked. Knowing she was triggering Raven into a feeding state. Raven's eyes turned black, and her fangs came out.

"It's been months. Stop trying to manipulate me," Raven said as she let out a soft growl. She regained control, retracting her fangs, and her eyes returned to normal.

"This is your true nature. You need to accept it. You can do God's work or be the lapdog for some white-haired princess who never leaves her palace. This is for you to do, or let her die," Veronica said.

"We'll follow them," Raven said. She returned to her feeding state, and Veronica joined her. They used the ether to follow the pair as they traveled along on their way to a private flat.

***

The couple stepped into the flat, and passion ignited between them as the man secured the door. He removed her clothes, determined to undress her completely, even as she attempted to reciprocate. Unexpectedly, his grip tightened around her neck, and he strangled her. In a desperate struggle, she fought back, trying to free herself and avoid losing consciousness.

Raven and Veronica stood frozen in the hallway, acutely aware of the escalating struggle to unfold within. The disconcerting symphony of gasps and strained heartbeats filled the air. The victim's pulse raced in a desperate crescendo as the oxygen dwindled. The inevitable finale drew near.

Raven burst through the door, shattering it from its frame. A deep visceral growl escaped her as she moved with the vampiric slipstream speed, forcefully separating the man's hands from the woman. With swift efficiency, Raven seized the man by the throat and pressed him against the wall.

Meanwhile, the woman, taking advantage of the disruption, retrieved her clothes and quickly dressed.

"I'm not with him. I just came home with him tonight. Whatever your business is with him, I want nothing to do with it. Can I leave?" The woman asked.

"Get out! Speak to no one. You'll remember nothing from the last hour. Go home," Raven compelled the woman. The powerful resonance waves almost knocked the woman to the ground. The women seemed not to notice Raven's black eyes or fangs. She dressed and left.

"Sleep," Raven commanded the man. He went limp, and she bit into him. Veronica joined in on the feast, biting him on the wrist. She alternated between kissing Raven and feeding on the man.

"See, my love. We are the sword of God. You saved that girl's life. Did you miss me?" Veronica asked.

"Terribly. I wondered if I would ever see you again," Raven replied. Veronica unbuttoned Raven's dress. Veronica caught a subtle shift in the ether. A small ripple she had not seen before. Then, a familiar smell she couldn't quite place.

"I warned you," Aysun said. She and Caria stepped out of the void. Caria had her axes in hand.

"Wait, Your Majesty, this is not what it looks like," Raven pleaded. Raven retracted her fangs and her eyes returned to normal. The man's body slumped to the floor.

"It's exactly what it looks like. We're not here by accident. I heard about the murder Countess LaRue committed last night. I came to see for myself, so there was no misunderstanding. There in front of me is a murdered man. Murdered without provocation," Aysun sieved with anger.

"Please let me explain, Princess. He was going to kill her," Raven replied.

"It looked to me, it was just a little rough play," Aysun said.

"No, you don't understand," Raven said.

"Stop, this is not a discussion. The two of you are banished from the Great Tree and the lands of Stormhaven. You have three days to settle your affairs. Then leave my lands," Aysun said.

"Do you want me to brand them?" Caria asked.

"Try it," Veronica said. Her eyes changed back to black, and she bared her fangs. She dropped the transformation she used to hide the corruption in her face. She took on a demonic look.

"Stop, Ronny, don't make this any worse," Raven said. She stepped in front of Veronica.

"Standdown, Caria. They're too powerful. We're done here," Aysun said. She grabbed Caria by the arm, and they slipped into the void.

"Did you see that? What she changed into was a monster. They're demons. We should kill them," Caria said.

"I've passed my judgment for now. Keep them under surveillance until they leave. Let's go," Aysun said.

"This is terrible. Why do I listen to you? I was doing great here. You're here for two days, and you've ruined everything," Raven said as she sat at the table.

"You can't blame me. How was I to know she had a Cosmic Fae bodyguard?" Veronica said.

"It was her, not the bodyguard. I saw her eyes change before they disappeared. Anyway, that's not the point. What am I going to do now?" Raven asked.

"This is a blessing. You can have your pet manage the vineyard here and accompany me up north," Veronica replied.

"No, I told you I'm not following you into some type of battle. There is so much blood on my hands. I will use the time the Princess has given us to get our affairs in order here, then I will go back to France. Come with me. Forget this battle," Raven said.

"I can't. I gave my word. You mean the world to me, ma chérie. I will come find you as soon as it's over," Veronica said.

"Promise?" Raven asked.

"I promise," Veronica replied.

***

The color in the trees faded to crimson and ochre. Over the summer, Elnara had spent much of her time working with architects, landscapers, and other tradesmen to continue construction on the massive estate at Stormhaven.

It's been over four months since construction started. She and Marcus had stolen away time to visit the construction site and be together. However, Marcus could only stay for a couple of weeks at a time. This time, he returned with Edric. Elnara was directing artwork being hung up in the main house. Marcus came over and embraced her, kissing her on the lips.

Aysun and Caria approached the estate from the Great Tree. The night sky gleamed with a full moon. They flew along and went up to the back door. Their silhouettes crossed in front of the moon as the guards watched them approach the house. Aysun and Caria walked in the back door, where Elnara and Marcus were.

"Well, this is better than what we walked in on before," Caria said.

"Oh, my, my, I wasn't expecting you two. Unhand me, human. What brings you out here unannounced and so late?" Elnara asked as she pushed Marcus away.

"Your Majesty," everyone said in unison as Aysun entered the room. Everyone in the room stood up and then kneeled to Aysun. She waved them up.

"Remember those two vampires I told you about?" Aysun asked.

"Yes," Elnara replied.

"I banished them today," Aysun said.

"Really, dish-dish," Elnara replied. Tetyana and Emira were playing a game on a nearby sofa. They stopped playing to listen in. Edric and Drifa were also present.

"The vampires killed two people. They killed a man right in front of us. We got there too late to stop them," Aysun reported. Mizzy walked into the room.

"Dinner is ready. I'll set two more places. Welcome, Your Majesty, Caria," Mizzy said as she kneeled.

***

At the dinner table, Sebeli and Mizzy served the food from the kitchen. Sebeli kneeled before the princesses.

"Caria, can you pass the potatoes? Did you really see a vampire, like in real life?" Tetyana asked.

"Yes, a blood demon seven feet tall, with black eyes and claws. Her face was pure evil. She was called the Vampire Demonica! RAWR!" Caria said as she made a clawing motion toward Tetyana, imitating a monster. Tickling Tetyana, and she laughed.

"Stop, you know I'm a Lightning Fae?" Tetyana asked.

"I thought you had that under control?" Caria responded.

"Maybe, I guess. Did you fight the vampires?" Tetyana asked.

"No, we didn't, Tetyana. I don't know what it is, but there is something about them. Countess Raven seemed sincere about not killing. She lived in that vineyard for months without incident. It's that Countess Veronica that concerns me. I feel like they deserve a chance for absolution. A chance to make amends or to be cured. Just not here. Besides, they're powerful beings. They move almost faster than you can see. They're very dangerous," Aysun replied.

"Where's rat face?" Caria asked Tetyana.

"Her mom doesn't want her to come out here because of Auntie Elnara getting kidnapped," Tetyana replied.

"Aysun, how long are you staying for? What do you think of the grounds and house? The other master bedroom is all decorated," Elnara asked.

"Just for the night, but at my house. I think it's time for you to return to the castle. The Harvest Market is coming soon. The progress you've made on the estate is quite impressive," Aysun said.

"I'll begin preparations to return. Sebeli is here, you should stay. Marcus, you should go back on the trolley tomorrow with Aysun," Elnara suggested.

"No, my place is with you. I'll ride at your side when you return," Marcus replied. He looked at her submissively with care.

"Oh God, he's got it bad, too. Are you two sharing an ah?" Aysun asked.

"Shut up and pass the potatoes. Marcus has his own room. Whatever are you insinuating? Besides, I have Emira to watch over my honor," Elnara replied.

"The morality police that's so pregnant she can barely get off the couch?" Aysun replied with a laugh.

"Hey! Come on, I do my job," Emira replied. Everyone laughed.

***

The Lightning Privateer had finished repairs, and, once again, set sail on the high seas. The mast and railing were fully repaired. Over the summer months, the Lightning Privateer worked itself around the coast to the north. They came within a week's travel of approaching the inlet known as the Goblins Strait, leading to the much smaller Orc Sea to the north. A major storm brewed.

The captain took the ship away from shore and further out to sea, attempting to skirt the storm. The storm reached cyclone level. Dinner was difficult for the ship's galley to serve. The boys got a bowl of chili and a small loaf of bread each. It was challenging to eat in the galley. One had to be mindful to hold the cup, plate, and utensils; otherwise, they would fly off the table.

The ship leaned heavily from side to side. The hammocks remained mainly stationary as the ship tossed back and forth around them. It was quite nauseating if you tried to watch the room swinging around you. Many people were feeling sick, but it was not safe to be above deck. Sam was thankful that he had finally gotten used to being out at sea. The bow crashed through the waves.

Before entering the storm, the mainsail had been reefed (loosened) to reduce the stress on the mast. The boys had secured the topsail. After dinner, Augie and Pavlo played a sea shanty as Augie improvised the lyrics. Volkov joined the group with a violin. He struggled to stand and play as the ship swayed back and forth.

Song
Verse 1:
I fell in love with Reyhan's charm,
A woman with a heart so warm,
Her smile could light up any place,
And her grace could match any pace.

From the moment we met,
I was drawn to her like a magnet,
And as fate would have it,
She left me feeling quite stricken.

Chorus:
Oh, Reyhan, my love, my heart's desire,
In my heart, you'll forever inspire,
Through the storms and the raging sea,
Your memory will always be with me.

Verse 2:
But one fateful day on the ship,
A sea monster attacked with its grip,
Its tentacles reaching up high,
Our ship was left on the verge of goodbye.

As the railings splintered and shattered,
And wooden shards filled the air,
I knew that I had to live,
For Reyhan, my love, I couldn't bear to leave.

Chorus:
Oh, Reyhan, my love, my heart's desire,
In my heart, you'll forever inspire,
Through the storms and the raging sea,
Your memory will always be with me.

More of the crew had joined to help sing the chorus, but the song was soon interrupted. The deck officer came down the steps looking for Volkov.

"Petty Officer Volkov, man the sea and anchor detail! The winds are shifting, and the topsail is loose!" the deck officer yelled below.

"You heard him, mates, man your stations!" Volkov yelled. Everyone scattered to grab their rain gear and then struggled to put it on with the ship swaying back and forth. The boys ran out of the hatch to see the unholy tempest of swirling clouds only visible when backed by any one of the frequent lightning strikes. As they got out on the deck, Volkov ordered them to retie the riggings. Then he sent them aloft to re-secure the gaskets of the topsail.

The perilous climb was terrifying as the ship pitched and swayed. Slowly, the boys inched their way to the topsail. The rain fell hard in sheets. Dugan and Gunay flew, holding on to Sam's raincoat in case he slipped. As they neared the top, the ship dropped into a trough and started climbing the next swell. The ship tipped backward. Sam laced an arm and a leg into the ratlines.

"Hang on!" Sam yelled at Augustus. Augustus did as Sam did to hang on to the rope ladder. Then they continued their ascension until they reached the topsail. Sam helped Augustus to get out onto the yardarm. Augie had gotten to the yardarm first and crawled out to the further end. Ivan and Pavlo also reached the yardarm on the other side of the mast and made their way out along the footropes.

The wind and rain made their task difficult. Sam was also concerned about being struck by lightning. He finished tying his second gasket as the ship pitched upwards, then suddenly to port. Sam grabbed on quickly to the yardarm. He looked to the right at Ivan and Pavlo as they held on. Sam looked over to Augustus, but he was not there.

Sam looked down in horror to see. Augustus plummeted down, striking his head on the railing before he dropped into the sea. Dugan followed him in pursuit. Man-overboard was sounded as the bells rang out. Sam knew there was nothing the ship could do for Augustus. If he had survived, Dugan was his only hope. Gunay secured the second gasket to replace Augustus so Sam didn't have to and then returned to hanging on to Sam in case he fell. As Sam descended, Ivan caught up to him.

"What happened?" Ivan yelled over the sound of the wind and rain.

"Augie fell," Sam yelled back. They continued their descent until they reached the deck, where Volkov awaited them.

"What happened?" Volkov demanded.

"Augie fell. He was there one second and gone the next. He was tying the second gasket, and then he was gone," Sam reported. Volkov was upset as he turned and left toward the direction of the captain's cabin. He swore indistinctly in the wind, throwing his hat. For whatever a profiteering snake Volkov was for spying on them. Sam realized he took his job seriously, and this was a severe loss of a crew member. It was all on Dugan now.

***

Dugan took human form when he passed the railing and was out of sight of the crew. He dove into the water and began searching for Augustus, searching all angles from underneath the water. When the ship was far enough away, he took flight at mid-height to continue the search from the air.

After a short time, Dugan found Augustus floating face down in the sea. He quickly dove in and brought Augustus's head out of the water. Dugan tried waking Augustus, but he was gone. The head trauma he suffered had killed Augustus instantly.

Dugan stayed with Augustus for a little while, remembering the moments that they had shared over the past months. Playing cards or just joking around. He and Gunay couldn't help but interact with the boys occasionally. Dugan had lost a friend. He wept for Augustus. Dugan pushed Augustus under the surface deeper into the deep black. Eventually, Augustus continued to sink on his own. He let him go to rest in the deep.

He returned to the ship before it vanished from sight. Sam was reading in his hammock. He waited for Dugan to return. Dugan peered out of the shadow at Sam. Sam caught his gaze hopefully, but Dugan shook his head, confirming the worst. Sam put his book aside and rolled over to face Ivan and Pavlo.

"Augie's gone," Sam said. The boatswain's whistle trilled the tune for lights out. Ivan and Pavlo also settled into their racks to comprehend the loss. The lanterns were gradually put out near them.

***

The Harvest Market had started. It was a week before Aysun's preemptive attack plan began. She walked through the part of the market where her family's spot used to be. A family was set up there. Aysun and Elnara walked together. The father barked for attention to sell his goods, just as Aysun's father had done. It was reminiscent of their childhood. They were on their way to address the troops arriving through the tunnels.

She stopped to buy some apples from the stand. She saw a young blond-headed girl sitting behind the stand with her mother, playing with a doll. The girl sat on the exact spot behind the cart where her stepmother would look after her at the same age. The cheap doll was made from a potato sack and some discarded cloth. Aysun handed Elnara an apple.

Elnara was distracted as Mehmet approached. Mehmet whispered something to Emira, and Emira quietly reported to Elnara. Elnara headed back to the castle. Lost in her thoughts, she dropped her apple.

Aysun went around the stand and approached the little girl. She looked at the mother, seeking her approval to address the young girl. The mother smiled and offered no objection.

"I like your doll. May I see her?" Aysun kneeled, examined the doll, and then returned it to her. The girl curtseyed to Aysun. Aysun offered the young girl an apple. The girl looked at her mother before accepting it.

"You know, when I was a little girl around your age. This was my family's spot, and we sold our vegetables here," Aysun said. The girl looked confused.

"But you're a lady from court," the girl said.

"I have my own court now, in the land of the fairies. I am the Fairy Princess Aysun of the Moonlight," Aysun said as she put her finger over her lips and winked at the girl. She nodded to the mother before returning to Caria, and that's when she noticed Elnara had left and returned to the castle.

"Where did Elnara go?" Aysun asked Caria. Aysun saw the barely eaten apple she had given Elnara on the ground.

"I don't know. Mehmet came and delivered a message, and she headed back to the castle with him and Emira. She didn't say a word," Caria replied. Aysun went to Hannah and handed her a few coins.

"Go pick out a nice doll from one of the vendors for that girl. Tell her it's from the Fairy Princess. Try to match her hair. Then meet me at the Tunnel," Aysun said.

"Okay, we must get to the tunnel," Aysun said to Caria. The king closed off the park so Aysun could amass her army. Aysun walked to the far section of the park near the tunnel entrance. A large camp was already being set up as a significant portion of the troops awaited her inspection.

As she approached, the troops cheered. Over the years, she had learned to accept the empty admiration of the aristocracy politely, but it touched her deeply, coming from the common person. She waved to the troops as she passed, and the troops reacted with more cheers. Officers brought the army to attention. She came onto the field and was greeted by General Emir and many other members of the General Council and other officers. She noticed the review stand.

"What's all this?" She asked Emir.

"This is your army," he replied.

"You mean our army?" Aysun asked, slightly confused.

"These volunteers signed up after your speech in the meadow. This is their graduation. They would be honored if you would stay as they present their final review. The rest of the regular army is arriving tomorrow," Emir said.

"Of course, I would be honored," Aysun said. Emir escorted her up the stairs of the review stand to her seat. She looked out at the thousands of troops. She was impressed at the turnout of the volunteers. Emir signaled the officer on the field, and the review began as battalions of warriors paraded by. The pipes and drums played, followed by the horns. The troops performed special marching maneuvers, waving flags as they passed the review stand.

"Where is Princess Elnara? I thought she was coming too," Emir asked.

"I don't know. She was called away," Aysun replied as she waved to the parading troops.

6

Chapter Six: The Sentence

***

Elnara met Marcus as he was about to mount a horse with a group of others, including some noblewomen from the castle. There were an equal number of guardsmen.

"Marcus, where are you going?" Elnara asked.

"I'm being sent on a mission?" Marcus replied.

"There is something I'll need to talk to you about. Please hurry back," Elnara said.

"I need to talk to you about something also, but not now. I have to go. The King has ordered me not to delay. We'll talk soon," Marcus said. He mounted his horse, and the group headed toward the South Gate.

"Do you think he's avoiding me?" Elnara asked.

"I'm sure he's just been busy. There is a lot going on lately, Princess," Mizzy replied.

"Where is he going with those girls? I know some of them. I know some of them are jealous of Marcus and me," Elnara said as they returned to Elnara's room.

***

"Mehmet, are you sure he asked for mercy?" Elnara asked as she was dressed in the dress she had worn when she had Jerimiah blinded. She knew that after today, the dress would be destroyed. There was no sense in destroying two dresses. Mizzy helped her get ready as Emira prepared her carriage and escort.

"Yes, since he made his plea to Princess Aysun. He's eaten nothing but bugs and a few berries. He's in agony. Last night, he broke. He's ready. Your Highness," Mehmet replied.

"Mehmet, check the sword and make sure it's sharp enough. It's in the cabinet over there," Elnara said. Mehmet went and retrieved the executioner's sword. He checked its edge to ensure its sharpness.

"It's very sharp, Princess," Mehmet replied.

"Ok, let's go," she came out dressed from behind the screen. Elnara took the sheath and sword and handed them to Emira to carry. She also wore boots instead of dress shoes. Valeria saw Elnara had a large guard contingent escort her out. She also saw Emira carrying the executioner's sword. Elnara exited the castle and climbed into her carriage.

This was her largest guard detail to date. Emira wasn't taking any chances with the Princess, not with hostile forces so close. She sent Mehmet on ahead to have Jerimiah moved into an abandoned barn inside the outer wall. Valeria grabbed her sword and followed at a discreet distance.

Elnara entered the barn with only Emira. Cinar and his two cohorts stood behind Jerimiah. Emira walked behind Elnara as they approached.

"Jerimiah, my Worm Prince, you've called for me," Elnara said.

"Yes, I have called for your mercy. Can we stop the theatrics? Please. If I am going to die, let me die with some dignity. Okay, maybe I denied it to you, but you've won. May I have a last request?" Jerimiah asked.

"I'll hear your request," Elnara replied.

"I want a proper last meal: a juicy steak, a potato, and a bottle of whiskey. Please show me that much mercy before you execute me. I've been beaten, blinded, and tortured on your orders. I submit to my execution. You said that stew was my last meal. That was shit. I ask for a proper meal. I don't want to die hungry, Princess," Jerimiah said.

"Emira, tell Mizzy to go to the nearest fine restaurant. Have a proper meal prepared with a steak and potato and bring it back here with a bottle of whiskey and wine," Elnara said. She handed Emira some coins.

"Yes, Princess," Emira replied. She left the barn.

A short time later, Mizzy entered the barn with another guard. The guard carried in the food. Elnara specified where to set up the food for Jerimiah. Mehmet led Jerimiah to the table. Mizzy went about setting up the food for Jerimiah. She put the food out and poured a glass of wine for him. Mizzy offered to pour a glass for Elnara, but she declined. Mizzy put the utensils into Jerimiah's hands and showed him where each food and drink items were. Finally, she pulled a pint of whiskey out of her apron and placed it with two shot glasses on the table. Mizzy stepped aside and waited for Elnara to tell her what to do.

"That's all, Mizzy. Please wait with the carriage," Elnara said. Mizzy and the guard went back outside. Elnara took a seat across from Jerimiah. She refilled his wine. He heard it.

"Thank you," Jerimiah said.

"You're welcome," Elnara replied.

"I'm sorry. Thank you, Princess. You know I was not always that way. I had to adapt in prison. My henchman, as she called him, was once my tormentor. I turned him to my side. I showed him we could curry favor with the guards if we managed the other prisoners. However, he had certain urges that needed to be managed. To prevent him from killing," Jerimiah said. He explained between voracious bites, each one more forceful than the last.

"Do you have a family that you would like notified?" Elnara asked.

"No, they've long since passed," Jerimiah replied.

"Is the meal to your liking?" Elnara asked.

"This is the best meal I've ever had in my life. Thank you for not letting me die hungry," Jerimiah said with a bit of huff.

Elnara opened the whiskey bottle and poured two shots. She set one glass near Jerimiah and then clinked the glass with hers.

"Cheers," Elnara said. They took a shot, and she poured another, then a third.

"You should make your peace with God now," Elnara said.

"First, I want to ask for your forgiveness. You don't have to give it, but I wanted to say it. I knew my actions were wrong," Jerimiah replied.

Elnara did not respond. She could not forgive him. She wondered who she could ask for forgiveness for what she was about to do. Elnara turned and looked at Emira and gave her a nod. Emira unsheathed the sword. She looked back at Elnara and offered her the sword.

Jerimiah reached for the whiskey bottle and took a hearty drink. Then, he stood up and walked away from the table a few steps. He took a deep breath.

"I'm ready. How should we do this?" Jerimiah asked. Elnara heard him say that 'he was ready.' She grabbed the sword from Emira. She walked up behind Jerimiah. Elnara swung the sword across his neck with all of her might. Jerimiah's blood splattered onto Elnara's face and dress. Jerimiah's body fell to the ground next to his head. Elnara dropped the sword next to the body.

"Bury him someplace respectful and bury the sword with him. When you're done with that, bring your men and come see me at the castle," Elnara said to Cinar.

"Yes, Princess, right away," Cinar replied.

Elnara went outside and climbed into the carriage as they approached the castle. She wrote out a note detailing sums of gold.

"Emira, take this note to the bank and give it to my mother. Use the carriage. Get three appropriately sized boxes and bring them to me. I need to lie down. Mizzy, see if Marcus is back. Tell him I want to speak with him if he is," Elnara said. When the carriage arrived at the castle, Elnara and Mizzy departed the carriage. Emira carried on to the bank.

***

Emira entered the bank and went and knocked on Ms. Sachin's door before peaking in.

"Oh, come in, dear," Defne said as she got up and hugged Emira.

"It's nice to see you. Where's my Esra? She didn't come?" Defne asked.

"Princess Elnara had other matters to attend to," Emira replied. She handed Defne the note from Elnara.

"Esra wants me to stay at the castle for the next week, but she doesn't say why, only that it's urgent and I must do it. Why does she want me to stay at the castle? Why does she want that? She doesn't say," Defne asked.

"She's arranged for an apartment for you in the castle. There are some things I am not at liberty to discuss, Ms. Sachin, but I think you should honor your daughter's request," Emira said.

"Fine, I'll come the day after tomorrow. I do like dining with the king. She's asking for a lot of gold and gems. What does she need so much for?" Defne asked.

"I'm not allowed to discuss it, Ms. Sachin," Emira replied.

"Everything is so secret with you, fairies. Let me put in Esra's request," Defne said.

***

Elnara poured a glass of wine. Mizzy returned.

"Marcus has not returned. I asked the king's valet, and all he would say is that Marcus is not expected to return for a couple of days," Mizzy said, as she could see Elnara's demeanor sank.

"What is it? Do you want to talk about it?" Mizzy asked.

"No," Elnara said. Mizzy helped Elnara get undressed.

"See that this dress is burned. Whatever remains of it is to be buried in the cemetery," Elnara said.

"I think I could get the stains out," Mizzy said as she examined the dress.

"It's essential that you do as I say in this matter. The dress is to be destroyed. Is that clear?" Elnara demanded.

"Yes, Princess," Mizzy replied. She put a robe on Elnara and then went to get water to fill the bath. Aysun, Caria, and Hannah entered the room.

"Elnara, is everything ok?" Aysun asked.

"Yeah, it's fine. How are the troops?" Elnara asked.

"You should have seen it. It's quite impressive. Are you sure you're okay?" Aysun asked.

"Yeah, it's fine," Elnara replied.

"Okay, I've got a lot of things to do. Let me know if you need anything," Aysun said as she left.

"Hannah, wait a moment," Mizzy said.

"Can you do me a favor and have this dress destroyed? Princess Elnara was very specific that she wanted the dress burned, and any remains or ashes buried in the cemetery. She was very insistent it be done properly," Mizzy said quietly to Hannah.

"Give it here. Aysun already let me go for the day. I'll see to it straight away. What happened? Where is the blood from?" Hannah asked quietly.

"She's carried it out, the execution, that is. She had me fetch a fine meal for him and everything. He was bathed and dressed all proper. She wouldn't let me stay to witness, but it's done," Mizzy replied. Hannah nodded.

"Maybe you should make sure she's not alone tonight. Make sure she's okay," Hannah said, and Mizzy nodded in agreement as she led Hannah out the door. Emira came in shortly after. Two guards accompanied her. They each carried a small chest.

"Princess, I brought the gold you requested. Your mother was disappointed you didn't make the request in person. I told her you have arranged for an apartment for her here in the castle. She said she would come the day after tomorrow. I should go report to Caria," Emira reported.

"Ok, thank you. Leave it on the table in front of the couch. I want you to find Valeria. I want you to ask her to tell me if there is any word on Marcus and when he will return. Then you can have the rest of the night off. I'm not planning to go anywhere else tonight," Elnara said as she finished her glass of wine. Mizzy prepared the tub for Elnara's bath. She helped Elnara to take her bath and then get dressed for bed.

A short time later. Cinar and his group were announced at the door. Mizzy led them in. The men all kneeled, and Elnara motioned for them to rise.

"Thank you for coming to my aid in carrying out this unfortunate sentence. I know it wasn't easy," Elnara said. She picked up the first box and opened it to display its contents to the unknown Fae.

"Actually, I rather enjoyed it. The human got what he deserved, Your Highness," he said.

"I think we are overdue for an introduction," Elnara said as she handed him the box.

"I am Private Vladimir of the Inferno. It's been an honor to serve you, Your Highness," Vladimir said.

"So, you're not from the Great Tree?" Elnara asked

"No, Your Highness. I moved here only a few years ago. Looking for an opportunity. I joined the military, hoping to serve on the guard of the returned princesses. Cinar asked for volunteers for the branding duty, and I jumped at the chance to serve," Vladimir said.

"Cinar, he has my endorsement to join our guard, but run it by Emira," Elnara said. She picked up the second box and displayed it for Mehmet.

"Thank you, Mehmet," Elnara said.

"Your Highness," Mehmet accepted the box.

"Mehmet, I have another small task for you. I want you to go to my estate at the Great Tree and retrieve Mia's armor. Put it in her stable, and when the battle begins. I want you to suit her up in case I need her," Elnara said.

"Very well, Princess. I'll go directly there," Mehmet replied.

"And now you, Cinar, for leading this task and taking care of the third. I've added a little bonus. Look inside the pouch," Elnara said as she opened the box. Along with the coins, there were a few valuable gemstones, including diamonds and rubies. It was a small fortune for each of the men.

"Should you ever need me again, I will gladly carry out your will," Cinar said.

"I will never brand another person again. The gold I have given you three is in appreciation for carrying out your task and your silence. I do not want you to disclose details of the torture or execution. File your official reports and let it end there. Can I ask for your discretion?" Elnara asked.

"Yes, Princess," they all replied.

"Do yourself a favor before you bring those boxes into a bar. Go deposit it in the bank. The bank to the south of the castle. My human mother works there. Tell her nothing, or bring it to the bank in the Great Tree. You're all dismissed," Elnara said. They bowed, and Mizzy showed them out. She returned and filled Elnara's wine glass.

"Thank you, Mizzy. I think I'll be ok from here. You're excused," Elnara said.

"Maybe it's better if I stayed. I could just sleep on the couch," Mizzy suggested.

"Unless you can conjure up Marcus, then you're excused. I want to be alone," Elnara said with some annoyance.

"Of course, Princess," Mizzy bowed, left, and closed the door. Elnara got up and locked the door behind her. Elnara sunk to the floor and cried.

***

Emira found Valeria. She was in her room reading a book. She had hurried back after witnessing the execution through the spaces between the boards on the barn wall. Emira knocked on the open-door frame.

"Come in," Valeria said. Emira approached and sat across from Valeria.

"I'm looking for information on Marcus. Well, the Princess is. She knows he's been sent on a mission, but wants to know when he will return. Failing that, she wants to know the minute he is back," Emira said.

"Has something happened?" Valeria asked.

"Valeria, I'm not stupid. I know you were there. I could smell you and hear you breathing on the other side of the wall, looking in. You saw it," Emira said.

"Okay, sorry. I forget how amazing you Fae are," Valeria said.

"Besides, if you want to pretend you're reading a book, you are about fifty pages behind your page fold. Seriously, I'm worried about Princess Elnara. She's cracking at the seams and wants to talk to Marcus. Can you get word to him?" Emira asked.

"No, I don't think so. I can try to ask the king, but I could tell Marcus left with the noble women of the court. I am sure that the plan to keep them protected is above me. Maybe if the Princess asked the King directly," Valeria said.

"Okay, I have to go make a report. Let me know if you find out anything," Emira said.

"Okay, I will," Valeria said.

***

Emira went to Caria's room and knocked.

"Yes, who is it?" Caria asked.

"Emira, I must speak with you," Emira said.

"Come in," Caria said. Emira entered the room and stood in front of Caria, fidgeting. Caria sat in meditation. She took her time to extinguish the candle in front of her.

"What is it, Emira?" Caria asked.

"It's done. She did it," Emira said.

"She's done what?" Caria asked.

"She's carried out the execution of Jerimiah," Emira replied.

"No," Caria said.

"I witnessed it," Emira said.

"Okay, don't say another word, come on," Caria put her uniform on, then she grabbed Emira by the hand and led her to Aysun's room. Caria and Emira entered Aysun's room. They kneeled. Aysun motioned them to stand.

"Tell her what you just told me," Caria said to Emira.

"Your Majesty, Princess Elnara has carried out the execution of the human known as Jerimiah," Emira said.

"What, when?" Aysun asked.

"Earlier today, about an hour ago," Emira said.

"Why am I just hearing about this now?" Aysun demanded. Emira kneeled.

"I, I carried out her orders. I reported to Captain Caria as soon as I completed her orders. The princess only wants to talk to Marcus, but he's been sent on some secret mission. Even Valeria doesn't know the details. I beg your forgiveness," Emira reported.

"Relax, Emira. I should have picked up when she said it was fine. It's never okay when she says, 'it's fine.' Come on," Aysun said as she got up and walked over to Elnara's door. She knocked on the door.

"Elnara, it's Aysun," Aysun tried the door, but it was locked. "Elnara, come open the door," Aysun said.

"No, I want to be left alone. I want to talk to Marcus and only Marcus," Elnara responded.

"Don't do this alone, Elnara. Not you, not with all you've been through. Don't shut me out," Aysun said.

"I said leave me alone. Leave me alone!" Elnara yelled.

"Ok, Elnara, I'll find out what I can about Marcus. This is not your fault. You did what you had to do," Aysun said.

"Leave me alone! I don't want to hear it anymore!" Elnara yelled. She kicked the door.

"Elnara, I'm going to leave you alone, but I'm here if you want to talk. I'm worried about you, and I love you," Aysun said, but there was no reply. Aysun retreated to her room.

"Caria, I want constant surveillance on her. There should be no intrusion into her room, but everything else is in play. She is to be considered a risk to herself. If anything happens to her, I'll hold you personally accountable. You'll allow no harm to come to her!" Aysun said.

"I've sworn my life to it! Your Majesty. Do you really think she would hurt herself?" Caria replied.

"I don't know, but I don't want to take any chances," Aysun said.

***

Hannah returned to the Inn where she and Mizzy were staying. She grabbed a shovel and a basket. Hannah placed the dress in the basket. She went out the back of the hotel. Hannah approached a couple of fae soldiers sitting around a fire. Hannah walked over to them.

"Hi, can I use your fire? I need to burn this dress," Hannah said. She picked the dress out of the basket.

"If you're going to burn it, can I have that ruby? That's not going to burn anyway," one man said. Hannah looked at the relatively large center blood ruby. She thought to herself. He was probably right that it wouldn't burn. Mizzy said Elnara was specific. She removed the ruby. Hannah would bury it with the ashes from the dress. She removed the ruby and placed it in her pocket.

Hannah then moved some hot coals from the fire off to the side. She placed the dress on top of the coals. The dress ignited. She sat and watched as the dress burned.

"Damn shame," Mizzy said. She walked up and sat beside Hannah.

"I thought you were going to spend the night with her?" Hannah asked.

"I planned to, but she all but threw me out! This business with this man changed her. Not for the good," Mizzy said. They sat there until the dress burned away. Hannah moved the coals away and collected the remains of the dress in the basket. She and Mizzy walked to the cemetery and buried the remains. Later that evening, as Hannah prepared for bed, she realized she had forgotten to put the ruby in the hole. She put it in a box and placed it inside her bedside table. She would bury it in the hole tomorrow.

***

The next day, after breakfast, Aysun and Hannah returned to her room. A maid exited Elnara's room.

"Hannah, can you talk to Mizzy and see what she says about Elnara?" Aysun asked.

"No, Princess Elnara sent her away as soon as we arrived. I can tell Mizzy is quite worried," Hannah said.

"Princess Elnara is letting the maids in. Go talk to that one and see what she can tell us," Aysun said. Hannah shuffled off to catch up to the maid. Aysun went out to her balcony, shrunk down, and flew over to Elnara's balcony. Emira had a vantage point from a chair-side table. Aysun landed beside her.

"What do you have to report?" Aysun asked.

"Not much. I think she is largely staying in bed. She sleeps for a few hours, then wakes up, paces the floor, and then goes back to bed," Emira said.

"So, there are no signs she's trying to hurt herself?" Aysun asked.

"No, I think she is just waiting to speak with Marcus," Emira replied.

"Okay, you can stand down from the extra watch. I'm probably over-reacting. I think we should wait for her to get a chance to speak with Marcus. She has never shut me out before. I don't know why she won't confide in me," Aysun said.

"Me either. When you went to dinner last night, I pleaded with her to let me in. I sat against the door and tried talking to her. She kicked the door hard and told me that if I didn't stop talking and go away, I would regret it. I have a knot on my head. She's never spoken to me like that before," Emira said.

"Yeah, I don't know. I guess the only thing we can do is give her space. She is letting the maids in. Get reports from them from now on. Let me know if something changes," Aysun said.

＊

Elnara approached the mirror. She removed her hat and veil. The corruption was set deep in her face. How orc-like she had become, she thought. How hideous. Gray hair outlined her face. She blew out the candle and put her hat and veil back on. She limped back to lie on the bed in the dark.

It was three days before Elnara would leave her room to take regular meals. The corruption had softened in her face, but she appeared to have aged from the experience. Marcus had still not returned from his assignment. Elnara remained withdrawn.

7

⊱❦⊰

Chapter Seven: The Attack

The night before the battle, Aysun slept in her bed. A voice spoke to her.

"She is going to need you," the voice called out. A figure appeared with long white hair. They both stood facing each other in a lunar landscape. The older fae woman wore a white, flowing dress.

"Mother?" Aysun asked.

"No child. Nuray has gone beyond," the voice replied.

"Inanna?" Aysun asked.

"Yes, my beautiful Aysun. My Moon Goddess. Why do you turn away from my gift? You are not the Goddess of Death. The moon brings balance, light, and peace. That is why I have chosen you," Inanna replied. She approached Aysun. Aysun kneeled.

"I'm sorry, forgive me, Goddess. It doesn't come as naturally as my other abilities," Aysun said.

"There is nothing to forgive. You were born a Cosmic Fae first. I chose you at such a tender age. I am deeply sorry for that. Nuray was taken from us far too soon. That left me little choice. Your bloodline is the future," Inanna tenderly reassured her.

"Did she suffer?" Aysun asked.

"No, I brought her here before the end. I held her until she disappeared. She felt no pain. Nuray only spoke of you, not of her own fate. She felt she had let you down. Nuray loved you so much. She made me promise to watch over you before she moved on. I've watched you your whole life," Inanna said. Aysun wept. Inanna leaned over and kissed Aysun on her head.

"You are chosen, Moon Goddess. Embrace your gift, or she will die," Inanna said. Aysun awoke.

"Who is going to die, Inanna?" Aysun sat up and looked around. Was that a dream? She wondered. Aysun tried to go back to sleep, but the experience overwhelmed her. She got up and went into Elnara's room. She went in without knocking. Elnara was sleeping. Aysun crawled into the bed with her, waking her up.

"Marcus? Oh, Aysun. Are we having a sleepover? I think we're getting a little old for that. Did you have a nightmare?" Elnara asked.

"Sorry, I just needed to get out of bed and think. It wasn't a nightmare, more like a visit. How are you doing?" Aysun asked. Elnara sat up.

"I'm fine. I don't want to talk about it. A visit from whom?" Elnara asked.

"Inanna," Aysun replied.

"It was just a dream. Go back to sleep. We have to be ready for battle in the morning. We need our rest," Elnara said as she laid back down. She grabbed Aysun's arm and pulled her in closer by rolling over.

"Don't let them put salt in that pond," Aysun said.

"Goodnight," Elnara said sharply.

"Goodnight," Aysun replied softly.

***

The next morning. Elnara looked for Marcus. She wore her full armor and had her helmet on to hide the corruption on her face and the change in her hair. She hoped he would understand and be able to look past it. Elnara searched franticly. Would he still love her?

Finally, she spotted Marcus on the castle's north side, but he was talking to another Fae girl. He handed the girl a small box the size of a ring. She opened the box and was so excited. She jumped up and hugged Marcus.

It took the wind out of Elnara. She stumbled backward momentarily. This was her worst fear realized. She would have feelings for this human only to be betrayed. She should never have trusted the human. Cinar caught her arm and steadied her. She turned and left and went out the western door toward the pond in the forest. Elnara met up with Caria on a small raised command platform. Caria stood with a spyglass, looking for any sight of the enemy troop's movements.

"Princess Elnara, you have command. I'm glad to see you wearing the helmet I had made for you. Do you like it? How are you feeling?" Caria asked as she kneeled. The helmet bore the resemblance of a dragon's head.

"I wish people would stop asking me how I'm feeling. Yeah, it's great, thank you. Let me see the telescope," Elnara said rather flatly.

"Is something wrong?" Caria asked. She handed the telescope over to Elnara.

"No, everything is as I expected it to be," Elnara replied.

***

Miray ran up and handed Marcus a small box.

"Marcus, Marcus, Marcus, I have it! I'm so happy I found you before the battle. I just got here with the last supply run. Tetyana made me promise not to open it. You had to be the first! I'm dying, though. I have to see it. Please, please show it to me," Miray begged. She was an explosion of energy. Marcus unwrapped the package and opened the box she had handed to him.

"Wow, this is nice. Tetyana is really skilled," Marcus commented. He closed the box for the ring and handed it back to her. She opened the box to view the ring. Miray was unaware that Elnara had walked in and was observing her.

"Oh my god, are you fooling me? Wow, Marcus, Princess Elnara is going to love this. I'm so happy for you two," Miray said as she leaned in and hugged Marcus.

"Can you put the ring in my room and tell Tetyana it's perfect when you see her? My quarters are on the second floor. Just ask any of the guards on the floor. Tell Tetyana that she can make the final version," Marcus said. He politely broke the hug.

"Oh, sorry, I'm a hugger. Of course, Marcus. Good luck in the battle today. Stay safe," Miray said as she departed.

***

Nearer to the north gate, the Fae and human generals waited for the full morning light. As the sun broke over the treetops to the east, the forest opened up with the songs of the birds. The King rode out in front of the generals.

"Major General Emir, are the Fae ready?" Alex asked. Alex sat atop an armored horse with General Emir and the king's lead general next to him.

"Front Gate Ready?" Emir called out. Aysun responded by lighting and raising a torch. Aysun wore a new custom suit of armor. Shining silver with white leather and purple cloth. She carried a white and steel war hammer with her. The sign of the Great Tree and the Moon emboldened on her chest and the hammer.

"Forest Ready?" Emir called out to the top of the west wall. A soldier raised and lowered a torch. Caria tapped Elnara to point out the torch. Elnara lit her torch with her hand and held it in the air. The west wall raised its torch again to show the defense was ready.

"The Fae are ready!" General Emir called to Alex.

"General, the west and south gates?" Alex asked the human general. The General gave the signal. A series of torches were lit in return. Valeria led the defenses at the two gates. She lit her torch and raised it in the air.

"Everything is set, Your Majesty. The defense is ready," the General responded.

"Let's hope Emira got into position. Princess Aysun. Signal the attack!" Alex called to her.

"Gladly! Light the fires!" Aysun called out. From atop the north wall, they lit a large fire. The fire sent up a smoke signal.

***

Emira saw the signal. She ordered the attack to begin on the ships off the coast. Emira rose out of the water and let out a shriek. The water glowed a bright blue beneath her. The other water elementals surrounded the three ships present at anchor. She wore a crown and some light mail armor around her shoulders. Emira also had mail armor around her belly to protect the twins. She was in the late stage of her pregnancy. The costume distracted the orcs and goblins. The captains and crew clambered onto the decks to meet her parlay.

"Trespassers! I demand you leave these shores! Return to where you came from, and do not come back," Emira shouted. This was just a diversion. The attack had already begun. The captains and crew were transfixed on her, laughing. Fae boarded and began sabotaging and looting the ships at anchor during the distraction.

"I am the Goddess of the Sea, and I demand my tax," Emira shouted.

"Go away, mermaid, or you'll be on the menu tonight," one of the ship's captains answered. The crews laughed, and with a wave of his hand, he ordered his archers to fire.

"You will pay one way or the other!" Emira proclaimed. She sunk back beneath the waves. The Fae opened barrels of oil and dumped them below decks. They lit the oil by smashing lanterns. They fought back to the top deck and fled over the side. The three ships out at anchor gradually caught fire and sank.

***

Elnara lit the first arrow and fired it at the forest. It didn't feel right to her. She felt nauseous.

"Light the forest on fire, and Caria, stand your ground. If one spoonful of that salt goes into this pond, you'll answer to me. You have command," Elnara said as she turned and left and headed back inside the castle.

"But Princess, I thought you were staying?" Caria called after Elnara, but Elnara didn't respond. She proceeded through the castle and then out to the stables, where Mehmet was waiting for her. Mia was already in her amour.

"Princess Elnara, Mia is ready as you requested," Mehmet said as he kneeled. Elnara motioned for him to stand.

"Thank you, Mehmet," Elnara said. As she passed Mehmet and approached Mia.

"Mia down," Elnara commanded. Mia complied, lowering herself to the ground. Elnara cast her cane aside and mounted her. Mia stood back up.

Elnara rode back into the castle. She merged with all the other riders, preparing for the attack on the supply convoy. Mehmet and Cinar accompanied her. They mixed in with the enlisted humans and Fae. Elnara had thought about how Felix fell in battle and how Valeria had said, 'he died a warrior's death.' Was it worth it? She considered the thought.

In the distance, near the north gate. Marcus called the troops to attention and then announced the charge.

"Riders ready? Charge!" Marcus called out. He did not see Elnara at the back of the pack. The riders charged out of the North Gate. Emir and Aysun, saw Elnara pass by.

"Elnara!" Aysun called to her, but Elnara ignored her. Emir ran to Aysun.

"What does she think she's doing? Emir demanded.

"The opposite of what she was told. Can you send some more guards after her to protect her?" Aysun asked.

"Everyone is in battle. There is no one left to send. Oh, this is a nightmare," Emir said as he wrung his hands and paced about.

"She'll be fine. She can take care of herself," Aysun said.

Elnara rode hard as they approached the shoreline. The morning sun glistened off the whitecaps. The lead group had stopped to free the prisoners. Elnara passed behind Marcus. He was dismounted and fighting hand to hand. Elnara stood up in the stirrups, firing fire arrows at the supply wagons. The human riders threw bags of pitch. The supply convoy was soon all ablaze. Aysun could see that her plan was going well. Elnara pulled out ahead of the pack.

Elnara rode on past the road where the troops were supposed to turn to retreat. She rode on toward the siege equipment. Ahead, the orcs had three trebuchets and a battering ram lined up. Elnara ran out of arrows as she approached. She dismounted Mia and drew her sword and shield. Cinar and Mehmet did the same.

"Tie your horses to Mia's saddle! Mia, stay," Elnara called to them. The noise of the battle soared as fires raged and swords and shields clashed. The screaming of men and orcs rose in the air. Elnara, Cinar, and Mehmet fought their way to each piece of equipment. Elnara glowed as she set them on fire with her hands, one after the other. Flames wafted out of her armor and from her hands. She pushed herself to her maximum output level. The equipment submitted to her fury. Cinar and Mehmet kept her from being flanked.

***

Marcus and the rest of the forces retreated down the fire road and back to the castle. He had not seen Elnara destroying the siege equipment before returning to the castle. Aysun flagged him down before he passed her.

"Marcus, did you see Elnara?" Aysun asked.

"No, I only saw Caria when I passed the pond. I assume she's retreated to the castle," Marcus replied.

"No, she rode out with your group," Aysun said.

"What? No, I didn't see her," Marcus said. They watched as the last of the riders returned to the castle.

"I'm going back out to find her," Marcus said as he turned his horse around. Aysun took Moon form and grabbed the reins of his horse. The horse tried to pull free. Marcus was stunned seeing Aysun. Her taller white form was hard to believe, a moving marble statue. It was so much more than Elnara had described to him.

"If you go out there, you're going to die. We've lost the element of surprise," Aysun said. The freed prisoners ran past Aysun, when the last one had passed.

"Raise the wall!" Aysun commanded.

Unable to stop their momentum, orcs impaled themselves on the spear wall. The archers cleared the remaining orcs from near the spear wall. Aysun returned to human form and fired her bow. Marcus retreated into the gate.

****

Elnara finished destroying the remaining equipment and supplies.

"Back to the horses. Retreat!" Elnara called out. They made their way back to the horses and mounted. An arrow struck Mehmet's horse through the eye. The horse fell over dead. It fell on its side and landed on Mehmet's leg. Cinar and Elnara dismounted and pulled him free. They put Mehmet on the horse with Cinar. His leg was injured in the fall.

Elnara rode on, and they followed the path to the fire road. The fire road was filled with orcs and trolls. The seaside path was their only option. They still had to push past the remaining forces when they cleared the tree line. They encountered a large troll.

The troll surprised Elnara as she rode by. It was just as surprised to see her pass by. The troll threw his hip into the side of Cinar's horse. Mehmet and Cinar were thrown off. The horse got up and ran away. The troll went to smash the downed riders, but Elnara had already turned around. She attacked the troll with a sword and shield.

"Get him out of here, Cinar!" Elnara yelled.

"My duty is to protect you, Princess!" Cinar yelled back.

"Go, that's an order! I'm right behind you," she yelled. Cinar picked up Mehmet. They shrunk to Fae form and flew towards the gate. Aysun saw them coming. Then she saw Elnara battling the troll.

"There she is!" Aysun called to Marcus.

"What the hell is she doing?" Marcus cried.

"She's fighting a troll," Aysun replied.

"We have to help her," Marcus cried.

Elnara continued to fight the troll at close quarters. She took several strikes on her helmet. The troll finally caught her with a solid swing, tearing her shield's bindings. Elnara pulled away from the troll and galloped a distance away. She rode toward the castle.

Elnara caught her breath. Her helmet suffered heavy damage. While it protected her from being knocked out, she suffered a cut to her face because of it. She threw the shield to the ground and removed her helmet. Marcus looked on, confused. He stared at her. She saw Marcus atop his horse, looking back at her. Elnara threw her sword down, sticking it into the ground below. She grabbed a nearby spear sticking up from the ground. Several freed prisoners were helping wounded soldiers around the edge of the battlefield. Elnara knew if she let the troll go, it would go after them.

"What is she doing now?" Marcus asked.

"She's not backing down," Aysun replied.

"That's crazy. Has she gone insane?" Marcus yelled to Aysun.

Elnara looked at Marcus. She was overwhelmed with rage and emotion as she thought about witnessing Marcus propose to the other girl. Having Jerimiah tortured and killed, the nightmares she constantly had about Jerimiah and her imprisonment and torture. The scars she would have to live with. Her father's death!

The thoughts and emotions washed over her. Fueling her anger. She pulled the spear out of the ground and then turned around and looked at the troll. She didn't like the feeling that the troll had bested her. Elnara turned Mia back around to face the troll. Elnara remembered the conversation she had with Valeria.

"He fought well until he fell," Elnara said. *"Then he died a warrior's death,"* Valeria responded.

Marcus flew past Aysun on his horse and jumped over the spear wall. He grabbed a spear that was stuck in the ground when he landed.

"Hey, over here! We're not done yet," Elnara yelled at the troll. The troll roared back. Elnara charged.

"Doesn't anyone follow orders anymore?" Emir asked.

"I think where those two are concerned, the answer is no. I think they will do what their hearts tell them," Alex replied.

Elnara aimed for the heart as she charged. The troll moved to the side at the last second. She stabbed the troll in the shoulder. The troll swung his club at Elnara. She made a mistake, and she knew this was the end. Elnara had used her sword and shield to skillfully avoid the troll's powerful swing.

Now, at spear length, she was exposed to the troll's full-force strike. Mia reared up, and they both took the strike. Elnara was sent flying, and her body struck a nearby tree. Mia was knocked to the ground. A gasp fell over everyone who witnessed it. Cinar dropped to his knees, taking Mehmet with him. Everyone looked on in horror. Aysun picked up her war hammer. She mounted a nearby horse. Cinar also mounted a horse.

"Lower the spear wall!" Aysun ordered. They lowered the wall, and Aysun, Edric, Yusef, and Cinar rode out.

"Defend the Princesses!" Emir yelled. Those still on their horses rode after Aysun, both human and Fae alike. Others remounted and followed. One of the human generals called out to the human troops to assist, but they didn't need instructions. They had already leaped into action.

Elnara pulled herself along the ground to get to Mia. Mia was still lying on the ground. Elnara noticed that Mia, though still breathing, couldn't get up. She crawled with all her might. Her right arm was broken from where the troll struck her. Elnara's left leg was broken again when she hit the tree. She had a hard time breathing. Still, she used her remaining strength to reach Mia. Blood spouted from Mia's neck.

"I'm sorry. I'm sorry," Elnara cried. She put pressure on the wound to stop the bleeding. Her hand trembled. Marcus rode up as the troll finally removed the spear Elnara stuck in him. Marcus threw his spear and stuck the troll in the abdomen. The troll retreated. Marcus dismounted and ran to Elnara. Mia's jugular vein was spilling blood. Marcus could see Mia's front leg was collapsed and broken. Elnara heated her hand to seal the wound and stop the bleeding on Mia's neck. Marcus grabbed her by her wrist and pulled her hand away.

"What are you doing?" Elnara shrieked.

"Elnara, it's too late," Marcus said.

"No, I can save her. I can stop the bleeding!" Elnara screamed.

"Babe, her leg is broken. I've got to get this armor off of you so I can carry you," Marcus said.

Elnara looked over and saw Mia's leg. She knew Mia was beyond saving. She rolled over and allowed Marcus to remove her armor.

"I'm sorry, Mia. Marcus, wait, I burned off all of my clothes," Elnara replied.

"Now is when you are worried about modesty?" Marcus said.

"No, Aysun is the modest one. Don't let people see my back," Elnara said.

"I'll do the best I can," Marcus replied. He covered her as he removed her armor.

Seeing an opportunity to attack, a group of orcs charged them from the nearby forest. Marcus was unbuckling her armor when he noticed they were almost on him. He stood up, drew his sword, and picked up his shield. He took down the first two, but was about to be overwhelmed.

Aysun dismounted at full gallop and used the horse's momentum to propel herself forward in her weightless moon form. She glided along above the ground to them. Then she took a heavier form. Aysun swung her massive hammer, sending an orc flying. She smashed another's shield. Her sheer overwhelming power was impressive to behold. The troll approached Aysun. He swung his club, which met her hammer in defense. She jabbed the troll in the face, which put him off balance. Aysun made a full swing at the outside of the troll's left leg. She shattered the knee of the troll, causing him to fall on his side. Aysun brought her hammer down on the head of the troll.

"Get her out of here, now!" Aysun ordered Marcus. He resumed trying to get Elnara's armor off. Elnara sobbed. Cinar, Yusef, and Edric arrived with the rest of the forces. They immediately helped Marcus to get Elnara's armor off. Marcus tore segments of cloth he scavenged nearby and some sticks and improvised some splints for Elnara. Marcus attempted to lift Elnara, but she clung to Mia's mane.

"Elnara, it's time to go. She's dead, babe. Let her go," Marcus said as he yanked her free.

Mia had already stopped breathing. The downed horse and injured princess noticeably saddened and angered the Fae fighting around her. There was not one Fae from the Great Tree who did not know of Princess Elnara and her horse, Mia. They mourned Mia's loss but fought on.

"Mia, I'm sorry!" Elnara called back. She kept repeating it until she passed out. Marcus ran as fast as he could toward the castle. As the battle raged on, she slipped into delirium, reliving a nightmare of killing Jerimiah. Elnara came around a few moments later.

"Marcus, you're here?" Elnara asked.

"Yes, I'm here. You're going to be okay," Marcus said, but he wasn't sure. Her body was bruised over.

Marcus carried Elnara as fast as he could until he reached a cart to place her on. He placed her on the cart and covered her with a blanket. He escorted the cart as it went back into the castle.

"I'm cold, Marcus," Elnara said. She went in and out of consciousness. He tucked her in tighter and rubbed her arm to comfort her. Marcus brought her into the castle. Drifa was there to greet them. She climbed into the cart and examined Elnara.

"No, no! Why did you do this to her? Stupid humans! Hiss," Drifa said, and she looked Elnara over.

Drifa extended her hands over Elnara's torso, allowing a gentle cold mist to envelop her. The frost formed on the outer layers of the blanket, creating an insulation that cooled Elnara's body while simultaneously providing the soothing benefits of Drifa's unique ability.

"Is she going to be okay?" Marcus asked.

"What does it look like to you? It's bad. We need to get her to the infirmary. We need a stretcher. Hiss," Drifa said. Valeria entered the room.

"Get a stretcher!" Valeria shouted.

"Where's Caria? Marcus, has anyone called to relieve Caria's position?" Valeria asked.

"No, Elnara was injured. See to Caria's relief," Marcus replied.

"What's happened to her? Will she be ok?" Valeria asked.

"She's taken a club strike from a troll. I don't know. It's bad," Marcus replied.

"I'm taking half of the east guard and all the south guard positions. The enemy forces to the east have retreated. The South Gate is clear," Valeria said as she put her helmet back on.

"Do it. Take the troops," Marcus replied. Valeria ran off.

***

Valeria emerged out the western side door with troops. She could see the devastation on both sides of the line. There were heavy casualties. She approached an officer standing near the many salt carts.

"What's the situation, Lieutenant?" Valeria asked.

"The lines are about to be overrun. We are waiting for the signal to release the salt into the pond," the Lieutenant replied.

"What's the signal?" Valeria asked.

"The Fae Captain, the Troll Killer, said we cannot put any salt in the pond until she goes down or gives the word. Otherwise, If I did, she would... well, let me just say it wouldn't be polite to repeat," the lieutenant said.

"Yeah, that sounds like Caria," Valeria replied. Valeria's troops assembled to the south of the pond. She paced them and yelled.

"I heard some of you complaining about missing the action on the North wall. Well, here's the action. Make me proud. Relieve the front line!" Valeria screamed. They drew their weapons and ran around the pond, shouting their battle cries, which grew into a collective roar. The humans and Fae on the line cheered.

"Lieutenant. I'm giving you new orders. Take your men and help get the wounded to medical," Valeria said.

"What about my orders to salt the pond?" the Lieutenant asked.

"Those orders are still valid, but only if our line falls. Until then, help with the wounded," Valeria replied.

"Yes, ma'am," the Lieutenant replied. Valeria sprinted over to where Caria was. Caria sat with her back to the archer's wall, clearly exhausted and disheveled. Valeria kneeled to face her.

"Caria, are you okay?" Valeria asked. She handed Caria her canteen.

"Yeah, you're late. Where's Marcus?" Caria asked, drinking from the cantina.

"Something's happened. Princess Elnara is down," Valeria said.

"What, how? The last time I saw her, she was heading back to the castle," Caria asked.

"It looks like she rode out with Marcus on the main assault. She took a club strike from a troll. That's all I know. They're moving her to the infirmary. I think it's bad, Caria. I think you should go," Valeria said.

"You sure you can handle this?" Caria asked.

"Yes, I have an excellent teacher. Go," Valeria said as she offered Caria a hand to get up. Caria took her hand and pulled herself up.

"Not one spoonful of salt hits that water," Caria said.

"You have my word. Now go," Valeria said as she drew her weapon and joined the fray. She looked back and saw Caria dive into the pond in full armor. A blue streak shot away from her underwater.

***

Elnara awoke in a bed in the infirmary. Drifa was attending to her. Elnara's head was fuzzy, and her mind was unclear.

"Have I been drugged?" Elnara asked.

"Yes, I've given you medication for the pain and to help you sleep. Don't try to get up. Go back to sleep. Hiss," Drifa replied.

"I don't want that. I didn't ask for that, and I don't need it!" Elnara protested.

"When you're a healer, Princess, I'll consider your opinion. Now shut up. Let's have her moved. Let's move her to her room," Drifa growled. Elnara faded back out of consciousness. They moved her past Aysun and the rest of the people waiting.

"Will she be okay?" Aysun asked Drifa. Drifa just gazed at her as they passed by. Elnara was placed in her room. Drifa came out and closed the door.

"Is she going to be okay?" Marcus asked.

"Does she look like she is going to be okay? Hiss," Drifa replied.

"What are you saying, Drifa? Give me details," Aysun said.

"She's dying. She's bleeding inside, and I can't stop it. All I can do is give her potion for the pain. I've done all I can do. If you have something to say to her, you should do it before morning. I don't expect her to survive the night. She needs to rest now. I put her to sleep so I can set her bones. Come back in a couple of hours. Hiss," Drifa said.

"No, it can't be. There must be something you can do. You were using magic. I saw you," Marcus asked.

"I should have shrunk her and kept her away from you humans. Now you've killed her," Drifa growled.

"No," Marcus said.

"Drifa, enough of that! Come and get me when I can visit with her. I'll be in the war room. Do all you can," Aysun said. Marcus sat down on the couch in Elnara's room.

"Yes, Your Majesty," Drifa replied. Drifa curtseyed to the best of her ability. Aysun and Caria went to the war room.

Aysun and Caria entered the war room. Caria announced Aysun. The Fae officers kneeled. The human officers also kneeled. Aysun waved for them to get up.

"Princess, any word on Princess Elnara?" Emir asked.

"She's resting. Give me a report," Aysun said as she approached the table.

"Your Majesty, the orcs have regrouped in the forest to the west, west of the road. As you predicted, they haven't boarded the ships, so we believe they're regrouping for an attack. We are fortifying our defenses. Is Princess Elnara accepting visitors?" Emir reported.

"No, she's not," Aysun said.

Emira entered the war room in high spirits. She kneeled before Aysun. Aysun signaled her up. Emira was still wearing the crown Aysun had lent her.

"I'm the Goddess of the Sea, and I come bearing tribute to the Moon Goddess," Emira said, as she sang with glee.

"Emira, report and take off my crown," Aysun said as she waved her up. She removed the crown.

"Sorry, Princess. We successfully attacked the fleet at anchor. Three ships were sunk. Two were left at the port as ordered. I also had the captain's chest looted from all three of the sunken ships," Emira reported. She had one chest brought in and opened it for Aysun to see.

"Give it to Shamus. Well done, Emira," Aysun said. Aysun went back to talking with the Generals. Emira moved next to Caria.

"What's going on? What did I miss?" Emira Fae whispered to Caria.

"Come with me," Caria said as she led Emira out of the room and into a nearby hallway. Caria turned to face Emira but was obviously tearing up.

"What is it, Caria?" Emira asked.

"Princess Elnara is injured. She rode out into battle and took a serious hit from a troll. Drifa said she's bleeding internally. She won't survive the night," Caria said. Emira broke down and cried. She slumped down and sat against the wall. Caria kneeled next to her and embraced her.

****

A few hours later. Elnara woke from a medicinally induced sleep. Her vision blurred as she struggled to regain her senses.

"Drifa, is that you?" Elnara asked.

"Yes, Princess. Hiss," Drifa replied.

"I want to get up, but I can't," Elnara said.

"You're drugged, stupid. You're dying, Elnara," Drifa replied. Elnara looked for her cane as she attempted to sit up in bed.

"What? Don't be silly, I'm fine," Elnara said. Drifa took a mirror and showed Elnara the extensive bruising on Elnara's chest and abdomen.

"There's nothing I can do. Some things are beyond my abilities. Elnara, I love you like you're my own daughter. Hiss. If there were any-thing more that could be done for you, I would do it. If you are up to seeing people. Aysun asked to be informed when you awoke. You need to let them say goodbye to you. Are you in pain?" Drifa asked.

"No, is there really nothing that can be done? How much time do I have?" Elnara asked. She relaxed into the bed as she realized her efforts to raise herself were futile.

"There is nothing to be done. I'll see that you are comfortable. The next time you fall asleep, I am not sure if you will wake up in this world. Any more time than that will be a gift from the gods. Hiss," Drifa re-plied. Elnara took a few moments to weigh the gravity of her situation. She had saved lives with the destruction of the siege equipment.

"I understand. I'm ready to see Aysun. Please find Marcus. I need to speak to him, too," Elnara said.

***

Aysun entered the room and sat next to Elnara on her bed.

"I'm sorry, Aysun," Elnara said.

"You never have been one to do as you were told. You don't have to be sorry. Are you comfortable?" Aysun asked.

"Yes, Drifa is making me take the pain medicine. We've had a glorious adventure, didn't we, farm girl?" Elnara said with a chuckle.

"Yeah, we did, fairy princess. Listen, I can't stay long. I had your mother sent for. She should be here soon. Marcus is waiting to see you. I'll send him in," Aysun said.

"Wait. I saw him with another girl before the battle," Elnara said.

"Who?" Aysun asked.

"I don't know. I've never seen her before. She's Fae. She's military. Marcus gave her a ring. That explains why he's been avoiding me," Elnara said.

"Do you want me to send him away? He was the first to get to you and carry you back. I think you should see him. I would have heard something if he were seeing another Fae," Aysun said. Elnara nodded.

"I need to see him," Elnara said.

"I'm sorry about Mia. She was a good horse," Aysun said.

"I loved her. I can't believe she's gone," Elnara said sadly.

"Send for me if you need me. I'll be back after the battle," Aysun said. She got up and went into the hallway.

"Marcus, she'll see you now," Aysun said.

"Thank you, Princess. Is she doing any better?" Marcus asked.

"I don't think so, Marcus. It's just a matter of time. Try not to upset her," Aysun said as she made her way into her room.

"I'm going to take a nap. Caria, keep an ear to what's happening. Wake me if there is any change in the orc's position or if there is any change with Elnara," Aysun said. Hannah helped Aysun get out of her armor and into bed.

***

Marcus entered the room and went over to Elnara's bedside.

"Hey babe, how are you feeling?" Marcus asked as he pulled a chair closer to her bedside.

"Marcus, who was the girl you were with earlier? What did you give her?" Elnara asked.

"Ah, you saw that. The girl was Miray, Caria's cousin. I made an arrangement with Tetyana to have an engagement ring made for you. What Miray gave me was a prototype from Tetyana. I thought having something that she made would mean more to you. Now the surprise is ruined. Is that why you did this? Is that why you went back after that troll, jealousy?" Marcus asked.

"You were planning to propose to me?" Elnara asked.

"Yes, you silly fairy. Don't you know how much I love you?" Marcus asked.

"You've been gone so much. I needed to talk to you. I thought the worst," Elnara said.

"The King had me under orders to move his family out of the castle. I was under strict orders to tell no one. I'm sorry I wasn't here for you when you needed me, but I'm here now," Marcus said.

"What does the ring look like?" Elnara asked.

"It's beautiful, just like you. I'll get it so you can see it. I want you to get stronger so I can propose to you properly. After we rescue your cousin," Marcus said. He waited for her to reply, but Elnara lay there silently, staring blankly. She began convulsing.

"Drifa, come quick!" Marcus yelled. Emira, Drifa, and Elnara's mother came running into the room. Drifa began attending to Elnara. She turned Elnara on her side and propped her head up with a pillow.

"Oh, my Esra! What's happening to her?" Defne demanded.

"She's dying. Emira, go get Princess Aysun," Drifa said.

"O-h-h-h-h," Defne cried. Elnara's mother fainted. Emira caught her. Emira and Mizzy moved her onto the couch.

***

"Am I dead?" Elnara asked. She stood in the fiery landscape outside the castle. She could see Valeria talking to Caria.

"Not yet, Elnara, or is it Esra?" the man asked.

"I am Princess Elnara of the Forge from the nation of the Great Tree. Who are you?" Elnara asked.

"I am Utu," Utu replied.

"The God of Fire and Judgment? Am I here to be judged? I killed him. I admit it. He deserved his sentence. I regret doing it, but not why

I did it. I will face your judgment for the execution of Jerimiah," Elnara said as she kneeled before him.

"Jerimiah? Who is that, a human? I don't care about them. Inanna asked me to look after you after your mother passed away. There was nothing I could do when you were in prison, but I can help you now. You can choose my help, or you can choose to go beyond. There, you'll feel no pain. No more guilt or doubt. You'll find peace at last; no more fighting. Sarah will be there. You can meet your mother. What's your choice?" Utu asked. Elnara thought about it for a moment.

"All Fae are warriors. I choose to go back and fight!" Elnara said.

"I can give you the power, but I cannot heal you. That you must do. If you want it, you must become the Phoenix and resurrect yourself from the flame. You can only do that through the flame. Burn bright Elnara of the Forge from the nation of the Great Tree. I choose you to be my Fire Goddess. He placed his hand on her head.

***

Elnara was resting peacefully. Her mother sat next to her on the bed, crying. Aysun entered the room.

"Is it time?" Aysun asked.

"She's had a seizure. I don't think she'll wake from it. It was bad. It's better to give her the nightshade now, so she doesn't suffer anymore, Hiss," Drifa said.

"Over my dead body, you psychotic fairy!" Defne growled.

"That can be arranged. I have more than enough," Drifa growled back.

"Alexandra, please get Esra a proper doctor," Defne pleaded.

"You two knock it off. Ms. Sachin, Drifa, is Elnara and my personal physician. There is no one we trust more. Drifa put the nightshade away," Aysun said. Marcus smelled smoke.

"Is something burning?" Marcus asked.

The bedspread near Elnara's hand caught fire. Marcus saw it first and put it out by stamping it out with part of the blanket.

"What's going on, Alexandra?" Defne asked Aysun.

"She's a fire elemental. Her abilities must have triggered. I'm sure it's normal," Aysun replied.

"No, no, it's not. She shouldn't be able to use her powers if she's not awake. Hiss," Drifa said.

Elnara's immediate bedding surrounding her ignited. Her mother screamed. Caria dashed in and pushed Aysun out of the room. Elnara's heat increased as other things in the room caught fire. Marcus tried to put it out.

"Everyone out!" Emira yelled.

"Esra is trapped in the fire!" Defne yelled hysterically.

"Esra, I mean Princess Elnara is the fire, Ms. Sachin. We have to get out of here," Emira said as she forced Defne out of the room. Everyone gathered in the hall. The king approached.

"What's happening here?" Alex asked.

"Elnara's dying. Her abilities triggered a fire," Aysun replied.

"I'm sorry to hear her injuries are so grave," Alex said.

Everything in Elnara's room was on fire. A bucket line formed, attempting to put out the blaze. Marcus stood at the head of the line. The fire was getting too hot for him. Edric relieved him.

"We can't put out the fire. She's too powerful. She going to bring down the castle!" Edric yelled. The water seemed to evaporate before it could reach her.

"Major, evacuate the castle!" Alex called out.

"Alex, wait. I'm meant to do this," Aysun said. Aysun remembered what Inanna told her. 'Embrace your gift, or she will die,' Aysun recalled.

"What can you do?" Alex asked.

"I'm a Moon Goddess," Aysun said as she took Moon form and entered the inferno. The flames reflected off her skin. Everyone marveled at her as she passed, a marvelous titan of gleaming white marble. Dressed only in her nightgown. Aysun walked through the flames. The heat coming off of Elnara was intense and seemed to keep growing. Aysun picked her up and carried her toward the courtyard.

Aysun carried Elnara out of the room and onto the terrace. She stepped onto and then over the balcony ledge. Aysun stood in mid-air, holding Elnara. She and Elnara's clothes were on fire. Aysun looked back at Caria.

"Meet me in the courtyard," Aysun said. Caria ran into Aysun's room and ripped the blanket off the bed.

"Mizzy, Hannah, grab clothes for them and get down to the courtyard!" Caria yelled.

Aysun descended into the courtyard as if on an invisible set of stairs. Aysun brought Elnara into the courtyard and laid her down on the stone path. Just in time, as Elnara increased her heat output again, generating visible flames from her body.

Elnara rolled over and curled over into a kowtow position. Elnara screamed. Aysun backed off. The heat was becoming too much, even for Aysun's Moon form. She backed away until she was far enough away to return to human form. Hannah rushed to cover Aysun. Mizzy helped to put another nightgown on her.

Trees near Elnara steamed and hissed. The trees creaked and popped as they dehydrated. The water on the edge of the nearby pond boiled. Elnara's bones cracked and popped. Elnara screamed in pain. When Marcus, Hanna, and Mizzy attempted to get closer, the heat pushed them back. Defne fainted again when she saw Elnara on fire.

Elnara stood up as she bumped up her heat again. Now, in the middle of the flames, she appeared to glow like a white-hot ember, with her red eyes glowing from the center of the flame. Her eyes locked with Marcus's. Marcus thought she looked like a phoenix with fiery wings projecting from her.

Elnara collapsed. Marcus, Hanna, and Mizzy attempted to get closer. Once again, Elnara was too hot to approach. Caria filled a bucket from the pond and dumped it on Elnara. Emira did the same.

"Sorry, Princess," Emira said as she poured her bucket out on Elnara. When Elnara was cool enough, Mizzy and Hannah dried and dressed her. Marcus held up a blanket.

"Her scars are gone. All of them," Mizzy said.

"How's that possible?" Emira asked. Drifa came over and looked over at Elnara. She felt Elnara's leg.

"There's only one explanation. She's a Fire Goddess. Utu has chosen her. There hasn't been one in three hundred years," Drifa said.

"She's a Phoenix. She rose from the ashes," Marcus said.

"The Phoenix Princess. I like that," Emira said. Marcus picked up Elnara and carried her back into the castle.

***

Elnara woke up to see Marcus staring back at her. They were in a new room.

"What are you doing here? Where am I? This isn't my room," Elnara said.

"No, babe, you destroyed your room," Marcus said. Elnara sat up.

"I thought I was dreaming. Aysun carried me through the air?" Elnara said.

"Yes, you nearly destroyed the castle. Aysun did some Moon thing and carried you down into the courtyard. She levitated," Marcus replied.

"I didn't know she could do that," Elnara said.

"There's more," Marcus said. He handed her a hand mirror and positioned it before her face.

"My scars are gone. The corruption is gone," Elnara said. She sprang out of bed. Happiness overwhelmed her.

"My leg, it's healed!" Elnara said as she jumped out of bed and ran over to the full-length mirror. She exposed her back to view in the mirror. The scars on her back were gone.

"Am I dreaming, Marcus?" Elnara asked.

"No, you're here with me," Marcus replied.

"What happened? Tell me everything. I can only remember bits and pieces," Elnara said.

"What's the last thing you remember?" Marcus asked. Elnara thought for a moment.

"Wait. Something about a ring, I seem to recall. Presumptive of you.

What makes you think I would ever marry a human?" Elnara laughed as she danced mockingly and then jumped onto the bed. Marcus moved around the bed poles.

"I only told you because I didn't want you to get upset about Miray," Marcus said.

"Oh, is that so?" Elnara asked.

"You know what I mean. I thought you were dying," Marcus said.

"What else happened?" Elnara asked.

"You had a seizure, and you started the bed on fire. You were getting so hot that you threatened to bring down the castle. Aysun carried you into the courtyard. We all thought you were dying, but you rose up like a phoenix," Marcus said.

"Like a phoenix, Utu. I remember now," Elnara said.

"What is Utu?" Marcus asked.

"Nothing, Fae stuff. Tell me more," Elnara said.

"I should go and tell Princess Aysun you're up," Mizzy said. Aysun knocked on the door and let herself in. Hannah and Defne followed behind her, carrying a couple of dresses.

"It's ok, Mizzy. Elnara get down from there. Everyone is waiting for you if you're up for it. Alex is hosting the dinner in your honor. So, you're all healed?" Aysun asked. Elnara jumped off the bed.

"Yep, and now I can go home," Elnara said gleefully. She shrunk down to Fae form and buzzed a lap around the room. She returned to human form and landed in front of Aysun.

"Oh, Esra!" Defne said as she looked on with amazement. She sat on a nearby couch.

"That's wonderful, Elnara. We'll have a grand parade for your return. Now get ready for dinner. Mizzy and Hannah help her. How did you heal yourself? I've seen you test your powers before. You've never been as powerful as you were today," Aysun said.

"You and I have both had visitors, it seems. I'm the Fire Goddess now, Moon Goddess," Elnara replied.

"Utu?" Aysun asked.

"Yes, he said Inanna asked him to watch over me," Elnara replied. She looked at Aysun humbly acknowledging their shared gifts.

"Get ready for dinner. Our night is not over," Aysun said.

***

"Her Grace Duchess of Stormhaven Elnara Sachin," Mizzy announced Elnara's entrance into the dining hall. She was met with a standing ovation. Her miraculous recovery was well known.

Elnara walked to her seat with a bit of a strut. Marcus pulled her chair out for her. Those in attendance openly discussed her appearance. She wore an off-the-shoulder dress for the first time since her escape from prison. She also walked without the support of a cane.

"Elnara, I'm overjoyed at your recovery. I've grown quite fond of you and Aysun. I think of you two as my daughters. The thought of losing you was horrifying. Thank God you've recovered. The Fae never cease to astound me. Your recovery is nothing short of a miracle. You don't need to use your cane anymore?" Alex asked.

"No, Your Majesty. I'm completely healed, and even my scars have disappeared," Elnara replied. The king tapped on his glass and brought the room to attention. He raised his glass.

"A toast to Duchess Elnara. May she have a long and healthy life," Alex proclaimed. Everyone toasted Elnara.

"So, Marcus, what do you say about me now? Do you find me more attractive without all of my scars?" Elnara asked. She pulled her hair to the side and showed her back and shoulders to Marcus.

"Your Grace, ever since the first moment I saw you, I have never seen your scars. I've only ever seen you. It makes me happy to see you happy," Marcus replied.

"Yes, I'll second that, Elnara, my deepest condolences for your loss. I know Mia meant a lot to you," Alex said.

"Thank you, Your Majesty. I'm so happy to be alive and healed. I can't believe she's gone. She was my best friend," Elnara said. Elnara's mood seemed to turn dark. She took her seat at the table.

Caria and Valeria entered the room and approached the head of the table. They bowed to the king, and Caria kneeled to Aysun.

"What is it, Valeria," Alex asked.

"Your Majesty, the two armies are regrouping to the north along the coast. I've sent the remainder of the Western forces to reinforce the pond. The major force of the enemy is preparing for a frontal assault on the northern gate. I'm having the gate reinforced, but they have a battering ram. The weaker north gate won't last long," Valeria reported.

"I destroyed their battering ram myself," Elnara said.

"They've repaired it. Your Highness," Caria replied.

Elnara's eyes glowed red. She pounded her fist on the table. Marcus could feel the heat generated by Elnara's fist. The sudden reaction startled Caria, Valeria, and most of the others seated nearby.

"Elnara! That's inappropriate," Aysun stated forcefully. Scolding her for the outburst.

"I apologize, Your Majesty. I don't know what came over me. Caria, I've lost my armor and my sword. Have Emira to find me replacements," Elnara said. Valeria looked at Caria. Caria returned the glance. They both knew Emira had not taken the events of Elnara's near-death experience well. Her emotions were on a razor's edge in her advanced pregnancy state.

"I can replace the Princess's sword. Just worry about the armor," Valeria said.

"Yes, Princess, right away. Valeria, she requires a special type of sword," Caria responded.

"Caria, you're dismissed. Valeria, I'm very particular about the swords I wield. Perhaps you should seek Emira's council on it," Elnara said. Caria bowed and headed to the door.

"I'm aware Princess. I ordered some swords from Caria's parents. Including a Fire Elemental Dao sword, very similar to yours. You may have it," Valeria said.

"The Arms Dealers?" Elnara asked.

"They're diplomats, Your Highness," Caria called out

before she exited the room. Elnara rolled her eyes at Valeria. Valeria and Elnara laughed.

"By your leave, Your Highness, Your Majesty," Valeria said.

"Thank you, Valeria," Alex replied. Valeria bowed and exited. She caught up to Caria as they went to speak to Emira.

***

"How do you have a Fire Elemental sword? I'm guessing Emira put you in contact with my parents," Caria asked.

"No, your cousin Miray procured a set of Katanas and a Fire Elemental Dao for me. I bought the Dao as a decoration. I was jealous of the one she carried. So, I got one for myself. They were delivered today. I found them leaning against my door. I need to find Miray to pay her," Valeria said.

"I didn't know she was here. We'll grab Emira and go find Miray together," Caria replied. Caria knocked on Emira's door.

"Emira, it's Caria and Valeria," Caria said.

"Go away!" Emira replied. Caria opened the door, anyway. They both went in. Emira lay on her bed, crying. Valeria went over and sat on the bed. She pulled Emira's head onto her lap.

"Hey, hey now, Emira. It's over. Princess Elnara is fine. She is better than fine. What's got you all broken up?" Valeria asked.

"I don't know. I can't stop crying. Why is she so reckless?" Emira asked.

"It's been a lot to take in today. Here, sit up and drink some water," Valeria said. She helped Emira to sit up. Caria poured a glass of water and handed it to Emira.

"She almost died again today. How can I protect her if I'm like this all the time?" Emira asked.

"You're pregnant, Emira. Your priority is to take care of those babies," Valeria said.

"Emira, Princess Elnara wants you to find her some armor," Caria said.

"What? No way. She is not going out there again. I won't do it. I'm not helping her put herself in danger again," Emira said.

"You know you don't have a say in it," Caria said.

"Don't make me do it. I can't do it. If I am this much of a wreck and she's fine. What's it going to be like if she gets hurt again tonight? I don't think I can handle it," Emira said.

"It's ok, Emira. I'll take care of it. You're on light duty from now on. Administrative duties only," Caria said.

"Thanks, Caria, keep her safe for me," Emira said.

"If Emira is down. Let me step in and cover for her. I'll protect Princess Elnara with my life, at least until Emira is ready to come back. You know I can with your training," Valeria said.

"The rest of her guard won't follow your orders. You would be tolerated as a human contingent at best. Most of her guards are Unseelie. You know what that means, right?" Caria asked.

"Yes, I know. Marcus stationed Corporal Varus with you at one time. He's given a very detailed account of his time with you. He was keen to point out that securing a relationship with Master Sergeant Cinar was vital to his settling in among your Unseelie guards," Valeria replied.

"Then you know what he is capable of?" Caria asked.

"Yes, why keep such a dangerous individual near the Princesses?" Valeria asked.

"There is a philosophical divide between Seelie and Unseelie where interaction with humans is concerned. However, Unseelie or not, they would never hurt a royal. Besides, sometimes some things need to be done," Caria said.

"Like the torture of Jerimiah?" Valeria asked.

"Yes, like that. I am sure the Princess will not object. Stay out of Cinar's way. If you disrespect him, he will kill you. Come on, let's get her armor and a sword. She'll be expecting to be fitted after she's done eating. Are you going to be okay, Emira?" Caria asked.

"Yeah, I should go check on the wounded. I just need a few minutes. You two go. Keep her safe. I need her to be around after the twins are born for me to protect her. Valeria, don't let anything happen to her. Swear to me," Emira said.

"I swear on the honor of my family. I will do whatever it takes to protect Princess Elnara in your stead," Valeria said.

"Thank you, Valeria," Emira replied.

***

A Fae tent city had sprouted up in the park near the entrance to the tunnels. They made their way through it until they reached the military supply depot. Miray was there doing inventory. Valeria carried the Dao sword.

"Hey cousin, Hi Valeria. I see you got my delivery," Miray said. Miray hugged them both.

"Yes, thank you. I brought the gold I owe you," Valeria said as she tossed her a small pouch of coins.

"Is there something wrong with the sword?" Miray asked.

"No, I'm giving it to Princess Elnara. She lost her sword in battle earlier today," Valeria said.

"We also need to replace her armor," Caria said.

"Of course, follow me. I have some Fire Elemental armor over here. Are the rumors true? Did Princess Elnara set fire to the castle and heal herself? That would be really amazing if it's true. I heard she almost died. That would have been so awful, then Marcus could never give her... Oh, armor, right? What size is she?" Miray said.

"Give her what, Miray?" Caria asked.

"Oh, sparkles!" Miray said as she became frantic. She pulled pieces of armor out at random.

"Miray, out with it! Consider it an order," Caria said.

"I didn't say anything. Come on, Caria, don't make me. It's a secret," Miray pleaded.

"That's captain to you. Miray, you are the worst person to keep a secret. If it's something about the Princess, you have an obligation to tell me as the head of her guard," Caria demanded.

"Oh, come on, don't make me. It's nothing bad," Miray said.

"Out with it," Caria insisted.

"Sparkles! Marcus is having Tetyana make a ring for Princess Elnara," Miray said as she became deflated.

"An engagement ring?" Valeria asked.

"Yes, but you can't tell her. Marcus and Tetyana will kill me," Miray replied.

"Sparkles?" Valeria asked.

"My parents were strict about no swearing. So, I needed a different word. 'sparkles' worked for me when I was little, and it just sort of stuck," Miray replied.

"I like it. I might have to use it," Valeria laughed, and Miray smiled.

"So, what does this ring look like?" Valeria asked.

"The band looks like a dragon holding the main gem. It's very beautiful," Miray said.

"I'm the same height as the Princess. You can use me to size her armor," Valeria said.

"Okay, that'll help," Miray said as she assembled a set of armor. After loose fitting the armor to Valeria, she stacked the fitted pieces to the side.

"Caria, it's like the best I can do. I could see if I can order something from the meadows a little nicer," Miray said.

"This is fine. Have it delivered to the castle. Bring a second regular set for Valeria. Make sure you come with it to help with the fittings," Caria said.

"Really, no fooling? I get to meet her?" Miray said.

"Yeah, you don't think I'm going to carry all this armor all the way there? That's a job for a junior officer, Lieutenant," Caria said as she saluted Miray.

"I'll have it there right away. Thank you, Captain," Miray said as she saluted back. Caria and Valeria turned to leave.

"Caria, seriously, thank you so much! Ah ha, yes," Miray squealed with excitement.

***

Mizzy helped Elnara get out of her dress and into her under-armor clothing. Then she helped to braid her hair for battle. Mizzy was noticeably distressed getting Elnara ready for battle.

"You're not going out there again, are you?" Mizzy asked.

"Yes, I am," Elnara responded.

"You should sit this one out. You're going to give your mother a heart attack," Mizzy said.

"I don't know how to explain it, but I must go out and fight. It's part of who I am. I won't be locked away again," Elnara said. There was a knock at the door.

"It's Caria and Valeria," Caria said.

"Come in," Elnara said. Caria and Valeria entered. Valeria gave the sword to Mizzy. She and Caria both kneeled.

"Please accept this sword as a replacement for your sword," Valeria said. Mizzy presented the sword to Elnara. Elnara took the sword and swung it about. Its balance and measure seemed to meet her satisfaction.

"Thank you, Valeria, it's perfect," Elnara said.

"Princess, I have put Emira on light duty until the babies are born. Valeria has asked to be assigned to your detail. I see no issues as long as you approve. My cousin Miray will be here shortly with your armor. She is so excited to meet you," Caria said.

"This is the cousin working with Marcus to make my engagement ring?" Elnara asked.

"Oh, you know about that?" Caria said.

"Yes, I know. Yes, on Valeria, and how is Emira? When Miray gets here. I'll address her, and you'll be silent," Elnara said.

"Yes, of course, Princess. Be nice to her. She's very excitable. Emira is fine. Today was a lot for her. It's time for her to rest until she has the babies," Caria replied. There was a knock at the door.

"The armorer is here. A Lieutenant Miray of the Ocean,"

a guard announced. Mizzy showed her in. Miray came in, set down the armor, and kneeled.

"You may rise," Elnara said.

"Thank you, Princess Elnara, I'm..." Miray said.

"Did I say you could speak?" Elnara asked. She pointed the sword at Miray.

"No, Your Highness, forgive me," Miray replied.

"You're going to make her pee herself," Caria interjected.

"I thought I told you to be silent," Elnara responded harshly.

"Yes, Princess," Caria said as she sat down.

"I saw you earlier. I saw you groping and hugging my boyfriend. Do you realize who I am?" Elnara asked sternly.

"Oh my gosh, Princess, of course, I know who you are. Princess Elnara, Your Highness. It's not what you think," Miray replied.

"Now you would tell me what to think! Do you know what the punishment is for insulting the royal family?" Elnara asked. Miray dropped to her knees.

"Oh, sparkles. I know. I'd never insult you. There's been a misunderstanding. Caria, help me," Miray replied, as tears spilled over.

"Elnara, enough!" Caria demanded. She stood back up. Elnara paused and looked at Caria. She could tell she had taken her fun too far. Caria was angered to the point of insubordination. Caria knew she might have just thrown her career away, but she would not have her cousin toyed with like this further.

"So, I heard you're a bit of a hugger. I know all about your scheme to have my engagement ring designed. Marcus sold you out. Any family to Caria is family to me. Come and give me a hug," Elnara said, opening her arms.

"Are you serious, Princess? I think I might have peed myself. I love you. You're my idol. I started taking your archery class and everything," Miray said as she went over and hugged Elnara. Miray was still shaken.

"Oh, you poor dear, you're shaking. I'm sorry. I was just having a bit of fun with you. It's Marcus that will really suffer," Elnara said.

"May I speak, Your Highness?" Miray asked.

"Of course, Miray. You can just call me Elnara in my quarters," Elnara replied. Valeria and Mizzy put Elnara's armor on her.

"Elnara, he loves you. I've never seen anyone more in love. He spent hours with Tetyana drawing up plans for your ring. Have you seen it yet?" Miray asked.

"No, Marcus said it wasn't right anymore. I believe he is changing it from a dragon to a phoenix. I don't want to see it until he actually proposes," Elnara said.

"So, it's not official yet?" Miray asked.

"No, nothing will happen until we get my cousin back. Doing anything like that while he is missing would be disrespectful to Sam. Marcus understands that. Besides, I might say no," Elnara replied.

"You would say no to Marcus? Oh my gosh, I think that would kill him. He's so handsome. Why would you say no? Oh wait, that's not my place to ask. Sorry, Princess Elnara, ah just Elnara. I'll stop talking now," Miray replied. The sound of troops moving through the castle was intensifying.

"Miray, you're so gullible. Don't you have a battle station to get ready for?" Caria asked.

"Yes, I'm in the second reserve. So, I have time to ensure the Princess is happy with her armor," Miray replied.

"The armor is fine, Miray. You better run along and get to your battle station," Caria said.

"Okay, it was really awesome getting to meet you, Princess Elnara," Miray said.

"It was nice to meet you, too. Sorry again if I startled you," Elnara said. Miray bowed and exited.

"Princess Elnara, why did you do that to her?" Caria asked.

"I was just having a bit of fun. I didn't realize she was so sensitive," Elnara replied.

"Well, she is. What a disappointment you were. She was so excited to meet you. I need to check on her. She was still shaking when she left," Caria said. She was clearly angered.

"Caria, calm down," Valeria said.

"Oh, don't be so dramatic," Elnara said.

"You threatened to execute her. She's fresh out of the academy. Miray was home-schooled. She's always been delicate. I have served your family since you arrived at the Great Tree. I did not appreciate what you did to my family, Princess. By your leave, Your Highness," Caria said as she bowed and prepared to exit.

"Caria, don't leave angry. I'm sorry. I didn't know. What can I do to make it right? Put her on my guard," Elnara said.

"She is not ready for that, but I might hold you to that in the future. Don't do that again to her. I really should go catch up to her," Caria said.

"Very well go, and Caria, I'm sorry," Elnara said. Caria exited the room. Aysun, Major General Emir, and Hannah entered the room.

"Aysun, Emir, to what do I owe the honor of your visit?" Elnara asked.

"You won't be needing that armor. Aysun and I have decided that you're going to be evacuated to the Great Tree. Mizzy, can you help her out of that armor?" Emir asked.

"No, excuse me, but you do not tell my staff what to do, Major General," Elnara replied.

"No? Princess Elnara, I must insist. We've almost lost you twice. That's quite enough risk. It's time for you to sit this one out. Consider it an order," Emir said. Elnara laughed.

"You can't order me to do anything, and Aysun won't order me because she knows I'll simply defy her if I choose. Valeria is in charge of my guard now until Emira returns from having the babies. Please make future intrusions via appointment through her," Elnara replied.

"Aysun, please order her to stand down," Emir demanded. He looked at Aysun. Aysun looked at Elnara.

"You know my answer. I couldn't fight the first time. Sam's life was at stake. I made a mistake this morning, and I got Mia killed. I have to live with that. Look at me, I'm healed. Something happened to me. Like you, I've been touched for a reason, and my gut tells me I belong in this battle," Elnara said.

"I'm sorry, Emir. I tried. You heard her. Hanna, come help me get my armor on," Aysun said. She left the room. Emir followed her out with a huff. Elnara smiled.

"Valeria, assemble my guard. You'll find Cinar in the Fae encampment," Elnara said.

"Um, Princess Elnara. Caria said the rest of your guards would not recognize my rank. Maybe you should send a Fae messenger," Valeria said.

"Mizzy, go ask Emira if I can borrow her First Lieutenant rank insignia for Valeria," Elnara said.

"Yes, Elnara. I'll be right back," Mizzy said. She returned a few minutes later with Emira. Emira gave her a pair of rank insignia.

"Princess, why did you want these?" Emira asked.

"Valeria is taking over my guard until you come back to full duty. I thought I would make it official," Elnara said as she affixed the insignia to Valeria's collar.

"First Lieutenant Valeria Marcellus, I appoint you as head of my personal guard and member of the royal family's guard. My personal protector. I expect you to take charge of my guard. I've seen you training with Caria and Emira. You've come a long way. Cinar's men will follow him, and Cinar will follow you if he respects you. What would you do if someone in your command wouldn't follow your orders?" Elnara asked.

"I would put them on report, ma'am, and they would be subject to a judicial review," Valeria replied.

"What if there was not enough time for all of that bureaucracy?" Elnara asked.

"In the field, I'd put them on their ass," Valeria replied.

"You're in charge now, so take charge. I'd like my guard assembled right away. I'll be on foot," Elnara said.

"Yes, Your Highness. If you'll excuse me. I'll gather them right away. I'm sorry about Mia," Valeria said as she bowed.

"Do you want me to come with you?" Emira said.

"No, I got this, but thanks," Valeria replied.

***

Valeria and Sergeant Varus approached the Fae encampment near the Fae tent village inside the castle walls. She recognized Elnara's symbol of the dragon and the seal of the royal guard. Valeria recognized Mehmet and Cinar sitting near a fire. They were eating and laughing. Valeria wore the standard Fae armor and rank insignia.

"This is the place, Lieutenant," Lucius said.

"Thanks, Sergeant. Don't get involved," Valeria said.

"Yes, ma'am. I'd advise caution," Lucius replied. Valeria walked over and stood in front of Cinar. Cinar was eating a plate of food. Cinar looked up at her with disdain.

"Master Sergeant Cinar of the Grasslands, do you know who I am?" Valeria asked. Cinar looked around and saw Lucius closer to the entrance.

"Corporal Lucius, why is this human in my camp? Get her out of here," Cinar said.

"Master Sergeant. It's Sergeant now, and I can't do that. I think you should hear her out," Lucius said.

"I asked you a question, Master Sergeant," Valeria said.

"You're Valeria, Marcus' kid sister. If you know Lucius, then you should know that I am not the biggest fan of humans, and you are not welcome in my camp. Now see yourself out, sweetie," Cinar said, slightly more annoyed.

"I'm afraid we need another introduction. I am First Lieutenant Valeria Marcellus. Captain Caria of the Ocean has assigned me the role of personal protector to Princess Elnara. I am head of her guard until Lieutenant Emira returns to full duty. You report to me now," Valeria said.

"I ain't taking orders from some human. Caria's got to be having some fun with me! Where is she? I want to speak to her. Why don't you run along and go get her," Cinar said.

"Master Sergeant, your orders are to assemble the guard and follow me. Now!" Valeria ordered.

"And I told you I ain't taking no orders from some human. Now get your face out of my camp," Cinar said as he put his plate down and stood up. He licked his fingers clean as he leaned in on her.

Valeria punched him in the jaw and then kicked him over the log he was sitting on. Cinar tumbled backward over the log and recovered to his feet. He looked over at his bow, which was near a tent. Valeria saw him look at it. She drew her sword.

"I thought all Fae were warriors. I'll cut you down before you nock your first arrow. What's wrong with your sword? Afraid to face me?" Valeria said.

"So, you're looking for a lesson. Okay then, after I knock your face in the dirt. You can go back and tell Caria. That me and the boys will be along as quick as we can. This is going to be fun," Cinar said as he drew his sword.

He lunged at Valeria. Despite his rather large size, he was surprisingly agile. After a quick exchange, Cinar got in a punch to Valeria's eye. It staggered her. He saw the Fae rank insignia on Valeria's collar and armor.

"Hurts, don't it? You need to take that off. You ain't Fae. I don't care if your brother is Princess Elnara's play toy. He's way out of his league, anyway," Cinar said.

"My brother is twice the man you'll ever be. He doesn't need to torture and execute someone half his size to feed his ego. Come on, show me what you got," Valeria said.

Cinar swung several times, finding nothing but air as Valeria dodged each attack. Cinar took a last swing as Valeria ducked it, spun, and stepped to the side. She kicked Cinar in the hip, catching him off balance and knocking him face-first to the ground. Cinar scrambled to his feet again.

"You're not fit to guard her, human!" Cinar whined as he wiped the dirt from his face.

"I heard about how you abandoned her. She almost died because of you. You abandoned your post!" Valeria yelled back at him.

"No, she ordered me!" Cinar yelled back as he charged Valeria. Valeria caught his arm and threw him over her hip. He landed hard on his back. Valeria kneeled on his chest and placed her sword across his throat. Cinar reached up and grabbed a bare spot on her arm.

"Go ahead, do it, Cinar of the Grasslands. Poison me. Show everybody what a coward you really are, and I'll slice your neck clean through. We'll end both our problems!" Valeria seethed. Cinar took a breath and let go of his sword and her arm. Valeria stood up and put her sword away.

"You have two choices. Pack your stuff and get out of my camp, or assemble the men for combat and follow me," Valeria said. Cinar sat up.

"Mehmet, you heard the Lieutenant assemble the guard," Cinar said. Valeria offered Cinar a hand for him to get up. Cinar took her hand and stood up. He recovered his sword. Valeria addressed the troops.

"I'll have all of you know Princess Elnara put this rank insignia on me herself. If anyone else cares to challenge my leadership, step forward or fall in!" Valeria announced. Cinar took a position behind Valeria.

"Infantry or calvary, Master Sergeant?" Mehmet asked.

"Infantry," Valeria responded.

"Yes, ma'am," Mehmet replied.

* * *

In tiny form, perched on a leaf of a nearby tree, Miray and Caria observed Valeria and Lucius approach the encampment for Princess Elnara's guard. Caria passed Miray some popcorn.

"He's right about that. This is going to be fun," Caria said as she and Miray observed the confrontation on a nearby tree limb.

"She punched him! Oh, my gosh. Are you going to stop them?" Miray asked.

"Are you kidding? I would pay to see this. Besides, if she is going to take command, this is the only way she will gain Cinar's respect," Caria replied.

"Wow, he's angry. How does she move like that? Go, Valeria!" Miray cheered.

"I taught her how to move like that. She's using his emotions against him. It makes him sloppy," Caria said. Caria and Miray continued to watch the confrontation unfold between Valeria and Cinar.

"Oh my gosh, she won. Wow, she's awesome! Wait a minute. Did you take her on as a student before me?" Miray asked.

"I told you, you're not ready yet. Valeria is already a seasoned warrior. See how she manipulated Cinar into becoming angry. That's you. You're too sensitive. You need to learn to become a warrior. It's about more than just swinging weapons around. Princess Elnara put you into a bad spin. You can't let something happen like that on the battlefield. It will be your end," Caria said.

"I understand what you're saying. I think I have to work on that. Mom always said I have my heart on my sleeve. Princess Elnara seemed really upset with me. I felt if you weren't there. I don't know what would've happened," Miray said.

"You need to study under Emira first because she also struggled with her emotions. My problem is the opposite. I am too quick to go into warrior mode, and it's hard for me to turn it off. I would rather be blessed with your compassion. Princess Elnara overstepped herself. I serve the royal family, but I am not their servant. I told her I would not tolerate that behavior toward my family in the future. She apologized. She doesn't seem the same after what happened to her. I think she just needs time to find herself again," Caria said.

8

Chapter Eight: The Final Battle

***

A horn sounded on the enemy line, followed by a drumbeat. The enemy was organized into phalanxes with spears and shields. Reinforced by three armored trolls. They faced off against Aysun's spear wall, followed by rows of Fae archers.

Marcus couldn't help but be a little unnerved, but his confidence was renewed when he saw Aysun, Caria, Edric, and the rest of her guard approach in full armor. They passed the front of the ranks the Fae and humans cheered. Aysun headed over to Marcus. He was mounted on a horse in front of the frontline.

"The war hammer and armor are quite a change from when we first met," Marcus said.

"The hammer was my mother's. I still have my knives," Aysun replied.

"It seems you can use both well. Thanks for covering me earlier," Marcus said.

"Thanks for getting to her," Aysun replied.

Elnara walked up. She was followed by Valeria, Cinar, and the rest of her guard. The Fae cheered even louder.

"Marcus, are you flirting with Aysun again? I can have my new head of security execute you for such an offense," Elnara asked.

"Well, that would make the holidays awkward. What are you doing out here? You and Princess Aysun shouldn't be out here at the front," Marcus said. Elnara gave her hand to Marcus. He politely kissed it.

"Marcus, I'm not going to sit out of combat. I realize now more than ever that this is what I'm meant to do," Elnara said.

"Princess, stay close to me," Marcus said.

"Marcus, my hero. I have a full guard detachment, and I'm a fire elemental. Stick with your cavalry," Elnara said.

"Promise I won't have to rescue you again," Marcus said. Elnara winked back at Marcus.

"Valeria, when were you going to tell me about joining the Fae ranks?" Marcus asked.

"It's a recent development. Emira is sitting the rest of this battle out and then some until she gives birth. I figure the king wouldn't mind if I accepted a temporary assignment until she can return to duty," Valeria replied.

"I'll see it's official," Marcus said.

"Valeria, I want to switch Mehmet with Edric. Edric can stay closer to Princess Elnara if she goes all Phoenix again," Caria said.

"Yes, Captain. Mehmet, you're reassigned to Princess Aysun detail for this battle. Edric, you're over here with Princess Elnara," Valeria ordered.

They both complied and changed positions. Elnara, seeing the nervous excitement among the troops, paced the front line. Aysun followed her, walking in step with Elnara. Elnara let her eyes glow red as she raised her bow in the air. Aysun shifted into Moon form, holding up her war hammer before shouldering it. The troops cheered and then settled down as Elnara stopped to address them.

"May I address them?" Elnara asked Aysun.

"Of course," Aysun responded.

"Listen to me, brave warriors of the forest and the realm of man! I am Elnara of the Forge, a child born of both worlds. Today, we stand united as one. The enemy forces before us seek not just to conquer, but to kill and enslave us. They underestimate the fire that burns within us, our unity's strength, and our free, unconquerable spirit! We will not surrender to the shackles of slavery. We are the guardians of our homes, the protectors of our families, and the keepers of our freedom! I will not kneel to these intruders. We will fight with the strength of the forest and the heart of humanity, side by side. Remember the love of your kin, the beauty of your land, and the freedom that courses through your veins. Let the enemy feel the thunder of our determination and the storm of our resistance. For when they look back on this day, they will remember not the fallen, but the indomitable spirit of those who rose to meet them. Show them your rage!" Elnara yelled as she output a quick burst of flames.

The troops roared in reply. The orc army began its advance. Ram horns signaled the enemy's advance. General Emir answered with the chilling trill of the Fae carnyx horns.

A haunting chorus of the brass dragons screamed their haunting melody. The dragon horns stood six feet over the heads of the troops. They called the Fae to the ready.

"Then we fight. Archers ready!" Aysun yelled. She waited for the opposing army to get into range.

"Loose!" Aysun screamed.

The Fae archers sent out heavy waves of arrows. Elnara's skill with the bow bewildered those seeing her for the first time. As the return fire came in, the troops raised their shields. Aysun took Moon form. Elnara raised her hand and created a flaming heat shield. The arrows coming at Elnara and those in her vicinity were incinerated or deflected by the heat. Arrows bounced off of Aysun.

The two armies clashed. Elnara, Valeria, Cinar, and Edric fought as a unit, but Edric was the only one who could get close to Elnara as she was outputting so much heat. Even the orcs tried to avoid her. She melted their armor and swords with her sword and bare hand. Aysun fought alongside Caria and Mehmet.

"Caria, take out those trolls!" Aysun called out.

"On it! Valeria, you're with me," Caria replied. Caria flew at mid-height at the first troll. She dodged the troll's initial swing and delivered a spinning attack with her large battle axe as she had done against the first troll she fought.

She jumped on the back of the second troll and grabbed him by the collar, yanking him back and exposing his midsection. Valeria stabbed him through the chest with her claymore. Caria jumped off the troll, and it fell forward. Valeria could not retrieve her claymore before the troll fell on it. Caria tossed her large axe to Valeria.

"You really need to carry a backup weapon!" Caria yelled to Valeria. Caria pulled out her two hand axes.

"I didn't expect to have a giant troll fall over on my weapon. Thanks for the axe," Valeria replied.

The two of them charged the last troll. Caria threw one of her axes but missed the mark, and it bounced off the troll's helmet. Valeria spun and planted the large axe in the back of the troll's leg, sending it to the ground. Caria walked up and chopped the troll in the neck with her axe, killing it.

"That's bullshit. That one was mine!" Valeria said.

"Two to one," Caria said. She threw her other axe, killing an orc behind Valeria. Caria took out the small axe she carried on her back. It caught Elnara's attention, as Caria wielded it when they first met but had dropped it.

Caria unscrewed the two halves of the handle, and a long steel chain of the nine-segmented whip chain appeared. Caria spun the whip around, collecting it around her arm. She made the whip glow with an ethereal edge. She spun it around the back of her arm and swung it around, using her body to change the direction as she used it to dismember the orcs. The whip acted as an ethereal blade, dismembering limbs. The battle waged on until there was a clear swing in favor of the Fae and humans.

"Valeria, fallback!" Caria yelled. Valeria and Caria fell back to get a respite.

Aysun and Elnara met at the center of the front line. Taking over the forward position of Caria and Valeria. The Titan and the Phoenix fought back-to-back as they broke the remaining line. Eventually, the Fae archers turned the remaining attackers away.

The remaining orcs fled the battlefield. Their only option was to retreat to the two remaining ships. The human and Fae cheered loudly. Aysun and Elnara powered down. They strutted past the King, and the Generals as they returned to the castle.

"I told you both my plan would work," Aysun said as she passed the King and General Emir. They both bowed from positions up on their horses, acknowledging her. Aysun and Elnara retreated to their quarters. Mizzy and Hannah prepared bathes for them, respectively.

***

Caria entered the dining hall. She heard the whispers of "Troll Killer, she got three more," making her uncomfortable. Part of her laughed inside. Valeria will be furious not to get credit. She approached Aysun and kneeled.

"Report Caria," Aysun said as she waved Caria up.

"There is a delegation from the orc army; they are approaching the north gate," Caria said.

"Really?" Aysun asked.

"Yes, Your Majesty," Caria replied.

"This ought to be interesting," Aysun said as she sprang from her seat with the King, Elnara, and Marcus. Most of those in attendance also got up to investigate this recent development.

***

Aysun rode out with Caria, Marcus, and Valeria. Elnara reluctantly accompanied the group, riding a random horse. General Criel waited on the battlefield under a white flag. Aysun's delegation rode up to meet them.

"I am Princess Aysun of the Moonlight from the nation of the Great Tree.," Aysun announced.

"Major Marcus Marcellus. I speak for this kingdom," Marcus announced.

"I am General Criel, and I speak for my army. Moon Goddess, your presence in this battle was not anticipated. Why have the Fae sided with the humans? This fight was between us and the humans. We are not at war with the Fae, and there is a non-aggression agreement between Goblins and Fae," Criel asked.

"The short answer is that you became my enemy when you abducted Princess Elnara and my brother. I witnessed Fae imprisoned in your camp in my realm in direct violation of the treaty. I left you two ships. You should use them to flee and do not return. Be thankful I let any of you survive. Why have you requested this parlay?" Aysun said.

"The victory is yours. I do not have any knowledge of these abductions. This is below the rank of a general. Princess Elnara and your brother would not have been targeted. Not by our orders. We do not have the resources to make the crossing across the sea. The entire crew will die without provisions and water. We ask that you provide us with fresh water and some provisions. In exchange for our immediate withdrawal," General Criel said.

"No, that's not enough. I demand to know where my brother is! Princess Elnara, we've already rescued," Aysun demanded.

"Remember me? I know you do because I remember you," Elnara asked. She had only seen him from a distance, but she recognized Criel from the base.

"Yes, I remember you. I had nothing to do with your treatment there. I would need more information on your brother, as some prisoners were sent to different locations," Criel replied.

"My brother's name is Sam, and he is a Gem Cutter. I understand that General Ak'rah holds him in some regard," Aysun said.

"The Gem Cutter? Yes, of course, I know him. Everyone does.

He's General Ak'rah's favorite, but Your Majesty, He's a human," Criel responded.

"He's my half-brother. Tell me where he is!" Aysun demanded.

"He's at Remus castle or on his way there," Criel said.

"Remus lives? Where is his castle?" Aysun asked.

"No, well, no one knows what happened to Remus after he killed Queen Nuray and Princess Sarah. Sarah burned him badly, and he disappeared. It's presumed he died from his injuries. General Ak'rah occupies the castle now. I could show you on a map," Criel responded.

"I will make a case for his return to General Ak'rah. He will not want to quarrel with you, Moon Goddess. I am sure if Sam had said who he was, this could have all been avoided," Criel said.

"Princess Elnara identified who she was, and yet she was mercilessly beaten. I will give you the supplies you need to cross the sea in exchange for my brother's location if he is not returned in the cycle of a moon. I will come for him, and I will not be in such a generous mood. Come back in the morning. Caria, see to the provisions and the exchange," Aysun said.

***

"Listen up. Quiet down. I know you're all excited that we have reached our final destination," Volkov called out. The crew tapped their cups on the tables in approval.

"The captain and crew have selected those of you that will be offered crew roles from now on. Check your locker after breakfast. You all have a note in there saying if you're staying on as a crew member or not. If you are staying on as a crew member, congratulations. You'll be paid wages at the end of the month. You'll be granted liberty to go ashore after the workday is over. Those not staying on as crew. You may depart the ship when we are secure from sea and anchor detail. You will be compensated with five pieces of silver. Here at Pirate Bay, there are two sides to the opening of the bay. Where we are is the orc side of the bay. At night, this side of the wharf will be filled with pirates, thieves, and cut-throats for hire. I advise you to take the ferry over to the other side of the bay. There is a mostly human settlement there where you may find work. It's been a pleasure serving with you. I wish you all the best," Volkov concluded. The men resumed eating.

"Don't worry, Sam, you'll be offered a crew spot," Pavlo signed.

"I'm not Pavlo. I'm too valuable to Ak'rah," Sam replied.

"Well, there is no sense fussing about it now. Let's finish our breakfast," Ivan said. The boys finished eating and returned to their berthing. They checked their locker, and as Sam predicted. He was not offered a crew slot, but Pavlo and Ivan had.

"So, don't keep us in suspense," Ivan said.

"It was always going to be a no," Sam replied.

"Sorry," Pavlo signed.

"Don't be," Sam said.

Volkov came over and opened Augie's locker.

"Do any of you know who Augie's next of kin is? He left no name and address," Volkov asked.

"I know how to get a message to them. Ivan can deliver it," Sam said.

"I'll leave it to you, boys," Volkov said. He removed Augustus' lock and wooden number chip from the locker. Sam sorted through Augustus's things.

"I think Augie would've wanted you to have this," Sam said. He handed Ivan the concertina. Sam split the rest of the things he bought from the store. Sam laid Augustus's towel on the table. He placed his clothes neatly folded inside. Augustus had written several letters to Reyhan and his mother. He'd drawn some pictures and written some poems and songs. Sam packed them all up. He took Augustus's towel out of the locker. He laid it out and placed Augustus's coins into the towel. Sam took five gold coins from his locker and placed them with Augustus.

"For Augie's mother," Sam said. Ivan and Pavlo did the same. Sam rolled up the towel tightly, then tied it with twine. He closed up everything and tied it with more twine.

Sam sat down and wrote a letter.

Dear Ms. Macer,

It is with profound sorrow that I write this letter. A few weeks ago, a tragic event occurred at sea, and it is with the deepest regrets that I must convey the heartbreaking news about your son, Augustus.

During a violent storm, we lost him, and despite our best efforts, we could not recover his body. He bravely risked his life to save his ship and crewmates. Augustus was a valued member of the crew. According to naval traditions, Augustus was given a proper sailor's burial service. The ocean now holds the resting place of a man who spoke highly of his family, especially mentioning a girl named Reyhan.

You will find his belongings and wages along with this letter. Augie was cherished among us, and we will forever remember him.

My sister or her associate will deliver this message to you. I hope you can find some comfort in knowing that Augie had friends and found happiness during his time with us.

With heartfelt sympathy,

Sam Ekici

Ivan Bereza

Pavlo Bereza

Ivan and Pavlo also signed the letter.

"When you return to port if the Fae don't contact you, send this package to Princess Aysun at Seaside. She'll know what to do from there," Sam said.

"Oh, you girls are not going to start crying again, are you?" Ivan asked. The bosun whistled sounded, signaling the start of sea and anchor detail.

"I'm not sure I'll get the chance later. It was an honor serving with you guys. I hope we'll see each other again," Sam said. The boys, for the last time, shook hands and embraced.

***

Sam, Ak'rah, and a contingent of Ak'rah's guards mounted horseback to travel inland. Gunay and Dugan held back a safe distance. They traveled for two days before reaching Remus's castle.

As Sam and Ak'rah approached Remus's castle, the imposing structure loomed ahead, perched on a rocky outcrop, its towering spires reaching toward the sky. The castle's stone walls, weathered by years of history, stood as a silent witness to the many stories it held within.

As they neared the entrance, the heavy wooden gates, adorned with iron accents, creaked open to reveal a somber scene. Gunay and Dugan held back a safe distance. General Criel's head was mounted on a pike. It served as a gruesome warning to all who dared to approach. The air was thick with tension and a sense of foreboding.

Entering the Keep, Sam and Ak'rah passed through the stone archway into the echoing hall. The flickering light of torches cast dancing shadows on the cold, gray walls. The usual sounds of a bustling castle were conspicuously absent, no chatter, no clattering of armor, just an eerie silence.

Proceeding further, they found themselves in the heart of the castle, a grand hall that once echoed with laughter and celebration. Now, it was a solemn chamber, its grandeur overshadowed by the weight of its apparent neglect. The absence of any welcoming committee and the desolate atmosphere hinted at something wrong.

Undeterred, Ak'rah and Sam moved toward the dining room, the heavy wooden door groaning as it swung open. The room, once a place of feasts and meetings, now sat in stillness. The long, ornately carved table was filled with a lush banquet. A dark-haired female Fae of noticeable beauty sat at the table, eating next to Remus. Remus himself a Goblin Fae, his face deeply corrupted. The left side of his face was heavily scarred from burns. His left hand missing the two smaller digits on his hand.

"Lord Remus, My Lady. Sir, why is Criel's head on a pike? Where is everyone?" Ak'rah asked.

"I sent them away. Who's your friend Ak'rah?" Remus asked as he stuffed his face with food from the table.

"Excuse me, sir, this is Sam the Gem Cutter. He does exquisite work. I've taken great lengths to bring him here," Ak'rah said.

"Why didn't you return for the attack as you were ordered?" Remus asked.

"A sea monster attacked our ship. It required weeks to repair. This was the earliest I could get here to secure reinforcements," Ak'rah said.

"Sam the Gem Cutter, huh? You imbecile. This is the brother of Princess Aysun of the Great Tree, daughter to Nuray. The Moon Goddess! What were you thinking? She's declared war on us. Apparently, you also had Princess Elnara, her cousin, in custody. I heard she was nearly beaten to death. The attack on the human castle was a humiliating defeat! Tell me why I shouldn't kill you now!" Remus asked. Ak'rah threw a large bag of gems on the table.

"My delay couldn't be helped. I left General Criel in charge. He was fully briefed on the plan and should have been able to execute it. He had the troops, and we had the element of surprise. I don't understand how he could've failed. The plan was perfect, and he was a capable general. What happened?" Ak'rah asked.

"First, let me introduce my guest. This is Countess Veronica LaRue from Paris. My very dear old friend," Remus said.

"Countess," Ak'rah said as he bowed politely toward Veronica.

"General, human boy. He smells delicious. Don't you, little bunny," Veronica replied.

"Countess LaRue," Sam replied, indifferent to being called a boy.

Ak'rah sat down at the table and poured himself a drink. Sam sat down next to him. Remus raised an eyebrow. Ak'rah gestured to the kitchen staff for him and Sam to be served. He knew he had to make a choice whether to treat Sam as a prisoner or a guest. At that moment, he was hungry, and they had both ridden a long way to get there, so he would defer the decision for the moment.

"Criel told me that Aysun fought in the battle using her Moon form. In the battle at East Mill, she fought as something else. It could have only been because she was using cosmic form. Like her mother, she's a dual-elemental. Isn't that correct, Sam the Gem Cutter?" Remus asked. Sam just tilted his head in acknowledgment of the question.

"Want me to make him talk? I'm hungry," Veronica said.

"No, not this one, not yet, anyway. I already have my answer. She knew the prison well enough to stage the escape, and she knew where and when the attack was going to be. She ambushed our ambush. Veronica. I brought a snack for you, my darling. Guards bring her in," Remus said.

The orc guards brought in a young female. She stood just inside the doorway, shaking. Her shackles rattled. Remus waved the guards out. The guards left and closed the door.

"Oh, look at the poor thing. She's shaking. Come and sit down," Veronica compelled the young girl to sit. She poured a glass of wine for the girl.

She stood up, pulled the seat out for the girl, and pushed her in to sit at the table. Veronica stood behind, savoring the smell of the girl. Sam looked at Veronica, confused by her behavior.

"Drink up, little bunny," Veronica said to her. The girl's hands shook. Her shackles rattled as she drank the wine.

"Oh, Remy, you're so good to me. You know Gem Cutter, I don't like it when people stare at me," Veronica said. Her eyes blackened, and her fangs came out. The girl screamed. Sam averted his gaze.

"Please don't kill me!" the girl pleaded.

"Be quiet and hold still, little bunny," Veronica commanded in a demonic tone. The girl became silent and still. Veronica bit into the girl's neck and started feeding on her. The girl tried to scream and cry, though her jaw and lips would not move. Tears rolled down her face. Her muffled plea was nearly silent. Veronica had not compelled the girl to sleep compassionately. Rather, she relished in the girls' suffering. She had done it on purpose to put on a show.

The sound of the girl's muffled crying in terror was too much for Sam to bear. The sound of her blood dripping onto the stone floor was sickening. Sam could tell from the amount of blood the poor girl was losing, and the look of her, she would not survive much longer. The sight and smell of it sickened him. He lost his appetite. He went to stand up in protest, but Ak'rah quickly grabbed his arm and held him in his seat forcefully. Sam looked at Ak'rah, puzzled.

"Don't choose now to die," Ak'rah said to him quietly but firmly.

Remus and Veronica had been observing them. In fact, Veronica's eyes had not stopped staring at Sam. He was careful not to stare back, heeding her warning. Remus and Veronica laughed. They cackled widely. Veronica put her fangs away, and the corruption on her face disappeared. Her eyes returned to normal. Veronica let go of the girl's head. The girl's body slumped forward as her lifeless head hit the table.

"Oops," Veronica said. She used the girl's napkin to wipe the blood from around her mouth as she resumed her seat. Remus and she continued to laugh malevolently.

"Sam, tell me, do you have any Fae with you?" Remus asked.

"Of course not," Sam replied.

"Is he telling the truth, my sweet?" Remus asked.

"The little bunny is lying through his teeth. I don't even need to compel him or dig into his mind. I can smell the two Fae out in the hall. Do you want to know what they had for lunch?" Veronica replied.

"So far, I'm treating you as a guest, but I have a dungeon. Lie to me again, and your treatment will change. Call in your guards," Remus insisted. Sam considered the situation.

"Gunay, Dugan come out. Come have a seat at the table," Sam said. Dugan looked over at Gunay with concern.

"That's a vampire. We should run," Dugan said.

"No, our duty is to Sam. If our fate is to be a vampire's meal. We did it in service to our people. To the crown," Gunay said. He grew to human height and went and had a seat at the table next to Sam. Dugan reluctantly followed him.

"Tell me about your mission. Have a seat. Eat, drink, I'm sure you're all hungry from your journey," Remus said. He motioned for them to be served.

"I'd rather die than tell you anything!" Dugan replied.

"We're supposed to rescue Sam, if there is a safe way to do so," Gunay said.

"And if there is no safe way?" Remus said.

"Dugan was to return and report Sam's location. I would stay behind to protect him," Gunay said. Remus took a drink of wine and then whipped his mouth with a napkin. He stood up and walked around the table. Stopping to lift the deceased girl's head from the table.

"There is not a safe way," Remus said. He dropped the girl's head back onto the table. Sam and his Fae guards were noticeably disturbed.

"See, our goals are in line. Sam is my guest here and will remain so as long as there are no attempts to escape or for a rescue. If I sense Aysun has violated the sanctity of my castle in her cosmic form. I'll have Veronica drain Sam until he joins our other dinner guest. Mister Dugan, you are free to leave anytime. Report back to the Moon Goddess. Tell her I want the Heartstone for the Great Tree in exchange for Sam. I also want her to respect the truce and withdraw her army to the Great Tree. Take what supplies you need from the kitchen and take a fresh horse from my stable. I have plenty. Stay the night, if you like. I'll see you have comfortable arrangements," Remus continued.

"Sir, if it's all the same to you. He will depart immediately. Dugan go," Gunay said. Dugan got up and went into the kitchen.

"And you are welcome to stay here and protect Sam," Remus said. He took the keys from Ak'rah and unlocked the collar around Sam's neck. He removed it and placed it around Gunay's neck. Remus locked it.

"See, we all get what we want," Remus said. He retook his seat.

***

Raven strolled through the central marketplace. A jewelry shop caught her attention. A rosary in the window caught her eye. She entered the shop and perused the displays. She stopped to look at one of the more elegant rosaries.

"May I help you, madam?" the storekeeper asked.

"How much for this rosary? Raven asked. The man flipped over the tiny price tag. This one is £300, madam. If you are looking for something less expensive, I have a selection over here," the storekeeper said.

"Price is not an issue. Can you show me your best wares?" Raven asked.

"Of course, madam, but perhaps you should return with your husband. The private collection is very expensive and exclusive," the storekeeper said.

"Are you inferring that I cannot afford it or that I need a man to approve of my purchases?" Raven asked.

"Forgive me, madam, please come this way into the private viewing area. You are, madam?" he opened a curtain to the back room and motioned Raven to enter.

"Ravencroft," Raven replied.

"Marguerite, please come down and manage the front. I have a customer," the storekeeper yelled up a set of stairs. A lady came down the stairs. The storekeeper entered the lavishly decorated sitting room. Raven sat in a high-back chair with a table in front of her. He served her tea and then went about opening a cabinet. He laid out trays of jewelry of all kinds. They were all of exquisite beauty. Raven went through each tray. She selected several pieces of jewelry. Raven slid the pieces she wanted over to the storekeeper. She put a couple of rosaries off to the side.

"Are the rosaries to your liking?" he asked.

"I'm looking for something special. Something that will last a long time," Raven said. The storekeeper went and opened a secret compartment in the wall and took out a small strongbox. As he did, he told the tale of the rosary.

"I have a piece. It has a long history behind it. It's become a family heirloom at this point. You are the first person I have shown it to since I inherited the shop. Commissioned by a wealthy widow. She tasked my Great-grandfather with creating the most protective rosary he could conceive of. She wanted her family sparred from the plaque. He spent months researching and consulting with the clergy," he said. The storekeeper placed the piece on a pillow in front of Raven.

"The Hail Mary beads are all pure black onyx. Onyx is said to have protective properties. It's renowned for its ability to absorb and transform negative energies. The six semi-translucent blood-red Our Father's garnets are a beautiful contrast to the onyx beads. They symbolize the blood of Christ. The centerpiece and cross were hand-carved by my Great-grandfather. He molded and poured the gold for the medallion of St. Jude, the patron saint of impossible causes, and the crucifix with Jesus adorned on it. You can see the exquisite detail and the care that went into making this masterpiece. The bead connectors are 18-carat gold. The crucifix and centerpiece are also encased in a silver surround. To protect them from evil. After he completed it, he destroyed the original templates, so this is a one-of-a-kind piece that cannot be duplicated. The beads alone are worth the asking price. They are perfectly symmetrical spheres, thirty carats each. You won't find a flaw in them or the garnets. He finished this piece in 1348 and had it blessed by the Archbishop of Paris, Guillaume de la Roche Tesson himself," the storekeeper said as he laid out the documentation on the piece.

"My Great-grandfather made it in 1348?" Raven asked.

"Yes, madam, my Great-grandfather named it The Beacon of St Jude," the storekeeper replied.

"Impossible causes. That's me," Raven said to herself quietly.

"Madam, your eyes are bleeding," he said. He offered her a white handkerchief, but she used a black handkerchief she had in her purse to wipe the tears.

"Sorry, it's a condition I've had since childhood," Raven replied.

"How much do you want for it?" Raven asked.

"The price is £10,000 for the Beacon. This is the expensive inventory," the storekeeper replied.

"What happened to the woman?" Raven asked.

"She and her family succumbed to the plague before delivery or payment could be made. Over the years, the Vatican has made several offers on it, but the offers were too low. My father also had a priest, a friend in here who he lent or rented the Beacon to perform exorcisms, but you didn't hear that from me," he replied in a hushed tone. She reached out and touched the crucifix. She was not sure what to expect, but nothing happened.

"I'll take it. I'd like these also," Raven said as she moved a set of gold and onyx jewelry over in front of the storekeeper. The set included a large onyx necklace with a diamond surround, a pair of matching earrings, and two rings of a similar style. Raven removed the largest ring from its holder and placed it on her finger.

"What's the total?" Raven asked.

"£13,500, madam," he replied.

"I'll offer £12,500," Raven countered.

"I can go as low as £13,250, but that's the best I can do, madam," the storekeeper said.

"£13,000, and we'll go to the bank across the street and complete the transaction. I'll come back and collect the Beacon. The rest you can send to my apartment here in Paris. Last offer," Raven said.

"Deal," the storekeeper agreed.

***

The Lightning Privateer was still at port. Dugan sold a gem to book passage on the ship. He shopped for clothes and luggage appropriate for a first-class passenger. He boarded the ship and went and found his cabin. Dugan unpacked and went to dinner.

The first-class dining area was elegant yet intimate. Dugan saw Pavlo working at the bar, and Ivan was bringing plates of food out from the kitchen. He winked at Ivan as he walked by and sat at the bar.

"Hi, friend. Bourbon, please," he signed his drink order to Pavlo.

"Are Sam and Gunay okay?" Pavlo signed as he poured the drink.

"It's complicated. They are good for now," Dugan signed.

"We're not supposed to talk to the guests. Come to our room later. We are in the hall outside, near the kitchen. Our names are on the door," Pavlo signed. He handed Dugan a menu.

***

Dugan knocked on the door, and Pavlo let him in. Their room had a set of bunk racks, a table, and two chairs. The room was simple, but an upgrade from their previous accommodations. Dugan sat on the bed.

"Sam is fine. I need to get back to Her Majesty. It looks like you gents have moved up to proper accommodations," Dugan said.

"Yeah, the hours suck, but the job is fairly easy. No standing watch, no sea and anchor detail. No more climbing the riggings. The tips are good, too. We have access to the kitchen twenty-four-seven. If you want something, just say the word. I have Augie's stuff. Sam wanted it given to his sister. Volkov went through everything after Sam left. What about your upgrade, first-class?" Ivan said.

"I sold one of Sam's gems. I couldn't travel third class while Volkov is looking for me. In first class, he can't touch me. We'll probably never cross paths," Dugan replied.

"If you need anything, you let us know. Why did you say it's complicated about Sam?" Pavlo signed.

"An old enemy of the Fae has returned, and he has a vampire guarding Sam," Dugan explained.

***

Raven prayed quietly with the Beacon in the back pews near the exit at Notre Dame Cathedral in Paris. A priest approached her.

"You're a little late for mass, my child," the priest said.

"Sorry, Father, I don't go out during the day. I have a skin condition. I burn easily. Father, is it true that God will forgive all sins?"

"My child, God is indeed a merciful God. He welcomes those who seek forgiveness with a repentant heart. It is written in the scriptures that God's love and forgiveness are boundless. If you have sins to confess or burdens on your heart, you are always welcome to seek his forgiveness and find solace in his grace. I haven't seen you here before. I'm Father Thomas. What can I call you?" Father Thomas asked.

"My name is Mathilde, but my friends call me Raven," Raven replied.

"Is that a replica of the Beacon of St. Jude? I've held the original. The church has been interested in its acquisition for some time, but its cost is very high. Is that made from glass?" Father Thomas asked.

"No, Father, it's not a replica. I purchased it earlier this evening," Raven replied.

"That must have cost you a lot. What is it that you do?" Father Thomas asked.

"I own vineyards, and some other business interests," Raven replied.

"Some senior members of the church would wish to speak to you about your purchase. Could you be available sometime this week for a meeting?" Father Thomas asked.

"No, I'm sorry. I don't want to part with it," Raven replied.

"I might be able to have his holiness in attendance. He could give it the highest blessing," Father Thomas pleaded.

"I should probably go. I just came here to pray," Raven replied.

"My apologies about the artifact. My superiors would expect me to have tried. I'll ask no more about it. It's yours legally. Raven, would you like me to take your confession?" Father Thomas asked.

"I am pestilence. Father, my sins are horrific, biblical. I don't think I should," Raven replied.

"Whatever you tell me stays between me, you, and God. Come, my child, I'm sure I've heard worse," Father Thomas said. He led her into the confessional booth.

"Thank you, Father. My heart is heavy," Raven said. They settled into the confessional.

"Bless you, my child. You've come seeking solace and forgiveness. The confessional is a sacred space where you can unburden your heart. I am here to listen and guide you. Is there anything you'd like to confess or discuss today?"

"Bless me, Father, for I have sinned. It's been over 150 years since my last confession," Raven said.

"My child, this only works if you're honest with God and take this seriously," Father Thomas said.

"Father Thomas, I am quite serious. 174 years ago, I was born in a small town near Salisbury, England. Since I was 16 years old, I have managed many aspects of my family's diverse business portfolio. When I was 23 years old. I moved to Paris to branch out on my own. I moved in with my cousin Marie. A business opportunity finally presented itself; however, I found out later that my business partner was a 300-year-old vampire. She turned me against my will," Raven said. She flashed her vampiric eyes at the priest.

"The greatest of my sins is that I'm guilty of taking a life, many of them. I have killed so many over more than a century that I've lost count. While I have many regrets, I regret the last one the most," Raven said. Father Thomas bolted from the confessional. Raven could hear his footfalls running away.

"Father Thomas?" Raven called after him.

"The devil is here!" he called out as he ran.

Acknowledgments

The cover and back art were created using Microsoft Bing Image Center from Designer with input from the artist:

Brian Waitekus

https://www.bing.com/images/create?FORM=IRPGEN

Benjamin Goodwill is an adventure enthusiast and traveler. He was born in the early '70s. He grew up in the suburbs of Chicago, Illinois. Ben has experience as a scuba diver, pilot, and US Navy sailor. He has a great passion for the ocean. Ben grew up loving fantasy and science fiction. One day, the idea of telling this adventure story of a couple of Fae girls came to him. He was compelled to write it down.

Also from this author:
Fae Legacy: The Thief and the Dragon Princess

Contact Info:
Facebook: Benjamin Goodwill
Contact Info: faelegacy7@gmail.com
Instagram: fae.legacy